Delivered

A King David Novel
Book Four of the Davidic Chronicles

Greg S. Baker

Delivered
A King David Novel
Book Four of the Davidic Chronicles

by

Greg S. Baker

Copyright © 2020

ISBN: 9798630733832
Independently Published

First Edition

All Scripture quotations are from the King James Bible.

Other Books by Greg S. Baker

Biblical Fiction Novels

The Davidic Chronicles
> *Anointed*
> *Valiant*
> *Fugitive*
> *Delivered*
> *King*

The Rise of Daniel
> *Crucibles of God*
> *Children of the Captivity*
> *Revealer of Secrets*
> *Arising Wrath*

Adventure/Fantasy Novels

Isle of the Phoenix Novels
> *The Phoenix Quest*
> *In the Dragon's Shadow*
> *Phoenix Flame*
> *Rise of the Dragon Spawn*
> More to come…

Christian and Christian Living

- **The Generational Warrior** – *The Battlefield Manual for First-Generation Christians*
- **Fitly Spoken** – *Developing Effective Communication and Social Skills*
- **Restoring a Fallen Christian** – *Rebuilding Lives for the Cause of Christ*
- **The Great Tribulation and the Day of the Lord**: *Reconciling the Premillennial Approach to Revelation*
- **The Gospel of Manhood According to Dad** – *A Young Man's Guide to Becoming a Man*
- **Rediscovering the Character of Manhood** – *A Young Man's Guide to Building Integrity*
- **Stressin' Over Stress** – *Six Ways to Handle Stress*

www.GregSBaker.com

To my mother.

Her support, love, and involvement
continue to be a deep source of
motivation. I love you so much, Mom!

Acknowledgments

A work of this magnitude is rarely accomplished without the help and support of others. In this case, my beta-readers provided a pivotal role in the development of this novel.

I would like to thank my parents, particularly my mother who is always willing to read multiple drafts of the novel—truly a labor of love. Keith and Debbie Baker could not be more wonderful parents, even to their adult son. Marjorie Gibson gave a detailed review of the book that helped immeasurably. Diane Frazier, like always, enthusiastically put her own projects aside to assist me in mine, adding very thoughtful and helpful suggestions. Rachel Walter added a vital touch to the novel and certainly deserves acknowledgment.

To all of you, thank you.

My wife, Liberty, once again, proved to be the pivotal linchpin in the direction of this novel. She listened tirelessly as I bounced ideas and thoughts off her. Without her support, this would simply not be finished.

And, of course, our Lord Jesus Christ must be acknowledged. He is the Word, and in the Word, He has given us the wonderful story of David as an example and admonition (1 Corinthians 10:11).

Author's Note about Biblical Fiction

What Is Biblical Fiction?

Biblical Fiction can mean a variety of things, but essentially, for my purposes, it is similar in nature to historical fiction. In Biblical Fiction, the author takes the true events and people of the Bible and expands upon them into a fuller story of "what might have happened" that connects those events and people the Bible speaks of.

For example, David mentions to King Saul that he had killed a lion and a bear. The Bible does not describe those events, so in a Biblical Fiction novel, I might write the scenes surrounding those events as it might have happened while staying true to the biblical account. It is not to be Scripture or to replace Scripture. Instead, it is meant to bring to life a possible fuller picture of the characters and events that the Bible describes.

It is similar to what preachers do when retelling a Bible story from the pulpit. They embellish the story, add emotional responses or reactions to the characters, and extrapolate events and actions in ways that depict logically what might have happened or how biblical characters might have felt. It is fictional, but logical fiction.

In such a novel, I would bring together many of the historical facts mentioned in the Bible and present a possible fuller picture of what the Bible describes in a shorter context, often in just two or three chapters. An entire novel could be based on those few chapters, filling in fictionally all the blank areas.

Scriptural footnotes are added to show where a biblical fact has been incorporated into the story.

My desire is to ensure that the biblical facts are the mainstays and core of the story while the fictional aspects are forced to revolve around those facts to bring a cohesive narrative that remains true to the biblical record. Other biblical fiction tends to do the opposite in order to try and present a more entertaining story.

Again, to be clear, this is not meant to be Scripture or to replace Scripture of any sort. Except for what the Bible says, the rest of what I write is fictional—my best guess based on the information we have as to what might have happened.

These stories are meant to be fun and adventurous but remain true to the biblical account. These novels are not children's books, though they are suitable for children. I am writing for a more mature audience, teenagers and adults. I don't sugarcoat the men and women in the Bible. They were often thieves, liars, murders, adulterers, and blood-thirsty warriors. I decided not to cheapen the violence and other horrible deeds that the Bible describes. I aim to show you an entertaining story, true, but also one that will hopefully inspire you to see the Bible stories in a broader sense. These were real people, with real problems, who made real mistakes, but who lived real lives that God wanted us to study and know.

So, enjoy.

Map of Israel

At the time David flees from King Saul

PHILISTIA

Ramah

Aijalon

Gibeah

Ekron

Kesalon

Jerusalem

Nob

Gath

Bethlehem

Valley of Elah

The Jeshimon Desert

Adullam

Keilah

Mareshah

Lachish

Hebron

Ziph

Hachilah

Carmel

En-gedi

Maon

ISRAEL

The Salt Sea

Beersheba

AMALEK

Prologue

The short climb to the winepress gave Abigail time to consider how best to share her news with her new husband. Despite three months of marriage, she still did not know Nabal well. She had met him for the first time just two weeks before their marriage, an arrangement that left her family much better off, seeing as her father was a wily negotiator and had received over fifty sheep and a score of goats to replenish his diminishing flocks. Not that Nabal would notice the loss. Being a direct descendant of Caleb,[1] the man was by far the richest man in the region.

The traditional betrothal period had all but been eliminated in her case. Both Nabal and Abigail's father had been in a hurry to seal the bargain. So, before she even had time to adjust to the idea of getting married, she was. The deal had been struck in less than a day, and now at seventeen, Abigail was a married woman to a man nearing fifty. If she had had a choice in the matter, she would not have married Nabal, but her family had fallen upon hard times, and Nabal had taken a fancy to her after the death of his first wife—a mysterious death that had left him heirless.

Unfortunately, Nabal seemed less than satisfied with his purchase. Abigail tried to be the dutiful wife, following all the commandments written down by Moses in the law. She never disobeyed, sought to be attentive, and did her best to learn her

---

[1] 1 Samuel 25:3.

husband's business so that she might better assist him. Yet he frequently brought up the dowry price, pointing out his dissatisfaction that she was not yet with child.

If Nabal was disgruntled with his new wife, then Abigail was unimpressed with her new husband. He was cunning though not overly intelligent, shrewd though not diligent, and his wealth made him influential though not liked. He cared little for the opinions of others and cared only for that which would increase his wealth.

She climbed the limestone steps to the winepress, a shallow hole roughly twenty cubits square and about a cubit deep. A dozen barefoot men clung to ropes dangling from beams suspended above the press, crushing grapes beneath their stained feet amid the slippery floor of the winepress. Nabal oversaw the process from the edge, watching carefully as the juice flowed down a narrow trench through a filter of twigs that captured the pulp and seeds and then flowed on into a deeper pit where the grape juice would begin the fermenting process.

"You lazy dogs! There's too much pulp!" Nabal snarled, his rough voice snapping over the pressers like a whip.

Abigail hesitated. Nabal was in a churlish mood, his face a thundercloud as he watched his servants work. The men, none of them very large or heavy, knew their business as far as Abigail could tell. Human feet were soft enough to press the juice from the grapes without breaking the seeds, which if broken, would create a bitter taste to the wine that few could abide, but from what she could see, the men were being very thorough—there wasn't all that much pulp. The servants bobbed their heads in acknowledgment of the unnecessary order and continued to do as they had done before.

Perhaps she could give the pressers a break from Nabal's attention. "Husband," she called, stepping up to the stone platform above the winepress. "I bring news."

Nabal spun on her, his eyes snapping at the sudden interruption, but then recognition struck, and he grunted, "Wife." He said the word like a curse word. He never used her name. "What do you here?"

"I bring word," she repeated patiently.

"Say on."

She swallowed hard, knowing he would not be pleased with her news. "Raiders, my lord—Amalekites have struck south of Maon and robbed your flocks."

Nabal was not a robust man, and the news hit him like a blow against his chest. He staggered back, clutching at his left arm. Abigail, trying to be dutiful, rushed to his aid, but after a moment of bumbling attempts to help, he brushed her aside with a sharp shove and straightened. His thinning hair stood high like willows in a breeze, and his lower lip bulged unnaturally. "How much was lost?" he demanded in a wheezy voice that struggled for every breath.

"Seventy-three sheep, my lord, and one servant slain." Abigail attempted to keep her voice even, worried about what her unpredictable husband would do.

He clenched his fists tightly and cursed her, his face turning crimson. Spitefully, he added, "The loss is more than the price of an undutiful wife."

Abigail flushed in shame, and her eyes dropped to study the pitted, white rock beneath her sandaled feet. She knew he was upset over the final dowry price he had to pay to claim her as his wife. It didn't help that her father had gone around boasting about it to everyone who would listen. She vividly recalled the moment when her father had come home after striking the deal. "Daughter," he had said, his voice light with relief, "you have brought succor to this family. Your beauty has snared the eyes of a great man." Her family had been struggling. Their sheep herds had been decimated by disease and raids, so her father had turned to the only commodity he had left. Her.

"Where did these raiders go?" Nabal asked, his eyes already turning away from her and latching onto the pressers like a merchant spying potential thieves coming to inspect his wares.

Relieved that he wasn't so focused on her, Abigail visibly straightened. "They fled toward Amalek, my lord. Word comes that the raiders follow Haman, son of Agag."

Nabal snorted. "Trust a king to fail in such a simple task. If only Saul would have slain Agag's entire household!"

Before she could think better of it, she tried to explain, "But, my lord, King Agag hid his son from the eyes of King Saul. The Amalekites wander their desert in tents. They have no city to call their own. They scratch out a living where they can. The king did much."

"Yet enough remain to raid!" Nabal roared. "They have taken what is mine!" He visibly calmed himself with effort. "And where is King Saul now? When Amalekite bandits steal and murder, where is our king?"

Abigail thought furiously. She wanted to please her new husband, to be diligent in her duties as a wife, but she had to be careful. Her intelligence[2] often intimidated the men she met, so she had learned to try and couch her words in such a way that they would bring no offence. She was only ever partially successful. Licking her lips, she volunteered, "Perhaps there is another way."

Nabal turned toward her, intrigue warring with disdain on his face. "Say on, Wife."

"Could we not find another to defend your possessions, my lord? What of this David, the son of Jesse? Did he not deliver Keilah from the hands of the Philistines when Saul would not?"[3]

The moment the words left her mouth, she knew she'd made a miscalculation.

"David?" Nabal spat on the ground, though was careful to aim his spittle away from the winepress and the juice flowing into the fermentation pits. "If not for David, King Saul would have come to our defense." He shook his head. "There be too many servants fleeing their masters these days. David lures Saul like bees to honey. As long as the son of Jesse lives, Saul will have no peace." He looked at her sharply as she opened her mouth to respond. "Enough, woman! Speak not his name again to me!"

---

[2] 1 Samuel 25:3.
[3] 1 Samuel 23:5.

She snapped her jaw closed and bowed her head in submission. But it appeased him little, and he added, "The rise of banditry can be laid at the feet of David, Wife. If not for his rebellion, we would not have these cursed Amalekites stealing and slaying my servants. It's men such as this son of Jesse that brings all such problems to our doors. You mark my words, Wife. David will bring no good to us."

Abigail was dubious. She had heard many rumors of this son of Jesse. He was a violent man, surely, but he had won many victories for the Hebrew people and surely the hand of the LORD was upon him. He had slain the giant Goliath, defeated the armies of the Philistines, and married the daughter of the king. Surely Jehovah was with such a man.

Her disagreement with Nabal shown in her eyes as she met her husband's gaze. Not without cunning, Nabal had long ago learned to read the eyes of those he bartered with. His hand struck her upside the face. Pain exploded, her ears rang, and she tasted salty blood trickling down her throat. She found herself on her knees holding her head to stop the ringing in her ears. She blinked through tears and saw her husband standing over her, his face contorted in fury.

"I will not be mocked, Wife. Never again." Menace and threat filled his voice.

Since she was already on her knees, she summoned what humility she could find and bowed over her husband's feet, mumbling through blood-stained lips, "As you command, my lord."

The pressers looked away, pretending not to see.

1

Asahel crested the ridge on the run, weaving through cypress and olive trees as easily as a light breeze. David's nephew raised both arms to the sky and then flattened them straight out at the shoulders. David went cold despite the warm air of the valley. The air carried the smell of foul sweat and oiled leather that accompanied his army like well-worn sandals, but with the odor came the sharp sent of fear that spiked as six hundred men realized danger lurked nearby.

King Saul was close.

As if reading his thoughts, Adino hefted the spear he was named for and pointed to Asahel. "The king draws near, my lord."

David clenched his jaw tightly. A weary feeling had settled deep into his bones, and it seemed he walked the edge of exhaustion. He couldn't recall what being refreshed and energetic felt like. Ever since he had rescued Keilah from the Philistines, he had been running from Saul. Killing Doeg the Edomite had thrown the king off for a time, allowing David's men to escape before Saul could surround them, but Saul had been relentless, pursuing David every day since.[1]

Moving from place to place, David had found himself drifting farther south into Judah until they had entered the wilderness of Ziph.[2] There he had remained around one of the tree-topped hills

---

[1] 1 Samuel 23:14.
[2] 1 Samuel 23:14.

that dotted the grassy landscape of southern Judah.[3] This had given them a week to rest and recuperate, but always the knowledge that Saul was closing in had kept David up at nights. Lack of food had stripped David and his men of what little fat remained to them, and everyone had lost muscle mass. Everyone was on the edge of starvation and exhaustion.

And now Saul had found them.

"He is close," Adino repeated when David said nothing.

Blinking, David realized he needed to act. "Give the signal," he ordered his lanky commander.

Adino seemed to elongate as he stretched upward, lifting his spear. He pumped it three times in the prearranged signal, and six hundred men and some additional women and children scattered into the rocks, grass, and shrubs of the valley floor. Along the slopes, trees grew, and into these trees the rest of David's army disappeared.

David fell to the earth behind a shrub and peered through the branches and small leaves as Asahel darted down the slope of the ridge; the youth's feet scarcely seeming to touch the earth as he went. Then abruptly, he disappeared, and everyone held perfectly still, waiting.

Glancing around, David could pick out a few of his men hiding nearby. Joab, Asahel's brother, crouched just beyond a clump of brush. Joab was rarely far from David these days. He followed his uncle like a loyal dog, and David had begun to rely upon him more and more. His nephew was turning into an inspired battle commander.

Beyond him, he could see where Eleazar and Shammah lay amid the grass. The two, like bickering wives forced into the same kitchen, had formed a deep and unlikely friendship. Eleazar's constant predictions of doom were offset by Shammah's ready humor and selflessness.

Elhanan and Abishai, the latter being Joab and Asahel's other brother, could barely be seen higher up the slope from David. The

---

[3] 1 Samuel 23:14.

two waited, still as death. Others of David's small army dotted the valley floor and slopes, all hidden.

Then two strangers crested the ridge from where Asahel had first appeared, scouts for King Saul's army. They stood in silence, studying the valley below where David and his men hid. It seemed impossible to David that they would not spot some sign of David's army. Surely a stray piece of cloth would wave in the breeze, the smell of unwashed bodies would tickle their nostrils, the squeak of leather, the gasp of a child, or Shammah's oiled scalp glinting in the sunlight would give them away.

But after long moments while David held his breath, the two men turned away and began a ground-eating lope along the ridgetop until they disappeared farther to the north.

David let his breath out explosively, giving silent thanks to Jehovah for yet another deliverance. Standing, he gave a sharp whistle that would carry no farther than a hundred cubits. Men began standing or emerging from hiding places, all looking to David. He gestured toward the south, and everyone began making their way in that direction, except for those scouts tasked with keeping a wary eye on Saul's progress.

David's commanders began gathering around him as they walked. Each step cost David, like a part of himself was being pounded into the soil by the tread of a thousand feet. And if it wasn't for these men, David feared he would have long ago turned himself over to Saul.

"The king draws ever closer," Shammah rumbled. David waited for more, but the large man fell strangely silent. When he had first met the bald man, Shammah believed that any problem could be overcome with a sharp enough sword or a large enough warclub. But he had grown these past years. Wisdom had begun to bring caution—though he resorted to violence when it suited him or when he came to the end of said wisdom.

Gad, the seer, never lost his grin, as if someone had stamped it permanently upon his face. "You, my large friend, have the true gift of seeing what everyone else also sees. This is commendable."

Shammah blinked, his eyes narrowing. While he tried to decide if he should be offended, Gad pressed on. "Where we may hide is withering away. Ever do we flee southward. Soon we will be among the Amalekites, and I tell you truly, their hospitality is lacking when it comes to Hebrews."

Abishai, Joab's next oldest brother, was young enough to snigger at this, but everyone else nodded soberly. All knew of King Saul's attempt to destroy Amalek. Under the king's direction, the Hebrews had razed the cities, salted their fields, and slain a huge portion of the population. Those who remained were shepherds and warriors who had fled into the desert to escape the slaughter. Among them, reportedly, was King Agag's son. The remaining Amalekites had banded together, becoming nomads in their own homeland and had taken to raiding southern Israel and other surrounding countries for whatever they could steal or kill. They moved like spirits, nearly impossible to pin down.

David did not want to go to Amalek.

"But where else is there?" Eleazar demanded. The vain swordsman walked too erect as if he was trying to force himself to be the tallest man in the company. "We cannot flee north. King Saul's men are like fleas on a filthy dog northward. West? The Philistines?" He spat. "They would not give us succor, mark my words! East? Across Jeshimon?[4] The barren land will suck us dry and leave our corpses for the buzzards."

The swordsman's words struck David like blows from a sword. He shuddered at each option. North was out of the question, but where? Saul's scouts ranged to the west, leaving only east and south open to David. He tugged at his beard and then traced the scar on his left cheek. It had darkened over the years since a Philistine spear had kissed his skin. Once fair-skinned with a hint of red in his hair, the weather, sun, and hard living had darkened him to match the scar. His hands and forearms were crisscrossed with thinner scars, testimony to the many battles he had fought. He studied the scars,

---

[4] The Jeshimon desert is known today as the Judean desert. Another, rockier desert lies to the south of the Judean desert, known as the Negev desert.

old friends that sometimes reminded him of things best forgotten. He clenched his fists, making the scars along his knuckles show white. So many battles. So much death.

He was reminded of the story his father had told about the night the death angel had visited Egypt in Moses' day. Legends spoke of the wind whispering through the trees and a dark presence that crowded the door of each house, a weight that constricted the space within each home, making it hard to breathe. But the lamb's blood on the doorposts had protected the Israelites from harm that night.[5] When the death angel passed on, the weight lifted and breathing became normal. But nothing could protect the Israelites from the wailing of the Egyptians as each firstborn was slain that night without a mark left upon the body.

David felt that weight now, like being enclosed in a small space with no room to move. He could smell the presence of death as it shifted through the empty spaces between the men. He shivered, trying to refocus his thoughts. He picked up his pace to see if he could outrun the evil feelings upon his heart and mind. The other men automatically kept pace, trying to close the distance to him. Like death. Their voices pushed at him as they offered advice and opinion, walls that towered high and slid close like the narrowing walls of a cave.

Unable to take anymore, David stopped in his tracks and spun around. "Make room!" he shouted, breathing heavily. His voice carried further than he intended, and a spike of panic stabbed his heart.

Startled, his men backed off some, giving him space. David breathed in heavily, eying the confused and worried faces surrounding him as he fought to regain control of himself. Finally, he closed his eyes and muttered a desperate prayer to Jehovah. The act of the prayer itself gave him strength. Jehovah had never let him down. More than that, there was the promise inherent in his

---

[5] Exodus 12:23.

anointing. Samuel, the Great Seer, had anointed David to be the next king of Israel.[6] That had to mean something. It did mean something.

Feeling some better, he opened his eyes and studied his men. He found Abiathar, the young priest, standing in the background, watching with disapproving eyes. Somewhere along the way, he had replaced his ragged robe with a new one, but even with all the running and hiding, the garment looked in better shape than it had a right to. How he kept himself so clean was anyone's guess. David beckoned the priest forward. "What say you, Abiathar? What counsel do you give?"

A muscle twitched in the priest's right cheek as he moved forward, the others making room for him. He carefully kept his gaze on David, ignoring everyone else as one might begging dogs. "We are Hebrews, servants of the Most High God. We should not hide in Amalek. Our God demands obedience. It is written that blessings come through the keeping of the law.[7] This is our land—land given to us by Elohim, our God. We should stand fast upon it. Keep the sabbaths and the law."

"Yet we are pursued even on the sabbath," Adino drawled as he gnawed on one of his Elah nuts, his whip-thin body leaning casually against his spear. "Would we not be slain if we did as you suggest?"

"We must trust in God," the young and idealistic priest insisted.

"Our enemies claim the same God!" Joab blurted out. The young warrior reddened and snapped his mouth shut, but others took up the line of thought.

"Aye! The lad speaks truly," Eleazar added. "Our enemies pray to Jehovah as we do. They seek His blessings as do we. How do we know their prayers are less worthy in the eyes of the LORD than ours?"

"Our cause is right," Shammah rumbled, eyes alight with fervor. "Saul has defied our God. David is the anointed king. God will fight for us!"

---

[6] 1 Samuel 16:13.
[7] Deuteronomy 11:27.

Eleazar shook his head and turned to the young priest. "Tell me truly, Abiathar, does our righteous cause give us leave to disobey the commands of God?"

"It does not," the priest said. His words carried conviction, but they lashed at David's heart like a whip.

Many of the men in David's company had fought with him when he was their captain under King Saul. They had violated not a few sabbaths marching to engage raiding Philistines who regarded not the laws of Jehovah and often sought to use the sabbath against the Hebrews. The veterans understood that some duties conflicted, that right and wrong were not so easily defined, and that sometimes two rights were at odds with each other. They had broken the sabbaths so that other Israelites could keep it. Was that wrong? Had they failed their God?

David had to believe otherwise.

Sucking in dry air, David held up a hand. Instantly, the bickering ceased. "This argument is best left for another time." He speared each of his men with his gray eyes. "Saul is close. Unless we escape, it will matter not where we go."

Adino spat out the shell of his nut. "Aye. This is so. We are being shepherded." Everyone looked at him curiously. He shrugged, his eyes shifting away. "Saul knows we have but one direction left to us. He will be waiting in ambush." He tilted his chin toward the south. "There."

Stunned silence greeted this pronouncement, and the younger men shifted, checking weapons, while the older men fingered beards. Beyond them, the bulk of David's army, perceiving that their commanders had halted, were finding comfortable places to wait. Here and there, women and children moved close to husbands and fathers. David wished for his own father right then, but Jesse and his wife were safe in Moab. He wondered if he would ever see them again.

"We must flee into Jeshimon," Abiathar suggested.

"Into the desert?" Eleazar protested, stabbing a finger toward the east. "Are you mad? Naught but scorpions and vipers live there. Supplies run low. If we venture into the desert, we will all perish."

David was tempted. Saul knew David's men were being hard pressed, and he doubtless counted on the fact that fleeing into the western desert would bring a swift end to David and his men. Nothing grew in the desert. It was a series of rocky and sandy canyons. A strong, healthy man with enough water, could cross the desert to the Engedi oasis in a day, but six hundred men with their wives and children and little water or food would find the task beyond them.

"Then we fight!" Joab said, partially drawing his sword. "Will not Jehovah deliver us?"

David shook his head, feeling weary. "I would not have Hebrew slaying Hebrew unless there is no other way, and it hasn't come to that yet."

"But they are the enemy."

David frowned. "Perhaps. But Saul is also the LORD's anointed. We will not lift our hand against him."

This declaration caused uncomfortable shifting among his men. David tried to think. A decision had to be made. He was on the verge of asking Abiathar to bring forth the ephod, when a shout broke the stillness and the ring of metal on metal bore testimony to a fight.

Spinning toward the sound, David searched the eastern slope of the hill for the source. Someone cursed and another shouted, "We are undone! The king has found us!"

A ripple of fear washed over the men like a sudden, cold wind. David vowed to flay the man who had spoken thus. His men were on the verge of panic, and many darted away without discipline, their instincts to protect loved ones instead of forming up into squads to repel a hostile enemy. On the verge of spitting curses of his own, David leaped to where Adino and Shammah were staring at the hill.

"Rally the men!" he yelled, startling even Adino into motion. "Guard our flanks!"

The two commanders nodded and sprinted off. Adino's thin body seemed to mold itself to the landscape, evading bushes and rocks. Shammah simply plowed through or over anything in his path.

The ringing sound of clashing weapons pierced the chaos surrounding David's small army. He spun around, looking for the wave of Saul's men, knowing he was exposed and vulnerable in this small valley. But he saw nothing.

Confused, he looked back toward the eastern hillside. He could hear the clanging of sword on shield—that sound sometimes haunted him in his sleep—but the trees obscured the source. He heard, also, the familiar sound of spears striking against sword and shield.

What is this? David wondered. If this was not an attack by Saul's men, then all that racket would surely draw them like jackals to a carcass.

Drawing his own sword, David charged up the hill. His sandaled feet chewed up the ground, the hard leather soles protecting him from thorns and sharp rocks. The laces crisscrossed his calves, rising nearly to the knees, providing support. He carried a simple, round wooden shield with hard leather stretched over it. Like most of his men, he had no helmet. During the recent victory over the Philistines, David had been presented with some scale armor plundered from one of the dead enemy captains. The overlapping thin bronze scales protected his arms and torso and fell to just below his waist. It was the only set of scale armor found on the battlefield that day, seeing as such armor was rarely found among the Philistine army. Most of his men wore hardened leather vests over their tunics. Such armor wasn't sufficient to stop a direct thrust with sword or spear, but it could deflect glancing blows, and in battle, one took every advantage possible.

His heart pounding with the effort of charging up the hill and dodging around trees that grew thicker toward the top, David finally reached the scene of the battle. A lone warrior fought against two of David's scouts, dancing away and confusing their coordination by using the trees to keep his attackers at bay. But more men were arriving, and soon Saul's scout would be facing overwhelming odds.

Then something about the warrior struck David as odd. The man was not dressed in a way David expected of a scout. His shield was covered in metal, not leather. His sword was straight and double-edged, unlike the typical Hebrew single-edged curved sword. And the warrior wore scale armor and a metal helm. He moved fluidly in his armor, bearing the weight with ease and skill. This was no scout.

Two more spearmen arrived, spreading out to surround the lone swordsman, and three men emerged from a copse of trees with bows in hand. The warrior would shortly be overwhelmed.

At that moment, David caught a glimpse of the warrior's face. Shock sent energy flooding into his muscles, and he bounded over the last fifty cubits of white rock and through the sparse trees like a man possessed. He knocked one of his spearmen off his feet, sending the surprised scout flying. Spinning, David snatched the other's spear shaft just behind the head and shoved it harmlessly up. Stepping close to the other scout, he bellowed, "Hold! By all that is holy! Hold!"

The man blanched at David's angry face, and dropped his spear, stepping away hurriedly. Letting the spear fall to the ground, David glowered at everyone, forcing his men to come to a stop by the force of his gaze alone.

The enemy warrior approached from behind David. "You truly know how to make a man feel loved, David," he said laconically.

A happy grin replaced David's scowl, and he spun about to embrace the warrior. "Jonathan,[8] you should know well that sneaking up on an army would be folly!"

Jonathan's wide face split, showing teeth in a mirthful smile. "How else was I to gain your eye?" King Saul's eldest son asked, sheathing his sword. He nodded to the archers with his trimmed

---

[8] 1 Samuel 23:16.

beard. "Yon bowmen would have filled me with their quills if I shouted down to them."

They embraced, and tears stung David's eyes. It had been too long since the friends had last met. Jonathan, at nearly ten years David's senior, still retained an unscarred, if weathered face despite the many battles he had fought—unlike David, who bore more than his share of scars, including a nasty looking one that ran from his left ear and down into his beard. Of equal height, David could look into his friend's dark eyes and see the love Jonathan bore for him. They were bound by more than duty and trial. Oaths had been given and taken, creating ties stronger than any other earthly relationship David possessed.

Jonathan, in many ways, was David's rock, a gift from Jehovah that bound him to a fading dream of being part of King Saul's family. Having been married to Jonathan's sister and then being outcast and essentially put away by King Saul, his wife given to another man, David had struggled to understand his place with the family he loved so much. Only Jonathan treated him like family. Only Jonathan bore him the love that he had craved from King Saul.

Years had passed since the two had stood above the Elah Valley upon which lay Goliath's corpse and covenanted themselves to one another with a holy vow.[9] The passing years had been hard on David, giving him a rugged appearance. Gone was the ruddy, fair-skinned complexion and the youthful hopes. Now, two warriors in their prime faced one another. Time changed things, but their love for each other had remained constant.

Quivering with emotion, David stepped back and wiped away the tears that had gathered in his eyes. He gave Jehovah silent thanks for sending Jonathan. He very badly needed his friend right then. "Tell me," he said, smiling, "why are you sneaking around these hills?"

Jonathan sobered instantly, his eyes shifting to the men gathering around them. "I have word of my father. He will be upon

---

[9] 1 Samuel 18:3.

you soon. I can be of help and divert his purpose, but we two must speak alone."

2

Some of David's men began muttering the moment Jonathan insisted that he speak alone with his friend. David swept a dark look across the men, and the dissent died away. "So be it," he said to Jonathan. Turning to Joab who had followed David up the hill, he ordered, "Keep the men moving south for the moment."

"Nay," Jonathan interrupted. "It is to the south that Saul seeks to bring you to ground."

Trusting Jonathan implicitly, David amended his orders to Joab. "Have the men stand fast but be ready to move on my word. When it comes, we must make haste.

Joab cast a suspicious look at Jonathan but managed to hold his tongue. He turned and ran down the hill, as sure footed as an ibex, to carry out David's orders.

David indicated the woods around him. "Walk with me, my friend." Jonathan followed his friend into the trees atop the hill. The woods thickened along the hilltop affording David and Jonathan a measure of privacy. "What news of your father, the king?" David asked.

"He seeks to entrap you to the south. But fear not. The hand of my father will not find you. I will aid you in this."

Powerful emotions surged within David's breast. Despite everything that had happened, Jonathan's loyalty and love had never wavered, not for an instant. "Why would you do this? If your father discovers your betrayal, he will not lightly overlook it."

Jonathan reached out and clasped David's shoulder tightly. "My father fights the truth, David. You will be king over Israel, and I will be next unto you. My father knows this in his heart, but he cannot accept it. He would see me king after him—not you."[1] Shaking his head, Jonathan grinned. "But I would not be king. I leave it for a weaker man who loves the flattery of others."

Wiping away tears, David offered up a smirk. "Flatterer."

His friend's eyes twinkled with mirth but then sobered. "I would not have you or any here doubt my intentions. Let us renew our covenant before the LORD."

David immediately clasped Jonathan's forearm, and with tears anew freely running into his beard, he said, "Before the LORD, in Whom is my salvation and hope, I avow these words to be true."

"Aye," Jonathan agreed, "fear not, for the hand of Saul, my father, will not find you. You will be king over Israel. I will see it done."

For the first time since David had known Jonathan, his friend had verbally acknowledged and endorsed the source of David's conflict with Saul. With those words, Jonathan relinquished all claims to the throne of Israel and threw his considerable influence behind David. It was a profound moment and it shook David to the very core of his soul. If anyone should be upset that David had set his sights on the kingship of the nation, it would be Jonathan. But all David saw in his friend's eyes was love and a fervency that deeply touched David.

Swallowing, David said, "And you will be next unto me. This I vow!"

Jonathan's smile lit up the woods. "Aye, this also my father knows. I think he fears it, but in his heart, he knows it will be."

David could only nod.

---

[1] 1 Samuel 23:17.

"Heed me," the king's son continued. "My father seeks to entrap you to the south. You must do what he least expects. You must flee east."

"East? We cannot cross Jeshimon. We have women and children and little water."

"You do not have to go far. Transverse the first set of ridges and hide in the rocks. You need not attempt the entire crossing."

"When your father finds me not, he will search the desert. He will find us."

Jonathan shook his head. "Nay, my father is as a bear in a wine press, clumsy and irritable. We will convince him you have gone elsewhere. My father has set spies to watch me, thinking I will lead him to you, but I will lead them on a merry chase, giving life to rumors that you are elsewhere. In the meantime, you must aid this deception. He must believe you have escaped to the north and west."

David considered. It might work—if Saul could be convinced. "What do you suggest?"

Turning, Jonathan pointed toward the southwest. "My father is there, believing you must also go there. But beyond," he explained, pointing again to the northwest, "is where your salvation lies. Send some of your men there at night. My father has the smaller part of his army encamped there. He seeks to prod you as a herdsman does his cattle, pushing you to where he lies in wait. But an attack upon this smaller army at night gives you a single chance to break his lines and draw the rest of his men out of position."

"I do not wish to shed Hebrew blood," David protested.

Jonathan turned sober. "Blood *will* be shed, my brother. Either yours or my father's. Heed me. Send only your most trusted warriors to do this, those who are most hardy. Break through the lines. Create noise and sow discord. If you do this in the evening, it will seem as if your entire troop has descended upon them. In the meanwhile, the rest can hide just within the desert, and my father will be drawn aside like a moth to the fire."

"And those who break through can make their way around," David finished, thinking hard. "Come down through the desert east of Bethlehem and rejoin those already escaped into the desert."

Jonathan nodded. "Such is my plan."

"It bears praise. But what of you?"

"I will add to the discord as I've said. I will draw not a few of his men away as I travel north. I will also see that my father hears of sightings to the north and to the west. Then I will return to my own house. I would be with my wife." He paused. "Once your forces have rejoined, they can petition the nearby towns for supplies. They are of Judah and should lend you aid."

David wasn't so sure, but he didn't argue the point. "I will do as you say. Go with God, my friend. May Elohim watch over you and give strength to your seed."

Jonathan's eyes glimmered in the light. "Truly, you are a prophet. The word of the LORD is on your tongue, for my wife is with child. Word but reached me yesterday."

A surge of joy rushed through David. "Truly? This is so? You do not mock me?"

"It is true. If the child be male, I will name him Mephibosheth."[2] Meaning "idol breaker or the remover of shame."

David looked quizzical. "A goodly name, but do you not have a brother by that name?"[3]

"Aye. The son of my father's concubine. But these be evil days, and shame has been brought upon my father's house. It is my hope that should I have a son, he will expel it and return honor to my house."

Thinking that these were indeed evil days, David could only agree. "I am well pleased for you, my brother!"

---

[2] 2 Samuel 4:4. Also known as Merib-baal (1 Chronicles 8:34). This second name contains the name of the false god Baal and is thought to be his original name and changed to Mephibosheth to remove any connection to Baal.
[3] 2 Samuel 21:8.

Jonathan clasped David's arm in farewell. "Then I am content. Know also that Adriel and my sister have welcomed their third son."[4]

David blinked. "Three sons? Truly he is blessed." He kept his voice even. He still harbored uncertain feelings when it came to Adriel and Jonathan's sister Merab whom David once nearly married.[5]

Jonathan might have detected a hint of David's ambiguity, for he gripped David's arm hard. "Heed me, my friend. If, perchance, something befalls me and I fall in battle, do not forget my son. Show him kindness."

Tears once again sprang to David's eyes. "I swear before the LORD, God of our forefathers. I will not forget."[6]

Jonathan, nodded, his eyes saying all that was left to be said. Turning, he trotted off into the trees on his mission to mislead the spies and thus prepare the way for David's escape. David watched his friend go, knowing that his friend took a significant part of David's heart with him.

Despite being surrounded by six hundred of his men, he felt suddenly alone. He wished with everything in him that he could turn back the clock and somehow prevent Saul's mistrust. Perhaps then he could still be by Jonathan's side and by the side of his wife Michal, now given to another man.

With a sigh, he returned to his men to begin preparing for their attempt to escape the snare King Saul had laid out for him.

Fifty men followed David, easing their way like spirits through the darkening gloom of a wooded hilltop that overlooked the flickering campfires of one of Saul's main encampments. Veterans of David's time captaining the Indebted, he trusted each of these men with his life.

---

[4] 2 Samuel 21:8. In fact, Adriel and Merab had at least five sons. It appears that Merab might have died, and Michal helped to rear the five boys as it is her name mentioned in this verse, not her sister, Merab.

[5] 1 Samuel 18:17-19.

[6] 2 Samuel 9:1-13.

Leading the wedge-like formation through the darkness, he could only see a few of his men to his right and left. The rest were lost in the gloom, but each knew what to do and would not deviate from the plan. Ahead, three sentries stood lonely guard. They were spread out across the crest of the hill, forming a chain that stretched from Jeshimon to the east and worked its way in a half circle back toward the south where the main part of David's small army was trapped.

Tomorrow, the jaws of King Saul's trap would close. This moment was their only chance to break free. Jonathan was right. He only hoped Jonathan had been successful in thinning the Benjamite lines, because without doubt, David's small force would be outnumbered ten to one.

He slowed, and the men to either side of him kept pace. The wedge flattened into a straight line as all fifty men came to a stop among the trees. They had removed their armor for the most part, knowing that the sound of metal would alert Saul's sentries. At David's command, his raiding party had wrapped their weapons in wool, blunting them. He was determined to take no Hebrew life this night. Their purpose was not to kill, but to sow discord and confusion. He wanted to create enough of a commotion that Saul would be convinced that six hundred men were attacking his lines and come rushing to lend aid to his beleaguered army.

David gave a signal that quickly duplicated itself down the line. He waited ten heartbeats and then slipped ahead alone. He already knew where the Benjamite sentry stood. Elsewhere, two more of David's men slipped forward into the darkness, like wolves seeking unwary prey.

David's target occupied a darkened shadow near a conifer tree. In the dark, the sentry appeared as nothing more than a misshapen shadow with a pointy top. Easing his way through the underbrush, David utilized all his skill to keep from snapping a twig or making any sound. He had elected to do the job himself, over Eleazar's protests, mostly because he needed to do something other than fleeing and hiding.

Perhaps a sixth sense alerted the sentry, for as David tried to sneak up, the guard shifted to look in his direction. Rushing forward, David closed the gap quickly, fearful that the Benjamite might shout out a warning. He slammed his fist into the sentry's face hard enough that the fellow's head snapped back to hit the trunk of the tree behind him with a dull thud. The man groaned and slumped to the ground. David had to catch the falling spear and snatch off the helmet lest it roll free and make too much noise. As it was, when the body hit the ground, he feared everyone within a league could hear it, but praise Jehovah, no outcry split the night's darkness.

Sighing, he set the man's spear and helmet next to the unconscious sentry, turned and whistled softly. Adino was the first to emerge from the darkness, his spear seemingly to grow from his hand like a third appendage. He looked at the fallen sentry and muttered something that David chose not to hear.

"Are the other two sentries silenced?" he asked his commander.

"Aye," came the soft reply, "and they still live."

Gratified, David nodded, a gesture likely lost in the gloom. He turned to look down upon the encampment established at the base of the hill. He could see men moving, silhouetted by the cooking fires and hear voices raised in laughter and a few in anger—typical campfire talk for warriors who knew a battle was imminent but not yet at hand.

Lifting his hand, David moved forward, forming the point on the spear of men that filtered downward from the crest of the hill. Like most of the terrain hereabouts, the trees grew predominately atop the hills, leaving the land between to fill with grass, low shrubs, and large white rocks. Only a few of the more stubborn trees grew in the valleys, and it was there, between the hills, that Saul's commanders had chosen to make camp.

When David reached the edge of the tree line, he stopped, giving the rest of his men the chance to catch up and take positions in the darkened woods. No more than a hundred cubits separated him from the first tent. The goal was simple. David and his men would get as close as they could without making any noise and then rush through the camp, shouting and creating as much chaos as possible before fleeing toward the wooded hills beyond. Hopefully, Saul's captains would believe that David's entire force had assaulted him and send for the king. This feint would give the bulk of David's army with the women and children a chance to escape into the Jeshimon desert and hide. David had left Joab in charge of that part of the operation—over his nephew's strident protests. But David wanted men who could be trusted not to kill unnecessarily. Joab was too anxious by far for battle. Only those who had served with him in the company of the Indebted were permitted to accompany David on this mission.

When he felt enough time had elapsed, David took a deep breath and mouthed a silent prayer for deliverance to Jehovah. Strictly speaking, what David intended shouldn't work, but they had no choice. If even one of the Benjamites in the camp recognized the true scope of their attack, the entire plan would become as useless as swine raised for meat.

Abruptly, he stood up from his crouch and began a slow walk toward the tents ahead. Fifty men, spread out along the tree line, followed. Eleazar commanded the left flank and Shammah the right flank. Adino helped David secure the center. David had warned his men not to try to disguise themselves. He wanted to be recognized.

It was time.

David lifted a hand, and shortly a horn shattered the night air from David's right. With the name of Elohim on their lips, David's men attacked. Nearly five hundred Benjamites turned in stunned shock at the sound. Then David's men were among them, shouting, bashing them aside with blunted weapons, tossing burning brands atop tents, shouting out names of men who were not there, bellowing contradictory orders, and generally lending to the impression that upwards of a thousand men were attacking the Benjamite camp.

In the resulting melee, David lost sight of Adino and most of his other men. He ran through the camp, barreling over some of the men he encountered and shouting to others that the son of Jesse was following and that the Spirit of the LORD was upon him. That gave men pause, for this was the name of the man who had killed Goliath, the same man who had defeated three other Philistine champions, and the same man of whom women sang that he had slain his tens of thousands.

Chaos erupted and then spilled out to infect every corner of the camp. David grabbed one man, a captain by the look of him, and spun him around to face back the way David had come. "He comes!" he roared at the man. "The son of Jesse comes! Defend yourself!"

Instead, stark terror overcame the man, and he lashed out violently, knocking David aside and running off into the night. David shook his head, both to clear the ringing in his ears and to wonder at the man's reaction. Truly, the LORD was fighting for David this night.

Then he was beyond the camp with his fifty men, running hard toward the tree line of a wooded hill beyond the Benjamite camp. In astonishment, he realized men in Benjamite armor were running along with his men. Some of the Benjamites having seen David's fleeing company assumed their own forces had been routed and so had joined what they had presumed was a general retreat.

One of these men ran alongside David, looking fearfully back over his shoulder at the camp aflame with burning tents and even the clash of weapons as confused and frightened men stumbled upon each other in the chaos and darkness.

David casually measured the man and used the flat side of his sword to lay the Benjamite out. The poor fellow went flying off his feet and landed in a heap among some thorn bushes. David winced in silent sympathy and ran on. Once in the trees, David quickly took stock. All fifty men were accounted for, and only a couple were limping from injuries.

"Shammah, Eleazar, you know what to do," he said looking at his two captains.

Nodding, they quickly gathered a group of men around themselves and loped off into the night. David touched Adino on the arm, and they took their own group and moved as quickly as they could. They would walk all night, trying to make it seem that a large group of men had come this way, and then come daybreak, they would break off into yet smaller groups and begin to loop back around to the north and east, to rejoin the main body of David's troops in two days hence.

Map of Israel

The Jeshimon Desert and Maon Wilderness

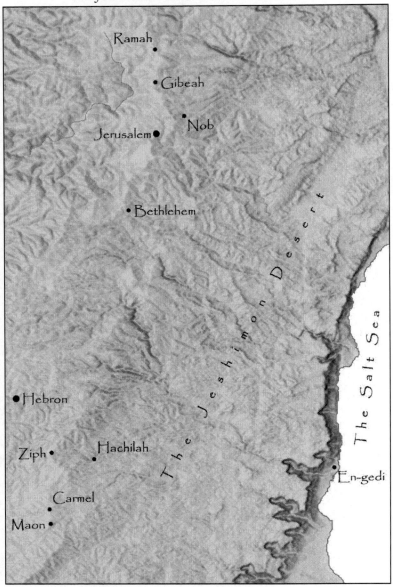

3

"The inhabitants around here call this the hill of Hachilah," Shammah rumbled, unconsciously rubbing his bald head. The big man stood next to David atop a ridge overlooking a steep, barren ravine that separated the hill from the more fertile mountains beyond the Jeshimon desert. A few scrub trees grew near the top and along the crest of the ridge, but otherwise, the land was nothing but rock and dirt. Even after two days since rejoining his men following the raid on Saul's camp, David still had little love for the barren and rugged landscape. It was nothing like the mountainous regions of his homeland in Bethlehem or the fertile slopes of Jerusalem.

Farther to the east, the desert properly started. Even the few bushes and trees disappeared into an expanse of rocky, broken ridges and steep ravines where little ever grew and even less lived. The very edge of this desert was a forbidding landscape that attracted only the hardiest of creatures, mostly lizards, scorpions, and the sturdy ibex.

Fortunately, winter was approaching, so the normally harsh temperatures of the desert had already begun to fade. The rains would come, helping to sustain David and his encampment, but he dared not rely upon the fickle weather to provide for a company nearly a thousand strong.

Shammah, who had grown up in the southern Judean mountains and hills, recognized David's internal war, and gestured with his long beard toward the west. "We must intreat with the

Ziphites, my lord. They have water and food, and we are in sore need of both. Hebron might have more in abundance, but Saul would surely know if you went there. It is doubtless being watched. I counsel seeking out the Ziphite elders."

The small town of Ziph occupied one of the taller hills to the west of Hachilah. That city along with a few others, Carmel and Maon, were the primary power in the region just south of Hebron. Being some of the most southern settlements, these three cities worked in harmony with each other, having often been the victims of raiding Amalekites from the south, roaming Edomites from the southeast, and the occasional Philistine incursion that wandered farther afield then normal.

A resilient people, they were well used to hardship and to being forgotten, being as they were far from the seat of power. David did not know how they would react to the presence of his small army encamped nearby. But in truth, he didn't see any way around the problem. He would simply have to approach the elders of Ziph and see if he could barter for food and water. He was desperate for both.

"What do you know of Ziph?" David asked his large commander.

"I know little, only what I have heard. Seek out the man Haroeh. He is the most respected of the elders in Ziph. It will be he who sways the others one way or another."

"Haroeh," David repeated. "I know him not. What manner of man is he?"

Shammah shrugged, the beads in his beard rattling with the motion. "Wealthy by most standards—but not by his. A man of means. A hard man, it is said."

"Choose men to accompany us to Ziph. We will see if the LORD will give us favor with this man." David scanned the horizon to the north where King Saul was reputed to be continuing the hunt for him. "Be discreet in your choices, Shammah. I want men of integrity who will not stir up the Ziphites against us. We can ill afford for them to send word to King Saul. This above all must be avoided."

"I understand, my lord." The large man hesitated. "There's much talk among the men. They like not this place, and some speak of leaving."

David grunted, a surge of anger tightening the skin around his eyes and lips. "Give them leave to depart. I would not stand with men who have not the heart or will to see this through."

"It is not about heart alone, my lord. They fear for their wives and children. Without food, the little ones suffer first. It is whispered that you have brought us to this wilderness to die."

"Such words are foolish! Have I not kept them from harm? Have I not kept them from Saul's hand?"

Shammah shrugged. "Do you wish for me to chastise them?" He flexed his ox-like muscles suggestively.

David was sorely tempted. Instead, he asked, "Are these the only words being spoken?"

The big man paused. "Most believe we cannot run and hide forever. Some seek a confrontation with King Saul in battle. They know that the LORD is with you, and that Samuel has anointed you to be king in Saul's place. There are questions. Why then do we not stand against Saul? This running is wearisome."

David realized he was hearing Shammah's own frustrations. His discourse had ceased to be about the rumblings of others and had switched to what he himself felt in his heart. This revelation rocked David and pained him deeply. If one of his most trusted commanders felt this way, then the discontent surely ran deep.

"Is this word shared by all," David whispered, turning to look out over the broken landscape.

"Nay. But many do hold to such words. I tell you truly, my lord, even my wife holds to such words."

That Shammah even had a wife had come as a shock to David. Apparently, after being released from his indebted service, the huge man had managed to convince a smith to give him his daughter in marriage. David had seen Shammah's wife, a petite little thing that would require three of her to even come close to matching her husband's bulk—but she was as tough as an old bullock's hide.

When Shammah had answered David's call, she had steadfastly refused to be left behind and had come along with her husband. David hadn't even known she was around until weeks later.

"It is more complex than simply confronting King Saul," David said, repeating an oft-heard argument. "He too is the LORD's anointed. And then there is Jonathan, the son of Saul. I could not look upon my brother's face if I was responsible for his father's death."

"Aye," Shammah rumbled. "So you've said." His eyes lit up as a thought struck him. "I tell you truly, that Jonathan is a mighty warrior. He has done great service to us. I think I will give my son this name. *Jonathan.* It has a princely ring to it, does it not, my lord?"

David warmed to the words. "Is your wife yet with child?"

"Nay. But when these dark days are behind us, we will look to the future."

And such a task of seeing that any of them had a future at all lay squarely upon David's shoulders. He straightened as if by doing so he could more easily carry such weight. "Select your men," he ordered Shammah, "and send Joab to me with the purse. We leave in an hour to bargain for food and water."

David's commander left on his errand, leaving David alone outside the main encampment. He knew the general character of the men who had come to aid him. Mostly, they had nowhere else to go. They were thieves, debtors, and generally discontented with their lot in life. They saw David as an out, a way to clean the slate and start over. But this did not change the nature of such men. They were prone to all sorts of character defects, ranging from laziness to outright greed. Shammah, among his other duties, had been tasked with instilling discipline in the troops. The bald-headed man took the most direct route available, and there had been more than one broken bone that needed mending.

The discontent was a problem, but not as severe as the lack of food and water. Much could be assuaged with a full belly and wet throat. And so, an hour later, David and a party of thirty men, including Joab and the prophet Gad departed. Elhanan the son of

Dodo came along to oversee the logistics of transporting any food or water David managed to procure. The young Hittite, Uriah, had also been invited to come, for which David was grateful.

Uriah was an oddity in David's troop. He never expressed discontent, anger, or anything other than total loyalty to David. A skilled warrior, Uriah managed to be well liked with everyone, able to dispel a tense situation with a softly spoken word. He never complained and his sincere, light-brown eyes could pierce bluster and anger like an arrow into flesh. In short, Uriah was a wonder, and David was glad for his company.

Ziph was built on a hill perhaps a league or two from the Jeshimon desert's edge. David set a fast pace, and they came into view of the small city while the sun still rode high in the sky. A short, but stout, rock wall surrounded the town, and a watchtower had been erected on a rocky outcropping atop the hill. Doubtless, the elders had already been apprised of David's approach.

Like most of southern Judah that wasn't desert, the trees tended to grow atop the hills, leaving tall grass and low shrubs to fill the troughs between. David paused at the base of a nearby hill. "Shammah," David said, "choose two men to accompany us to the city. The rest will abide here until we return. I would not have the Ziphites believe we mean them any ill."

Shammah selected Joab and Uriah. David's nephew, Joab, grinned at being selected, his smile not doing his flat face any favors. Not overly handsome, he nevertheless possessed a ruggedness and strength that would do him well as a warrior and leader of men. David already knew he would rely much upon his nephew in the years to come.

Without asking, the prophet Gad fell into step with the four warriors as they made their way toward the city gate. David gave him a quizzical look but did not forestall the seer. "Do you have any advice, seer?"

The ever-grinning prophet shrugged, his black beard waving in a stiff autumn breeze that had sprung up suddenly. "I once was the proud owner of a mightily foolish dog," he said. The small company fell silent to listen. "He was truly a sight to behold—muscular, sleek fur—and no challenger did he have. Surely, he was king of all canines, and I loved him much. One day, he chanced upon a lion which had stolen a lamb from my father's flock. The lion, a great and angry beast, was in the midst of his hard-won feast and in no mood for interruptions. They fought, my king of the canines and this most ferocious of mighty beasts. Great was the battle. The roars and growls echoed among the high peaks of the mountains. There was no quarter given and none asked. It was a battle to the death." He fell silent then, a wistful cast to his smile.

Joab, eager and entranced by the story, demanded, "What befell your dog? Was he victorious?"

"Alas, my young warrior, he was not. The lion enjoyed two meals that day. As I said, he was a mightily foolish dog."

Joab looked confused. "How so? Did he not do his duty? Was he not tasked with protecting the flock? Wherefore is this foolish?"

Gad's grin had grown wider with each question, until his smile fairly took up his entire face. "The foe was beyond my beloved dog."

David's nephew's face, if possible, flattened even more as his innate stubbornness rose within. "That is not foolishness. That was his duty. Did not David once face a foe mightier than he in the giant Goliath? Did not Elohim deliver the giant into David's hand? In my mind, your dog acted with wisdom."

"Except," Gad pointed out, "Elohim did not deliver the lion into my dog's teeth. In the stead, Elohim delivered my foolish dog into the mouth of the lion."

Joab snorted. "He was but doing his duty—what he was trained to do!"

"Ah!" Gad stuck a finger in the air. "How rightly you speak! But I still contend that my dog was a fool."

"Why?" Joab demanded, his face tightening.

It was Uriah who spoke up, his soft voice barely reaching the ears of the small company. "The lamb was already dead. There was nothing to save."

That brought Joab to a stop. He blinked, his eyes narrowing. "But would not the lion hunt again? Should not your dog have fought the lion?"

Gad nodded. "All you say is right." He clearly meant both Joab and Uriah.

David struggled to make sense of the moral. Was Gad warning him against fighting a lost cause? Was bargaining with the Ziphites something beyond David's ability? He mused it over as Joab continued to argue his points and Gad continued to agree with him without really agreeing, serving only to frustrate David's nephew as the circular conversation continued. Was David the lion or the dog in the story?

At length he gave it up and cast an angry scowl toward the prophet. "Why do you speak with such dark sayings?" he asked. "Can you not say it plain?"

Gad whose amusement seemed to know no bounds nodded. "Aye, my lord, but even if spoken plain, could you not still discover hidden meanings even in plain speech?"

David gave a curt nod, conceding the point. "I like it not, however."

Gad shrugged. "As you say. Perhaps one day you will have a son who sees value in such dark sayings."[1]

Uriah spoke up. "I wouldn't mind such a son." The Hittite looked sincere.

"You remain yet unmarried," Joab pointed out. "Is there no woman in Israel to suit you?"

Uriah looked thoughtful. "I wait for one of unsurpassed beauty." Everyone looked at the Hittite in surprise. This was a side David had not expected from the unusual young man. Uriah reddened from the attention. "I look yet," he admitted.

Joab let loose with a full belly laugh. David felt his own smile struggling to appear, and for a short moment, the weight he carried

---

[1] Proverbs 1:1-6.

lifted. But when he turned back toward the gate of the city, his mirth fell away. A group of aged men awaited him just within the gates.

They formed a half circle of judgment that caused David to miss a step, but the need of his troop asserted itself, and he straightened and strode forward as if going to battle. In a way, he was. He was fighting for the lives of nearly a thousand men and women.

Beyond the elders of Ziph, David caught sight of archers scattered about through the stone houses. Others doubtlessly crouched along the wall watching. He was not coming as an enemy then, but not as a friend either. Others, little more than boys or with gray in their beards, stood nervously behind the elders wielding spears. This did not surprise David. Most of the men able to lift a spear had been snapped up by King Saul,[2] so the city often relied upon aged warriors and boys not yet of an age for defense. Doubtless, they knew of David's small army and they knew that, should David decide to, he could easily overwhelm Ziph's poor defenders. It didn't matter that David would never consider such a course of action. That they believed it so was enough to generate fear.

The elders stood arrayed before David and his small party as they entered through the open gate of the city. No greetings were offered. No one so much as spoke as they waited upon David. Taking a deep breath, the son of Jesse stepped forward beyond his men and bowed deeply to the elders of Ziph. "I bid you greetings in the name of the LORD God of Israel under whose wings I find shelter. I am David, son of Jesse, a son of Judah. I come in peace and wish to bargain for food and water, for my men and I are in sore need of both." He scanned the impassive faces, most hidden in long, gray beards, but here and there one or two shifted, casting sidelong glances toward the elder situated in the very center of their arc. This then must be Haroeh, the elder Shammah had mentioned.

---

[2] 1 Samuel 8:11.

David turned his eyes to study this man who likely held the fate of David's small army in his hands. Taller than the average Hebrew, he nevertheless filled that height with such bulk as to seem short. His full beard reached high on his wide cheekbones, nearly to his eyes so it appeared as if two twinkling stones regarded him from a face of hair. A spectacularly long nose that also had dark hair protruding out the nostrils acted much like a divining rod, quivering as it aimed at David. His arms, like the other elders, were folded before him in a gesture that indicated he held no weapon, a gesture of peace, but his eyes said differently. Hostility and suspicion gleamed there, waiting much like quicksand, ready to suck in everyone and anything.

Noticing David's gaze upon him, Haroeh stepped forward offering only a slight bow, one bordering on disrespect, in response to David's. "You are known to us, son of Jesse. We welcome you to Ziph in the name of Jehovah. I am Haroeh, son of Micah, also a son of Judah. If it pleases the LORD, we will hear you and see what barter there is to make." The elder gestured to the hardpacked dirt of the ground. "Please sit and be refreshed."

So saying, he promptly did as suggested, sitting cross-legged on the ground with his hands resting comfortably on his knees. The other elders followed, sitting in a half circle before David. David also sat, knowing that the custom was to do business in the gate of the city before the people. This would be a collective decision, not something that one man decided. But David guessed Haroeh would be the deciding vote in any decision made this day.

When David and his men were seated, Haroeh raised his arm and a veiled girl appeared, bearing a pitcher of water. Starting with David, she went from man to man offering drink and water to wash the dust off their feet. When she came to David, he revised his opinion. This was no young girl, but a woman true, though perhaps on the short side. Her beauty caught him off guard and captivated his attention as surely as if Goliath had suddenly appeared in their midst. The thin virgin veil did not hide the symmetrical features, the grace with which she walked, or the gentle feminine lines that graced her form. Her long hair bore a rich gold color and her skin, what David could see of it, gleamed like pearls.

She noticed his scrutiny and meekly bowed her head, casting her eyes away. David was intrigued, a feeling he hadn't felt since first laying eyes on Saul's daughters. David raised a hand to halt her from moving away. "May I know your name?" he asked, letting his eyes drink her in.

The girl glanced at Haroeh who nodded ever so slightly. Turning back enough not to cause offence, she said so softly that David had to strain to hear her, "I am Ahinoam, daughter of Ishiah."

Ahinoam. A beautiful name, meaning "one of grace." She certainly was well named.

Haroeh spoke up, his ringing voice carrying easily to every ear. "She is of Jezreel,[3] my wife's cousin and has no other family and so came here." He paused, and David could see his eyes glittering. "Here to me," he finished, the sentence filled with meaning.

Looking at Ahinoam, David ignored the warning that layered the elder's words. A sudden desire to have this woman to wife nearly overwhelmed him. His own wife, Michal, had been taken from him and given to another man. He had not seen his wife in over a year, and the bereft had left him with a hole in his spirit. He wanted to fill that hole, but before this moment, he had thought to simply wait until such a time as he could demand his wife back. But seeing this woman, seeing her beauty, her grace...David wanted her.

With an effort, he put aside his desire and focused on the reason for which he had come. Perhaps later he could return to this beautiful woman and see about what it would take to make her his wife. As Ahinoam moved on to Shammah, David met the knowing eyes of Haroeh with iron ones of his own. David doubted the Ziph elder missed much.

Addressing the elder, David spoke, "I thank you for your hospitality. You say you have heard of me. You know then that I and

---

[3] There were two cities named Jezreel. One was located near the Sea of Galilee in what is also known as the Jezreel Valley. The other was located somewhere in Judah to the south. It is likely that Ahinoam came from this latter city.

those with me haunt the hills hereabouts. We need food and water and would barter for such with the noble people of Ziph."

Silence greeted this announcement. Finally, one of the elders with a long face and snow-white beard, cleared his throat. "What you ask is a hard thing, son of Jesse. All here know that your master, King Saul, seeks your life. You would call the king's wrath down upon our heads and snuff us out from the face of the earth. Nay, you must leave us in peace. Seek for sustenance elsewhere."

David's eyes narrowed and in a voice that bled with the heat of a raging fire, he responded. "And where should we go, elder of Ziph? I and those with me are unjustly judged, our lives in peril, and our women and little ones in jeopardy. I too am of the household of Judah as are each of you here. Why do you refuse aid to kin? Is this the will of Jehovah?"

Another of the elders, this one with skin so wrinkled that he resembled a dried grape, answered. "All here have heard what King Saul did to the inhabitants of Nob—how he cleansed the priesthood for aiding you.[4] Would you have us be as they? Would you see our houses burned, our wives slaughtered, and our children slain for the sake of your rebellion?"

White-hot anger flared to life in David's chest. He found himself standing, a violation of custom, but too many fears, too many worries and burdens lay upon him. He would not leave without the necessary sustenance his people required. "Clearly wisdom does not always belong to the old," he snapped, his anger getting the better of him. Shammah rose with him, laying a restraining hand on his arm, but David shook it off and addressed the sitting elders. "We have dealt with you in good faith. I have the strength and power to take what I want. Do not mistake that I must rely upon you. I and the men with me can be a shield unto you by day and night. We can defend your homes from bandits." He paused, looking meaningfully around him. "And I will deal with King Saul should he come to seek

---

[4] 1 Samuel 22:6-23.

me out. Heed me well, elders of Ziph, you would be wise to intreat with me."

Shammah reached out and applied pressure to David's shoulder. This time he allowed the big man to guide him back into a sitting position. But his glare was no less fierce. And he could see fear in the eyes of the elders, and to his shame, he found himself relishing this fear. They turned to each other and began whispering among themselves, all save Haroeh who stared hard and long at David, his hairy face giving nothing away as to what he thought.

Finally, Haroeh lifted his hand sharply, cutting off the whispering among his fellow elders. He waited until everyone fell still and then spoke in his ringing voice, "Do you then barter with threats, son of Jesse? Are you no better than the Amalekite raiders who take by force what they want?"

David struggled to regain his temper. He honestly didn't know what he would do if he didn't get the supplies he so desperately needed. Would he truly attack? He had thought himself incapable of such an action, but he had as much implied that he was prepared and willing to take such an action.

He let his breath out in a long sigh. "We would barter our swords, my lord Haroeh. We would stand as a shield for you. You would have but to call upon us, and we will deliver you out of the hands of the Amalekites. The king has taken your sons to him. Who is left to defend your families?" He gestured to those standing near. "Boys and old men? We offer our spears and lives."

"And what of King Saul?"

"If word comes that the king has learned of me, we will spread tales that we forced you to intreat with us. This will turn aside the king's wrath." He leaned forward, resting his hands on his knees, his eyes intent. "I will lead the king on such a merry hunt that he will not think of you."

The elders all fell silent, staring at David. Finally, Haroeh nodded. "So be it. I propose that we barter food and water with the son of Jesse. In return, he and his men will be a shield unto us to deliver us from the hand of the Amalekite raiders." He hesitated and then added, "And a promise to turn aside the wrath of our king when his gaze rests upon us." Not if. When.

The elder leaned over and began unlatching his sandal. David immediately understood. It was still the practice in the smaller, more remote cities to exchange sandals to confirm a bargain. Something similar had been done when Boaz had redeemed Naomi's inheritance and purchased Ruth to be his wife.[5] Reaching down, David begun unlacing his own sandal.

Removing a sandal each, David and Haroeh stood, facing each other. The elder spoke, "You are all witnesses this day to the bargain made with the son of Jesse."

The elders, some looking none too happy, murmured, "We are witnesses."

The two men stepped close and exchanged sandals, sealing the bargain. Kneeling and looking each other in the eye, they began relacing the sandals back on their feet. David detected a wariness in the elder's eye and a glimmer of something else—satisfaction, perhaps, or something more. David liked it not. He didn't trust the elder, but he was satisfied that a bargain had been struck.

Standing again, Haroeh pointed to the side of the gate. "We will bring what you require there. Have your men come to fetch it in one hour."

David bowed.

The elder then folded his arms. "Where do we send word when we have need of you?"

This was the tricky part. David didn't really want to reveal his hiding place, but in truth, he doubted he could keep it a secret even if he wanted to. It would not be hard to follow them back, laden down as they would be with supplies, and discover it for themselves. Besides, he had made a bargain. "We encamp on Hachilah in the south of Jeshimon."

The elder frowned. "I know of it."

---

[5] Ruth 4:7.

"Send word if you are invaded. We will come quickly and deliver you from the hand of all invaders."

"It is well then."

David turned to go, but not before scanning the faces of the people around him, looking for a last glimpse of Ahinoam. His desire still burned within him, and he fully intended to pursue the matter. But not now. Later perhaps. He looked but saw her not.

4

Haroeh paced across the hardpacked dirt floor of his house, pulling at his long, quivering nose. Sounds drifted to him from one of the adjacent rooms where his wife and Ahinoam labored over bread dough, their quiet murmuring and soft laughter a stark counterpoint to the turmoil raging in his mind as he tried to decide what to do about the son of Jesse.

For perhaps the hundredth time, he ran through the pertinent points in his head. First and greatest of the problems would be King Saul's reaction when he learned that the people of Ziph had aided David. He didn't believe for a moment that the king would overlook such a breach of loyalty—not after what Saul had done to Nob and the priests there. Oh, he had heard of Saul's justification for the massacre, that the Gibeonites had somehow polluted the priesthood. He snorted softly, dismissing the notion. Nob was destroyed simply because the priests had aided the son of Jesse.

He turned his mind to what might happen if he betrayed David to the king. If the young warrior found out, he would doubtless attack Ziph. With six hundred men, Haroeh had no doubt that David could easily burn Ziph and everyone within to the ground. The rumors of David's prowess had spread like wildfire. It was said that, with but a few men, David had withstood the entire Philistine army and slaughtered them nearly to a man. That large, bald man with David fit the description of Shammah, the son of Agee, another mighty man whose prowess in battle had already become something of a legend.

And if he did betray David, he doubted the king would bother to deliver the Ziphites out of the son of Jesse's hands, much less deliver them from the marauding Amalekites who had taken to raiding throughout the region. *Curse Haman!* he swore to himself. *Why did the son of Agag have to take to raiding now?*

He considered David's offer to shield the Ziphites from the Amalekites. It would be of great value and doubtless much property and many lives would be saved because of it. But what good would all that do when King Saul brought the full might of his army against Ziph? Not a man, woman, or child had survived the slaughter at Nob.[1]

He pulled at his long nose, brushing the hair of his beard away lest it tickle his nose and set him to sneezing—an unfortunately all-too-common occurrence. He then paused in his pacing to stare at the front door of his house. Now where was that greedy cousin of his? He had sent word to him the day before and had received a reply that he would come before the Passover began.

As if thinking about him somehow conjured him, a voice floated through the air from outside. "Ho in the house! Do we have leave to enter?"

Haroeh strode over to the wooden door and flung it open. His cousin and his cousin's young wife stood without. If Haroeh was considered robust, his cousin looked like something that had been lying too long in the sun. He looked shriveled, sickly—except for the eyes. A seething cunning lay in those orbs, like a pot set to boil. It was that intelligence that Haroeh hoped to invoke.

"Nabal!" he roared. "It's well that you have come. Please, my house is your house."

Nabal grunted, muttering something that Haroeh didn't quite catch, but knowing his cousin as he did, he probably didn't want to know. His cousin brushed past him, his wife in tow. Once inside,

---

[1] 1 Samuel 22:19.

Nabal rounded on Haroeh and demanded, "What's so urgent that I must be called away from my flocks and vineyards, Haroeh? I like this not. Bandits do roam the countryside, and if I am not around, the laborers grow lazy and will not even know when the flocks are stolen from beneath their very noses. By the eyes of Caleb, speak your peace, but do so quickly."

Nabal's impatience was nothing new, neither was his biting tone. Haroeh decided to ignore both. "The evening feast is nearly ready. Come, let us go to the table so that we may talk and fill our bellies."

The offer of food stole some of Nabal's impatience. "It is well," he answered.

Haroeh smothered a smile. Nabal would stay and then linger through the Sabbath.

Abigail, Nabal's wife, looked up. "Pardon for speaking, my lord. Does your wife require aid? I may be of service, if my lords are willing."

Haroeh didn't know Abigail all that well. He studied her briefly, noting the youth, the full, appealing figure beneath the richly colored halug. His cousin had made a fine choice in this woman. She was beautiful and capable. Her dark hair complemented her dusky skin and brown eyes. Yes, she was beautiful. Only Haroeh didn't like the way she had spoken out of turn without first being addressed. It was a small thing, but he liked his women to be able to anticipate needs and act on them without having to ask or being told.

Apparently, Nabal agreed. He scowled at his wife darkly. "Go," he ordered, "and give what aid the women may require."

Bowing, she scurried away, and soon a third voice mingled with that of the other two women. Haroeh beckoned his cousin to follow. They moved to the second level of the house, one of the few houses in Ziph that had a second story, climbing the white stone steps so that they might speak without the women overhearing. They sat upon mats around the table, and Nabal leaned back against a pillow and sighed deeply. "I tell you, cousin, this travel is growing wearisome," he said.

Haroeh nodded as if he understood. "The road grows longer as we grow in age."

"You speak truly. Now tell me, cousin, why have you requested my presence?"

"I wish to speak of David, the son of Jesse. Know you that he came to Ziph and made demands of us?"

Nabal's eyes narrowed and he leaned forward, his interest spiked. "Truly? What demands?"

"He seeks provisions for him and those misguided fools who follow him. They haunt the hill Hachilah just within the Jeshimon desert. Know you of this?"

Nabal shook his head. "What use have I for rebels? It is Haman, the Amalekite, I fret about. He has raided my flocks yet again."

"The son of Jesse has promised to protect us from such in exchange for provisions. What say you to that?"

"I say it is foolishness," Nabal snapped. "The son of Jesse has fled his master's table. He will not chase after bandits lest King Saul learn of it. He will not bestir himself for such little gain."

Haroeh paused. He hadn't considered that possibility. "I have heard that this David is an honorable man. Would he not keep his word?"

Nabal snorted softly. "He has forsaken his oaths to the king, and I hear tell that oath-breakers and the discontented comprise the bulk of his troop. Why should he keep such an oath?"

"And yet, if I do not aid him, he has threatened to take the provisions by force. If that happens, Nabal, we lack the power to withstand him. He could destroy my city and take all he wants. And there is more," he added quickly to forestall his cousin from speaking. "If King Saul learns that we have aided the son of Jesse, he may do to us what he did to Nob. No matter which way I turn, we may be sorely punished."

Nabal's pale face sagged as he considered the possibilities. "You seek my wisdom on this matter?"

"Aye, I do. We are cousins, you and I, of the house and lineage of Caleb.[2] This land is rightfully ours. This city is mine. Your lands are among the most plentiful in the region. The right of choice belongs to us—to you and me. What say you? Do we aid this David and risk the king's wrath? Or do we risk the son of Jesse's fury and betray him to King Saul?"

Nabal sat back again, his eyes lifted to the roof of the house as he considered. From below, the voices of the women rose as they moved near, bearing the food for the evening feast. His sickly-looking cousin nodded. "I understand the problem, cousin. But even if you do seek to sustain David, how long can you do so? Has he not above a thousand men, women, and children with him? How long can you provide for so many? He would consume more than the Amalekite raiders could steal." Nabal smoothed a scraggly, graying beard with one gnarled hand. "I say that we send messengers in secret to King Saul. Prevail upon him to come down with subtlety and take this David by surprise. In this way, you can avert the son of Jesse's wrath and gain the king's favor." He nodded as he talked, his voice growing more excited. "Indeed, perhaps with this favor, we can prevail upon the king to lend us aid to drive these Amalekite bandits from our borders."

Haroeh's face betrayed none of the inner conflict within. His cousin's singular care, it seemed, was these bandits who preyed upon his goods. He cared little for Haroeh's problems. But then this came as no surprise. Haroeh knew the character of his cousin, but too, Nabal possessed an unusual type of cunning that saw right to the best ways to turn negative circumstances to one's own favor. It was for this reason he had called upon his wealthier cousin. And the idea of having Saul come in secret did seem the most expedient means of surviving.

"I will do as you suggest," Haroeh said, lowering his voice as the women's voices drew closer. "I will go in person and seek the king's favor."

---

[2] 1 Samuel 25:3.

Nabal grunted, satisfied. "Then there is no more need of this talk." He raised his voice. "Bring the food. Let us feast!"

Haroeh's wife, his ward, and Nabal's wife arrived at each other's heels up the stone stairs, each expertly bearing a platter of food or a pitcher of wine. Nabal, naturally, took one taste of the watered-down wine that Haroeh favored and demanded something stronger. With an inward sigh, Haroeh nodded to his wife who pulled Ahinoam in her wake to fetch the stronger wine. Before the evening was finished, Nabal would be drunk. This too, Haroeh had expected. There would be little religious ritual for the upcoming Sabbath this day.

When the two women left to fetch the wine, Nabal leaned across the food and whispered none too softly. "Ahinoam has a beautiful countenance. Do you intend to take her to wife?"

Haroeh glanced at Abigail who seemed oblivious to the conversation as she spread the food around the table for the two men. Nabal's wife was young, younger than Ahinoam by several years, but carried herself as one who was older, and Haroeh didn't believe she missed much. But what harm would answering do? He had made little secret of his intentions. "Aye, when the time is right. My wife favors her, and it will do us both well to have a younger woman in the house." He tapped his fingers atop the wooden table. "And as you say, she is of a beautiful countenance."

Nabal grinned, his mouth already full of food. He swallowed. "Can you then afford to have her?" he asked, eyes twinkling with cunning mirth.

"My ventures have been profitable," Haroeh said stiffly. "I can well keep two wives."

"Then this is a time of rejoicing!" Nabal glanced at his wife, who continued to serve the food. "I find myself envious. A single wife is all I can afford."

Abigail who was moving mutton to within her husband's reach, stiffened ever so slightly which caused Nabal's grin to widen. Haroeh knew that Nabal, should he wish, could afford to keep several more wives in his large household. Nabal was, without doubt, the richest man in the region. He clearly wanted to deliver some insult to his young wife. Haroeh pushed it from his mind. How Nabal treated his wife was none of his business.

Already, he was turning his mind to the task at hand. He would leave after the Sabbath. It would take a couple of days to reach Gibeah,[3] and he needed to have every word exactly right if he intended to survive this mess between the two mightiest men in the land. There was one other reason to betray David that hadn't been voiced, one that might make it easier for Haroeh to provide for two wives. In times past, the king had offered a reward for news of the son of Jesse. Haroeh fully intended to claim that reward.

King Saul stood before his chair, impatiently awaiting the delegation from Ziph. Word had been brought by Ishui that the Ziphites knew where David had hidden himself. Saul still didn't understand how his one-time harper could have escaped the snare he had so carefully laid. Evidence suggested that he had broken through his lines, and rumors had come flooding in that David had fled to the north and west, but no matter where Saul had looked, David or any knowledge of David was nowhere to be found. It was impossible!

He growled low in his throat, causing some of his advisors who lined the wall to glance his way nervously. His moods had increasingly grown worse, he knew, but he cared not. Only when David was dead would he find peace. He knew this instinctively.

The door opened and four middle-aged men came in behind Saul's second son, Ishui. Because this meeting would be about David, he had ensured that Jonathan, his oldest son, was not present. Jonathan's love for David was well known, and Saul didn't trust his son not to interfere where and when possible. Abner stood behind the king; the flinty-faced battle commander watched everything in

---

[3] 1 Samuel 23:19.

the dim light of Saul's throne room. Saul had eyes only for the four men who bowed deeply before their king.

The obvious leader possessed an impressive amount of hair growing out of his face and, aided by the longest nose Saul had ever seen, gave the impression that someone had stuck a bush on top of the man's shoulders. Not willing to wait for the normal exchange of pleasantries, Saul, who easily towered over everyone in the room, took a step toward the men. "What news of David? Tell me."

The leader straightened while keeping his eyes humbly cast toward the ground. "I am Haroeh, chief elder of Ziph, my lord, the king. Does not David hide himself with us in strongholds?" Haroeh dared to look up then, but Saul was so excited that he cared not for this breach in decorum.

"Where?" Saul demanded.

"In the wilderness near the hill of Hachilah, which is on the south of Jeshimon, my lord."[4]

Saul fell back into his chair, astonished. Surely if that were true, he would have discovered David already as that was well within the trap he had set. It seemed impossible that David and those rebels who followed him could have so easily eluded his grasp. His suspicious nature reared its ugly head, and he fixed this Haroeh with a piercing look that caused the man to flinch. "Rumors abound," he said slowly, "of David's whereabouts. I grow weary of following false trails. How do I know this is not yet another such, and while I am seeking him in every cave and hill he is elsewhere?" Saul's mouth tightened. "I will not be mocked, elder of Ziph. Do you speak truly?"

The heavyset man brushed back some of his unruly beard and then pulled at his long nose. Saul liked not the look of it. The elder's eyes slid to his companions, but they seemed more adept at remaining anonymous than in helping. Haroeh cleared his throat before answering. "This is more than a rumor, my lord, the king. We have witnesses to his presence. He has been seen."

"Seen doing what?" Saul asked, sensing more here.

---

[4] 1 Samuel 23:19.

Haroeh hesitated. "Bartering, my lord. He seeks provisions for his troop."

Saul leaped from his chair and stalked toward the elder of Ziph, pinning him in place with the force of his gaze. Rage burned through his blood and colored his vision. It was all he could do not to ram his javelin into the elder's chest. He stood a few handspans from the quivering elder and took several deep breaths to regain control of himself. After a moment, he hissed to the elder, "The lives of all who aid the son of Jesse are forfeit—their goods and their families as well. Heed me well, elder of Ziph. I will see the son of Jesse dead and all those who bring him comfort. I want those who aid him hunted down and slain. Do you understand?"

Saul couldn't see the man's face beneath all that hair, but the eyes were wide and frightened. The elder swallowed and fell upon his face before Saul. "O King, come down according to all your desire. The son of Jesse abides yet in the wilderness of Jeshimon and Maon." After a moment's hesitation, the elder added, "Our part, O King, will be to deliver him into your hands."

Saul stilled, his anger evaporating as quickly as it had been born. This was an intriguing offer. No one in Judah had ever before gone so far. "Rise," he commanded, even going so far as to help the hairy man to his feet. He kissed those hairy cheeks, unbothered by the grisly bristles. "Blessed be you of the LORD for you have compassion on me." He meant it too. For too long had the elders of Judah subtly defied him. To find one willing to help end the source of all his problems nearly brought tears to his eyes. Perhaps the LORD was not yet finished with him. Perhaps he had at last regained Jehovah's favor.

"Thank you, my lord," Haroeh replied, his eyes filled with wonder.

"Go," Saul said softly, looking the elder in the eyes. "Go, I pray you, and prepare for my coming. Find where he hides himself, discover those who aid him yet. It has been told me that he deals very subtly. Take knowledge of all his hiding places, and when you know of a certainty where he is, return here to me, and I will come down with you."[5] Saul spun around and strode back to his chair, his body quivering with the hope and possibilities that the LORD hadn't yet forsaken him completely.

When he turned around, the elders were still there, their leader looking unsure. "You may go," he said as he sat, straightening his tunic. He rarely wore his royal robes these days, knowing that at any moment he might be called to take the field. "Hold," he commanded, freezing the Ziph elders in place as they were backing toward the door. "One thing more. When I come down to you, I will seek David wherever he may be, even if I must search throughout all the thousands of Judah." He stared at the Ziphites, letting his implied threat sink in. Satisfied that he had made his point, he leaned back and closed his eyes, effectively dismissing the delegation.

Soon, he thought, *soon I will have David in hand at last.* He could hardly contain his glee over the thought and over the idea that the tribe of Judah would be the instrument of David's downfall. He rubbed his eyes, trying to work some of the strain out of them. He knew how he looked—hollow-eyed, sunken cheeks, and skin a clammy-looking pale yellow. He knew, but he also knew that it would all turn around once David was dead and his kingdom secure.

He heard the door close behind the elders of Ziph, and he snapped his eyes open. "Abner," he called to his cousin, "heard you what the Ziphites said?"

"I did, my lord," the humorless general answered. He moved around to face his king, the weathered and darkened skin was beginning to loosen around the general's face and his hair now had speckles of gray in the short curly locks that peeked out from under the man's turban. Yet the man remained a formidable presence, and he could intimidate a mountain if he set his mind to do so.

"Gather the men. We will follow behind the Ziphites and be ready to snare the son of Jesse once they learn what hill or cave he haunts."[6]

---

[5] 1 Samuel 23:20-23.
[6] 1 Samuel 23:25.

Abner bowed. "As you command, my king."

Saul detected a sliver of doubt in his commander's voice, though nothing in the other's face gave anything away. "You have ought to say?"

Abner's face remained blank, but after a long moment, he ventured to say, "I fear only these reports that the Philistines are stirring. They like not that they were turned back at Keilah. I think they may try to strike again—and soon."

Saul nodded. "We have nothing to fear from the Philistines. They are weakened and distressed. They will cause us no worry."

"What if they learn that you have gone south to search out the son of Jesse? Will they not see an opportunity to strike to the north?"

The king growled low in his throat. "The Philistines will not bestir themselves, Cousin. Let your mind be at ease on that. The son of Jesse is the one who must concern us. See to the muster of the troops. We march on the morrow."

Abner bowed. "As you command, my lord." Spinning on heel, he marched to the door as if setting forth to do battle.

Saul watched him go. He then summoned his scribes, needing to record some of his thoughts and to send out orders to various garrisons throughout the land. Soon though, David would be undone, and Saul would find peace at last.

5

Picking his way around the broken rocks of the mountain slope, David eased along the edge of the ravine, moving toward his furthest outpost. For the last several days, he had been restless and irritable. He had tried playing his harp and singing praises to Elohim, but his frustration remained. He didn't like this hiding at the edge of the desert. He didn't like the murmurings and black looks that were hurled at him from every direction like spears whose barbs stabbed at his mind instead of flesh. And most of all, he didn't like being here while Ahinoam, the woman who had so ensnared his mind and imagination, remained yet in Ziph.

He had made up his mind to take her for his wife. Finding the best way to make it so was all that remained. Unlike Michal, whom he had wanted mostly because the marriage would bring him closer to King Saul and Jonathan, Ahinoam had no such ties that would prove beneficial. She was simply beautiful. And meek. He had seen that latter quality right away—so in contrast to his wife Michal—that he instantly felt drawn to Ahinoam.

Thus, his need to be alone. He had slipped out of camp and made his way toward the furthest watch post that protected one of the avenues of approach to the main encampment. He needed to be away, to think, to gather himself. Mostly, he just needed to be doing something before his restlessness consumed him.

He made his way over the rocky soil, making little effort to conceal his approach, but was nevertheless gratified when his sentry stepped out behind a short tree and took aim at him with bow and arrow. "Halt and be recognized," the guard challenged, his voice carrying just loud enough to reach David.

David would need to commend Joab. The young man had chosen the sentries well. More and more, he was coming to rely upon Joab. His nephew had a head for tactics and an ability to make split-second decisions under tremendous stress—and usually make the correct one.

"Well done," he replied. "Your caution does you credit." David moved closer, and the sentry lowered his bow with a start.

"My lord David! Forgive me. The sun behind you has shadowed your face. I knew you not in the bad light."

"Be at peace. You did rightly." Some of the tension seeped out of the sentry's shoulders. "You are Shallum, son of Joshah, are you not?"

The slender sentry drew himself up. "I am, my lord."

"How goes your watch, Shallum?"

"All is quiet thus far. No one has ventured this direction."

"Then you have seen others?"

The sentry frowned. "Only those traveling south. One or two north."

All thoughts of being alone fled David's mind. "Show me where."

Without hesitation, the sentry turned and moved catlike through the sparse trees toward the edge of the rocky peak that had been chosen as his outpost. David followed, wary of where he placed his feet to make as little noise as possible. The scout's news was worrisome. This watch post was set right at the edge of the Jeshimon desert. Small trees grew along the crest of the ridges, their boles and roots twisted and intertwined around the rocks.

When they reached the crest, they carefully moved around a boulder to slip into its shadow where they would be hidden from all but the sharpest of eyes. To the west, David could see lazy smoke that drifted up from cookfires to mingle with the thin layer of broken clouds that stained the morning sky. The sentry pointed at the smoke. "Ziph lies there, my lord."

"Where have you seen these travelers?"

Pointing, the sentry said, "They come down from the hills there and walk south, skirting the desert and then moving toward Ziph."

David considered. "Yet that is not an established route. I expected no movement here. What manner of men and women were they?"

"Men alone, my lord. They were dressed as farmers or shepherds."

"Do their flocks follow?"

"Nay. They come and go in twos and threes."

David studied the empty landscape before him. Finally, he turned to the sentry. "We are discovered."

"How so, my lord? No one has ventured in this direction."

"They do not wish for you to know," David said absently, looking more closely at the folds in the land. There was still enough cover to hide spies, and he felt sure some lurked where he could not see. He also believed they knew exactly where David's sentries were. But who were they? Saul's men? He ran his finger down the scar that dominated the left side of his face. Had Saul found him at last? It seemed impossible. As far as he knew, Saul had returned to Gibeah, and he had not heard any rumors that he had stirred himself to leave.

The sentry had been studying the terrain. "Are you sure of this, my lord? I still see nothing."

"Come. Let us put it to the test." Making no effort to stay hidden, David moved out of the shadow of the bolder and retreated toward the Hachilah encampment, the sentry following, bafflement plastered all over his face.

David moved quickly, forcing the sentry to trot just to keep up. Together they wound around the hill crest and set off along the top of a ridge. David could feel eyes on him, like an itch he couldn't reach between his shoulder blades. They arrived at the end of the ridge where it dipped down toward a gorge. The trees continued to thin here and hardly any grew along the next ridge over. Lizards scurried out of their way, and he even spotted a scorpion that scuttled quickly beneath a rock.

The path here cut steeply down to the bottom of the ravine. From there, they would follow the path through the gorges for a way before climbing back up to the top of the broken ridges. David started down, but he didn't go far, just enough so that he and the sentry disappeared from the view of anyone watching from behind.

Motioning the sentry behind another rock, he moved as close to the crest of the ridge as he could and lay down, waiting. To be seen here, someone would have to come right to the edge, close enough for David to apprehend.

They waited. Combat, David had discovered, was mostly waiting, interspersed with frantic moments of panic-induced melee where the fog of battle often created more confusion than actual combat. Thus, he had learned to be patient, slowly tensing his muscles and then relaxing them so they would stay loose and ready for that moment when action was required.

In this case, he knew that the spies watching this outpost would be cautious, also patient. The victors in many a contest often went to the one who could outwait the other. The difference here was that he knew he was being spied upon, but the spies, though they might suspect that David knew of their presence, could not be certain. At some point, they would come to see.

He grew uncomfortable as the sun rose higher in the sky, sucking the coolness from the ground and heating the air. David began to sweat, but he held himself rigidly still, listening for the telltale signs that someone was approaching the ridge crest.

A lizard, mistaking him for another rock, scurried over his body and disappeared into a crack between two stones. David didn't so much as twitch, continuing his ritual of slowly tensing his muscles and then relaxing them. The sentry, well-disciplined himself, remained crouched behind his rock, eyes on David as often as he searched his surroundings. Despite that, David could feel the man's nervousness.

After what seemed like hours, but was likely only minutes, David heard the scuffing sound of sandals slapping against rock, moving closer. Still he waited. Whoever approached had enough sense not to dart ahead and expose himself, but based on the amount of noise he made, David didn't think the man could be too practiced in the art of stealth—so likely not a warrior or one of King Saul's scouts, but a spy nonetheless.

Peering upward, David waited. When the top of a turban became visible to David, he launched himself forward as if from a sling. One moment he lay perfectly still along the path, and the next he was on his feet, charging up the short distance to the crest of the ridge.

The spy never had a chance. David hit him hard before he could even register the danger. With a startled cry, half of pain, half of fright, the man flew backward to land with a heavy grunt among the rocks of the ridge. Instantly, David stood above him, sword drawn, and the point poised over the hapless man's neck.

"Declare yourself," David hissed, anger at being right, that they had been discovered, bleeding from his very pores.

The man's eyes bulged, locked fearfully on the sword held rock still above his neck. A shepherd by the look of his dress, a graying beard, and an impressive number of wrinkles that lined his sun-worn face, David put the man in his middle years. Certainly, no warrior.

"Answer," David barked.

The man flinched, eyes widening. Recognition stained his face. "I am Reaiah, son of Zereth, a shepherd, my lord."

David's eyes glittered, weighing the words. "And what do you here? Speak truly, graybeard, for I will know if falsehood escapes your lips."

Swallowing, the man nearly nodded, but caught himself lest he accidently impale himself on David's sword. "I am a man of Ziph, my lord, set to watch this spot, to see what your man does and where he goes, and to report any comings and goings."

"To whom?"

"The elders of Ziph, my lord."

Anger continued to rise within David's breast, threatening to carry him away as a sudden storm does a fallen leaf. If he understood the spy's words aright, he and his men had been betrayed by the elders of Ziph. David's grip on his sword tightened to the point where his knuckles turned white and the tip quivered, brushing the spy's neck ever so lightly.

The spy paled. "Mercy, my lord! Mercy!"

"The elders seek to deliver me into King Saul's hands." It wasn't a question.

"Aye. The king comes with three thousand men."

"Where?"

"They are here, my lord! Even now they move through the gorges and ravines. They seek to entrap you at Hachilah."[1]

Despite the rising temperature, David's body turned ice cold. Trapped! Betrayed! White rage roared into being, brought to life by his incessant irritation and frustration over the circumstances that constantly conspired against him.

Without further thought, he plunged his sword into the spy's neck. The man's eyes went wide in disbelief, but then they drained of life as his blood poured out upon the sand and rock. David stared at the blood staining the ground, staining his soul. Despite his vow not to take the life of any Hebrew, he had just done so, and not just any Hebrew, a man of Judah, one of his own tribe.

He backed away, stumbling in his haste to put distance between him and the dead man, but the stain upon his soul followed him, mocked his vow, mocked his faith in his God.

Shallum caught David lest he fall into the ravine. "My lord," the scout said, his voice sounding higher than normal, "what are we to do? The king is upon us!"

The king. King Saul. Here. Betrayed by the Ziphites.

David fell to his knees, tears already leaving trails in the dust that coated his face. He was surrounded and betrayed, and the stain on his own soul throbbed like a spasming muscle. Unable to contain

---

[1] 1 Samuel 23:24.

himself, he cried out to his God, "Save me, O God, by Your name, and judge me by Your strength. Hear my prayer, O God; give ear to the words of my mouth, for strangers are risen up against me, and oppressors seek after my soul."[2]

The words rang in his ears and heart. At other times, such words had come, filled with the Spirit of the LORD and driven deep into his mind, heart, and soul. He would remember them for the rest of his life.

"Will we then be delivered?" Shallum asked, hope and fervor burning in his eyes.

"They have not set God before them," David affirmed, and seeing this man…this man who had put his entire life and future in David's hands, he felt the need to add, "Behold, God is my helper, and the LORD is with them that uphold my soul." Standing, he placed his hand on the man's arm. "He shall reward evil unto my enemies and cut them off in His truth."[3]

The words did something to the scout, infusing him with confidence and strength. But for David, they meant something more—something profound. Later, he vowed, he would deliver the words to a musician. This prayer would need to be remembered.

His eyes sought and found the dead Ziphite again. The man's face would haunt him for the rest of his life. *Reaiah, son of Zereth.* David shook himself, ripping his mind from the dead man at his feet and turning it to the more immediate problem. It cost him to do this, to put aside his guilt for what he'd done, to harden his heart against this atrocity of taking a Hebrew life. But if he failed to act now, he would condemn his men and himself to death.

"Make haste," he whispered to the scout. "We must make haste."

Spinning, he began to run. He honestly didn't know if he was running to or from something. He didn't look back, didn't know if his scout followed. He fixed his eyes forward. He had to return to his troop.

---

[2] Psalm 54:1-3.
[3] Psalm 54:4-5.

David never remembered the run back to Hachilah. The hill, sitting within the boundaries of the Jeshimon desert, was also part of the Maon wilderness. Maon—his dead brother's name. A small town near Ziph also claimed that name. All other rational thought fled David's mind. If he could get to his men, perhaps he could slip them out to the west before Saul's soldiers attacked. He could flee through the Maon wilderness, perhaps even lose himself in the mountainous region farther to the west.

Perhaps.

A shouted challenge brought David back to himself. He looked up, startled to discover that he had somehow already reached the encampment. Adino, leaning on his spear, his eyes looking half asleep, stood before him. David had to slam to a stop to avoid running over his commander.

"Rouse the men!" he shouted. "The king is upon us!"

Tents littered the hilltop, scattered among the rocks and sand like so much debris after a frightful storm. The hill formed a narrow wedge between two steep ravines and with only one route that provided ease of access to the top of the hill. The point of the wedge dropped away into a steep canyon, choked with low-growing shrubs and sharp rocks. When it rained, the water would run down off the higher elevations to the west and carve its way through the narrow canyons and empty out into the Salt Sea to the east. But the terrain only offered one clear accessible route to the hilltop and that was at the base of the wedge toward the north.

At David's cry, men stopped what they were doing and stared at him. For a moment, he couldn't fathom why everyone wasn't as frantic as he. King Saul was here! Why wasn't everyone scurrying about like ants to get away?

Adino hadn't so much as twitched, continuing to lean against the weapon that had become his namesake. "What is this, my lord? Do you jest?"

"We are betrayed," David roared, his voice carrying easily to the farthest part of the camp. "The Ziphites have delivered us into the hand of the king. We must flee!"

A shout from behind David spun him around. The scout with whom David had returned had lagged significantly behind, unable to keep up with his lord's punishing pace. The route they had taken had forced them to wind through the ravines and up and down several more. The scout had just begun his ascent from the bottom of the ravine, picking his way carefully around boulders and other obstacles.

The shout had come from beyond him. A score of men appeared from the rocks and low shrubs as if conjured. They all carried the short bows favored by King Saul's warriors. Taking aim, they let loose with a volley that arched into the late morning light. The scout never had a chance. Three of the arrows pieced him, and he fell without making a sound.

His men began to shout then, scrambling for weapons and issuing orders to wives and children. David, his heart thumping mightily against his chest, spun away from Shallum's body and began trying to organize his troop before all was lost.

Joab and Eleazar ran up to him. "More are cresting the next hill to the west," Joab reported. He swore then, his face angry.

David turned on his nephew violently. "Do not speak in vanity!" he hissed. "We must trust in the LORD to see us through, but do not let such profane words stain your tongue again!"

Joab's flat face went rigid. "The LORD is not with us, else we would not have been betrayed."

David struck him then, knocking his nephew backward. Joab staggered, his face betraying shock and not a little hurt. David followed him, moving in like a cat. "Do not speak so, my nephew. The actions of men are not the LORD'S doing. We must keep faith."

The young man returned David's glare, but meekly asked, "What would you have us do?"

David tried to regain control of his anger, but he lacked the willpower just then. "Gather the men. We will need to head north."

"Saul's men approach the height," Eleazar said, pointing. "We have only a few minutes before we are surrounded."

"Leave the tents!" David roared. "Abandon the supplies. We must flee."

The seriousness of the situation finally sunk in, and women trying to strike their tents left off and began gathering in a loose circle, herding the smaller children into the center. His men were strung out, uncoordinated and disjointed in their efforts to confront Saul's men.

And from further to the north, a squad of warriors breached the ravine and moved onto the wider part of the wedge, cutting off David's escape route. He swallowed and wondered if his nephew didn't have it right. Had God abandoned them?

The thought shook him, and he mentally clawed at this failing faith, trying to preserve some measure of it. "Abiathar, Gad!" he yelled, turning around in circles to try and spot the priest and prophet. They hurried over to him. "Seek Jehovah," he begged them. "Seek for our deliverance or all is lost!"

He meant it too. More warriors made it up the ravine to stand between David and his only real escape route. If the LORD did not intervene, David would have to stand and fight. He was outnumbered more than five to one, and unless something happened soon, Hebrew would be slaughtering Hebrew.

He thought of the Ziphite he had already killed in his anger. Was this then punishment? He did not know. Straightening his shoulders, he drew his sword and began barking orders. They would try to break away to the north of the hill. There was a narrow trail that led south, but only a few could take it at a time. Their only real chance was north. The bulk of Saul's army had yet to reach favorable ground as they struggled to transverse the ravine to the west. Sun glinted off metal shields, swords and spear points, but as of yet, only a handful of Saul's men stood in the way. That would change soon. He would need to strike now if he wanted to have any hope of breaking out before Saul could bring the full might of his army down upon David.

"Come," he said softly to Adino, Eleazar, and Joab. "Let us see whether God will deliver us."

Saul's grin, the first in a long while, would not leave his face. He could see David, and he knew his enemy was trapped. Trapped at last! And soon to be dead. There would be no escape this time. Jehovah had at last delivered the son of Jesse into his hands. He clenched his hands, looking at them and imagining them around the other's neck.

Glancing up, he fastened eyes on his enemy. No longer was David the hapless shepherd from Bethlehem, wide-eyed, and eager to please. He had become a warrior true, a worthy enemy indeed. Saul watched as David rallied his men to him, enraged that any Hebrew would have chosen to follow the son of Jesse instead of showing the proper loyalty to their king—a king chosen and ordained by Jehovah.

Abner stood beside Saul, as still as a rock, his face showing nothing. His commanders knew what to do. There was no need to be personally involved with the kill.

Then Abner spoke, his voice sounding as if he'd been practicing chewing rocks. "A messenger, my lord."

It took long heartbeats before the words registered in Saul's ears, and instantly a moment's disquiet speared his heart. No. He turned to see a young man, dressed in worn leather armor stumble to a stop, his breath coming in ragged gasps, and Saul didn't think he'd ever seen someone so red in the face.

"My lord!" The scout fell upon his face, his harsh breathing sucking in dust and dirt and blowing it out again in small puffs.

Abner stepped close. "What word do you bring the king?"

"The Philistines, my lord! They invade!"[4]

Saul felt his heart drop into his stomach, and he flinched as if the words were bee stings. Abner saw it and understood. He dragged the man to his feet and shook him. "How know you this?"

---

[4] 1 Samuel 23:27.

The scout gaped like a fish pulled from the water. "I beheld them, my lord. They strike directly for Gibeah!"

No.

Saul felt all his strength leave him in a single moment. If the Philistines had struck anywhere else, anywhere at all, he might have been able to ignore it, at least for a time. But not Gibeah. Not his home. Not Benjamin.

"This cannot be," Saul whispered into the air. He turned to look at the hill across the ravine. David's men were gathering, preparing to make an obvious push north to try and break through Saul's lines. Little did the son of Jesse know that another force, much larger, was already moving down from the north. David was cut off. Trapped.

The scout, taking Saul's words at face value, ventured to say, "The Philistines come in force, my lord. They must know you have left the city."

"Betrayed then," Saul hissed, his anger swirling through him like a whirlwind. "I will not be undone! I will see David dead!"

Abner, his stoicism broken for once, said, "And what of Gibeah? What of our home?"

Saul understood. He had no choice. If he was to intercept the Philistines, he would need to leave at once. David would not be put down easily. He had only six hundred men, but it would take time, time Saul didn't have.

"Call the men," the king said, sounding for all the world like a man stricken with a fever. "We march immediately. For home."[5]

Abner nodded to his armorbearer. The young man put a horn to his lips, a long ram's horn twisted and purple with age, and blew a long, deep blast. He paused for a count of five and then blew it again. Once more he blew it, and Saul watched in despair as his men turned immediately in obedience to the prearranged command and began moving swiftly back toward where Saul had set up his watch post.

---

[5] 1 Samuel 23:28.

In no time at all, David and his men had been abandoned to their own fate. For now. Soon Saul's commanders began gathering around the king. In precise words, Saul gave the command to begin the march back toward Gibeah and to intercept the Philistines. He gave David one last look.

The son of Jesse was staring across the ravine, having finally picked Saul out on the opposite slope. They locked gazes then, and for a moment, Saul felt a connection with David. Saul remembered then a time when only a few men had followed him, when he was beset upon every side with enemies and disbelievers.[6] Only after the defeat of Nahash the Ammonite had Israel turned to him fully.[7] A thought then struck Saul so hard he had to stand fast as the world spun around him. Was he, King Saul, David's Nahash? No, he would not let it. David, for all his prowess as a warrior, would die. Only then would the kingdom be strengthened, and Saul's line assured.

All of this was conveyed in a single stare. David, sensing some of it, still managed a deep bow, a gesture of respect for a respected enemy.

Turning away, Saul said to Abner. "Let us go. We will destroy the Philistines and then seek the son of Jesse to slay him. He cannot hide for long."

Abner made a hand gesture, and his commanders began barking orders. Soon, they melted away, leaving the desert to David and his men.

---

[6] 1 Samuel 10:26-27.
[7] 1 Samuel 11.

6

D avid could hardly believe his eyes. He stood rooted in place, staring across the ravine to the other slope to the spot King Saul had recently vacated, as if by staring at it, he could force it to provide answers.

Joab moved up to stand next to his uncle. "My lord, why has the king abandoned the attack?"

David's other commanders, confusion evident in their eyes, gathered about. "We were surrounded," Eleazar muttered. "Did I not say coming here was a mistake? Did I not say the king would find us?"

"Yet young Joab has it right," Shammah rumbled, the beads in his beard knocking together as he ran a hand through the hair. "We were surrounded. We were in the hand of the king. It is a deception."

Slowly, the rest of David's men began crowding close, weapons still firmly grasped and at the ready, eyes darting around, not fully accepting that the king had abandoned the field. David turned to look at them. Confusion and relief battled for supremacy on their faces. Elhanan, Uriah, Asahel, Abishai, and so many more all looked to David, waiting for him to speak.

David knew he had to say something, so casting about, he found a boulder he could clamber up upon and stood above the people. He surveyed them again, noticing Gad and Abiathar watching from the outer fringe of the crowd. Women and children also gathered about, moving in behind the men, all eyes lifted to David.

David spoke, lifting up his voice to be heard by all, "From henceforth, let this rock be known as Selahammahlekoth.[1] For here is a place of division with the king on one side and we on the other. I know not why the king has turned back from pursuing us, but it is clear: Jehovah has delivered us from the king's hands. Give praise to His name, Hebrews. This day, God has heard our prayer and seen our plight. Only the hand of Jehovah could turn aside the king's wrath. Rejoice, my countrymen! Rejoice in the LORD our God!"

A ragged cheer went up in response, though many of the men continued to emit confusion. Then Shobal pushed his way through the crowd, and men making way for him. His unhappy face was twisted with some unknowable emotion that acted like a battering ram. "Where do we go now?" he demanded. "The king knows our hiding place. Does anyone here truly believe that he will not come again? Surely, this is a trick, a trap. We trusted in you, my lord, and you have led us to this end. What now?"

A spike of anger sliced deep into David's brain. The insult was clear, and David saw Joab's flat face flushing with indignation, which mollified David a little. Lifting his hand to forestall his nephew from doing something foolish, he turned to Gad and Abiathar. "What say you? What says the priest of the LORD? The LORD's prophet?"

The young priest shook his head. "The LORD has not spoken to me. Do what is right in your own eyes, my lord."

David's face tightened. He didn't want to hear that, and the murmuring of the men simply increased. He looked at Gad hopefully.

The grinning prophet rubbed an ear, his face twisted in obvious thought. Finally, he lifted up his voice and said, "I once had a neighbor, a shepherd of truly unremarkable and lazy reputation. Yet he had in his flocks a most remarkable and cunning ewe. Contrary to its typical nature, this ewe possessed unusual wisdom for a sheep.

---

[1] 1 Samuel 23:28.

She would never stray far from her shepherd, knowing well that greater safety lay in the shepherd's hand than in wandering afar. When danger presented itself, she would flee to her shepherd while the other sheep scattered in panic." Gad paused and the silence was deafening. The prophet held everyone in his hand. "One day a lion sought to make a meal of this cunning ewe and she, as was her want, hastened to her shepherd for protection. Howsoever, my neighbor, being slothful, had fallen asleep and was not aware of the danger and so could not protect the ewe." He fell still then, a hint of his grin twisting his upper lip.

Shobal, his eyes glazed over in confusion, glared at the prophet. "What words are these, seer? Did the ewe then perish for the foolishness of the shepherd? Is this your moral?"

"Nay," Gad replied, "the cunning ewe, in her wisdom, hastened to the shepherd where the lion discovered a larger meal at hand, one not prepared to flee. It was not the ewe who perished, but my slothful neighbor. The ewe lives still."

David idly noted that so far, all of Gad's stories involved a lion. He wondered why that was. Shaking his head, he tried to understand the purpose of the story, to gain the wisdom that the prophet was trying to impart, but much like his first story, David could not grasp the full sense of it. "Am I the shepherd or the ewe in your tale," David inquired.

Gad shrugged. "You are a man."

That was hardly helpful. Yet there must lie some wisdom in the seer's words. Joab, obviously as perplexed as any, confronted the prophet. "Your words hint that we must sacrifice our lord to protect the rest of us from the king!" David's nephew studied the prophet's face, trying to read sense in the widening grin of the seer.

"I am an advocate of wisdom, young Joab," Gad countered.

Adino roused himself enough to look interested. "Then you propose that we flee somewhere that will distract the king, that will set him upon a new target. We, all of us, are the ewe then."

"Only if King Saul is the lion," Shammah rumbled. "Perhaps we are the lion, and it is we who chase after the wrong prey. We chase the ewe when it is the shepherd we should seek. Mayhap the king is the shepherd."

Arguments sprang up like weeds after a spring rain. Some thought as Shammah did and others as Adino. A few, with dark looks, obviously were considering Joab's words that safety lay only in giving up David. That so many different understandings could come from one simple story amazed David. He realized then that this was likely Gad's intent. By offering up such a tale, he had invariably focused everyone's thoughts on an action. The true moral, David supposed, was in the danger of doing nothing. The ewe had fled and found safety. The shepherd had allowed slothfulness to lull him into the jaws of the lion. Inaction was more dangerous than action. He had to decide, to give his men a focus, a goal.

Deciding abruptly, he raised his hands calling for silence. The noise died away as everyone turned to look at him. "We must leave here," he said, making sure everyone could hear. "We will go where the king will least expect." He pointed toward the east. "We will cross Jeshimon to the Salt Sea. There are springs at a place called Engedi that will sustain us.[2] We will go there for the king will not expect us to challenge the desert. He will look for us in places where we will not be."

"This is folly," Shobal protested. "We will perish in the desert."

"Nay," David replied firmly. He jumped down off the rock and moved forcibly toward the stalky man who dared challenge him. "It will be our deliverance. We will perish if we remain." David lowered his voice, moving right up to Shobal and pushing him back with the mere force of his presence. "Speak no more of folly lest your words discourage the people. I give you this one warning. Speak not again."

Shobal's close-set brown eyes widened as he realized David's intent, and he backed away to put himself beyond David's reach. "As you will, my lord," he said, offering a stiff half bow.

Turning away in disgust, David spoke to his commanders. "Gather our supplies and equipment. In one hour, we must begin

---

[2] 1 Samuel 23:29.

our march. Give thought to the women and children, for I will leave no one behind." He hesitated. "And fetch Shallum's body. I would not leave him for the scavengers." But with the scout's death, David was forced to realize that no one knew he had killed the Ziphite spy. Except for Jehovah, whose eyes saw everything. He turned to Asahel, Joab's youngest brother. "Asahel, my nephew, you are the fleetest among us. Run ahead. Find safe passage through the desert." He placed a hand on the slender young man's shoulder. "In this, I rely upon you."

The lad's eyes lit up, and his body quivered with energy. "I will not fail you, my lord."

"Then go. Mark the path. Lead us to Engedi." David watched the lad scamper off, his feet hardly touching the ground as he raced to gather up a few supplies.

Everyone scattered then, preparing as best they could for the journey through the desert and leaving David alone, an island atop the Hachilah hill in plain view of everyone, yet isolated from each. He stared off into the distance. Dark clouds were gathering to the west, driven in off the Great Sea. They were entering the rainy season. The hot, dry summer had passed, and winter's approach heralded a change in weather.

He didn't like the looks of the clouds. Storms often broke against the mountain range, lashing the peaks and hills with terrible force, but breaking before it could descend upon the Jeshimon desert. Yet rainfall in the Judean mountains brought its own kind of danger to the desert canyons and ravines. David's troop would need to be quick to avoid them.

Asahel had marked the way across the desert, and as David had known it would, the path tended to follow the dry riverbeds at the bottom of the steep gorges that cut their way down toward the Salt Sea and Engedi. It was by far the easiest way to travel the desert. Trying to travel over the top of the canyons would have cost too much time, turning a journey of a day or two into something much longer.

They hadn't gotten truly started until sometime after midday, and that meant they were now in the last watch of the day. They would need to spend the night in the desert, not a prospect he relished, but one he had known was inevitable.

The troop, over a thousand strong with six hundred fighting men at its core, was strung out behind him. The men had the task of protecting the women, children, and aiding the aged, but the charge slowed everyone down, and night loomed close at hand.

"Joab," he called back to his nephew, "search out a place that we may spend the night. Choose high ground away from the ravines."

Joab bowed, but looked doubtfully at the steep walls of the canyon on both sides of him. "There is no easy passage behind. Perhaps up ahead."

David nodded. "Make haste," he said softly for his nephew's ears alone. "I would not much like to be caught down here at nightfall."

"I understand," Joab acknowledged. He plowed ahead, his heavy body churning up the ground like a bull, leaping from rock to rock heavily, but with the unbounded energy of youth.

David watched him go. Asahel remained up ahead somewhere. Hopefully the young man had enough sense to turn back as darkness began to descend. The sun had long disappeared behind the dark clouds to the west, casting everything in shade and shadow. He knew what it meant. Rain was falling on the Judean mountains and soon water would be rushing down the ravines on its way toward the Salt Sea. The rocks around him were stained darker gray from previous flashfloods, scoured clean as a testament to the violence of the water. He did not want to be caught down here when that happened.

He glanced back at the string of men and women following him down the canyon. Shammah brought up the rear, herding everyone ahead of him as a sheepdog would his sheep. Adino and Eleazar helped control the center and David and Joab led. Others of David's trusted inner circle were scattered throughout the troop, lending aid where needed. Not far behind, walking together, were two of

David's older brothers, Eliab and Abinadab. The rest of his brothers were in Moab with his parents. Abinadab had chosen to follow David from Moab while Eliab had caught up to them later with two of his older sons, more of David's nephews.

David was surprised at the number of his nephews who had come to him. He had family here, though he was growing closest to his sister's sons, Joab, Abishai, and Asahel, than to the rest. Eliab, his brother, was a warrior true, but David would always remember how his oldest brother had scorned him when he had wanted to challenge Goliath. They had never spoken of it again, but the memory of it had not died completely. Abinadab was a leader, a man people easily followed and trusted. He commanded a portion of David's men, and David felt confident he could rely upon his brother. But his brothers would never become the core of David's inner circle. To that privilege went younger men, such as those who had fought with him when he was captain over the Indebted— though others, such as his nephews and men like Uriah, Elhanan, Benaiah, and more, were becoming more and more a part of the men David relied upon the most. They were mighty men of valor, each and every one, and he had even heard rumors that they were calling themselves David's Mighty Men.

A shout was raised from back within the canyon, echoing eerily off the walls and carrying far on down past David. He spun to look and saw everyone scrambling up the cliff face, searching for higher ground, using whatever was at hand to move as high as possible.

"A flood!" Eliab roared in warning, dashing for the side of the ravine. "Get clear!"

David paled, his worst fear coming to life. He scanned the side of the canyon, spotting a faint trail that was likely used by desert foxes and ibex to scale the steep sides. "There!" he called, pointing. Everyone not already doing so, rushed to get away from the dry riverbed that ran along the bottom of the ravine.

David sprinted to the trail. It was little more than a narrow tract that required four feet or hooves to navigate safely, but it was all they had. He urged Eliab and Abinadab up, looking nervously back up the ravine. He could hear it now, a roaring sound of water being compressed through the narrow canyon, a wave of death that not even the hardiest could withstand.

He took an extra precious moment to scan for anyone not safely away but saw no one. Hopefully, everyone had gotten clear.

"David!" Abinadab shouted from his precarious position farther up the trail, "climb!"

Reacting on instinct, David scrambled up the trail on all four. Ahead, his brother and nephew were clinging to shrubs some fifteen cubits up from the canyon floor. The low-growing bush was the only thing that grew in the desert, protected from the sun by the steep walls in the summer and high enough not to be swept away by the periodic flashflood.

David made it about ten cubits before a wall of water shot out of the mouth of the ravine from behind and crashed into the side of the cliff with enough force that David felt the rock walls quiver in response. The roar was deafening. The water rebounded, turning on itself and rushed forward with tremendous speed, mad with power, brown with dirt, and speckled with debris that could impale a man as surely as a spear could.

David instantly realized he wasn't high enough. With a desperate cry to Jehovah, he flung himself up the faint trail, bruising knuckles and scraping his hands on the sharp rocks. He leaped at the last moment and grabbed a rocky ledge. And not a moment too soon. The wall of water shot by, the spray soaking David and the swell of the initial wave reaching high to tug at his sandals. The narrow path he had climbed was obliterated, and David lost the bit of purchase his feet had.

He screamed in denial and defiance as the water snatched powerfully at his legs and tried to carry him with it. Only the hardiness of the rock he clung to kept him from being swept away. As it was, the force nearly wrenched his arms from their sockets. Pain lanced through his body, and he felt the skin of his calves lacerated, cut by debris and rock.

Then the initial swell passed, and the muddy water rushed by, if not with less rage then with a bit less momentum. The water level dropped abruptly, leaving only his feet being tugged by the rapidly moving water. His arms continued to ache in protest, but he had nothing to which he could stand upon. The path was gone. Tightening his lips, David held grimly on.

"Hang on!" Abinadab ordered from higher up. His brother's body was spotted with mud, camouflaging him against the cliff face. He lowered himself down to David, extending a mud-speckled sandaled foot. "Grab on!"

David measured the distance. If he could pull himself up a bit, he might be able to grab the laces that were wrapped around his brother's foot and ankle. It would take a mighty effort. The water continued to pull at him. Pulling his body out by his arms, which were now quivering with pain and effort, might be more than he could manage.

Just when he had determined to make a try, something slammed into his legs with enough force that he nearly lost his grip on the rocky ledge. He grunted as his arms screamed in pain and tears sprang to his eyes. He glanced down and tried to blink away the tears.

A girl, perhaps twelve years of age, clung to his feet, her fingers twined into the laces of his sandals. She must have been swept down from farther up the ravine and come close enough to David to grab hold. He recognized her, having seen her around camp. She was the daughter of Eliam, the son of Ahithophel.[3] David knew Eliam to be a stout warrior and a loyal man, one who could be trusted. But for the life of him, he could not remember his daughter's name.

"Do not let go," he called to her. He swallowed against the extra strain that the drag on the girl was producing. Her whole body was in the water except her head, and even then, the water would periodically crest to cover her chin and mouth, forcing her to spit out muddy water.

---

[3] 2 Samuel 11:3; 2 Samuel 23:34.

The girl's heart-shaped face and large, green eyes stared at him in something close to panic. Yet the girl didn't make so much as a sound as she clung to his legs.

Determining that she would not let go, David looked back up at Abinadab and Eliab. "Lend me aid," he shouted above the roar of the rushing water. "I cannot hold on much longer!"

"By Abraham's beard," Abinadab muttered, "you cause more problems!" He turned to Eliab who was perched higher up the trail. "You must use me as a ladder and fetch the girl. We can't pull David up until we get the girl clear of the water."

Eliab understood instantly. He quickly scrambled down and over Abinadab, who grunted when a knee or elbow found a tender spot. David's oldest brother clamored down, using rocks and bushes to help him descend. He then reached down and grasped David's left wrist firmly.

"See if you can reach the girl now," his brother said.

Trusting that Eliab would not let go, David reached down with his right hand, stretching as far as he could, but the girl remained beyond his grasp.

The strain on his left arm increased, and David gritted his teeth tightly against the resulting pain. "You must reach," he shouted down to the girl. "You must aid me! Reach!"

The girl stared at him, blinking rapidly to clear the muddy water from her eyes, but her hands remained firmly locked in place, intertwined in the laces of his sandals. He realized then that she couldn't do as he asked. The moment she let go, she would be swept away.

"Hurry!" his eldest brother grunted. "I cannot hold much longer!"

David glanced up. Eliab's face was red underneath the drying mud spots that dotted his face. Knowing that all three of them were in danger of tumbling into the raging waters, David prayed. He called out to Jehovah for strength.

God heard.

Strength flooded into David's muscles, infusing them with a strength that went beyond mortal ability. With a praise to Elohim on his lips, David drew his legs up, dragging the girl up and out of the rushing waters until he could grab her upper arm with his right hand. Taking firm hold, knowing his grip would likely leave bruises on her arm, he pulled.

As soon as she cleared the water, her fingers came loose, and she was free. Abinadab reached down, took the girl and pulled her, dripping, up to the meager safety of the narrow path.

"Move higher," David ordered. He didn't know how much longer the Spirit of the LORD would infuse him, and he wanted to reach higher ground before it gave out and left him weaker than ever.

Eliab let go of David's wrist and scrambled up to join David's other brother and the shivering girl. David rotated, grabbed the rocky ledge with both hands and pulled himself fully out of the water. Reaching up, he found another handhold and slowly climbed to where the others waited, clinging to the narrow ledge that served as a trail.

He reached a spot where he could stand and the Spirit of the LORD departed, taking the supernatural strength with it. Pain replaced strength. His muscles quivered in weakness. Eliab had to reach over and grab David, pulling him close to the cliff face lest he fall back into the raging, foaming waters below.

They stayed like that for a long time. Slowly, as full dark descended upon the land, the waters began to recede. Three hours later, a mellow stream ran down the bottom of the gorge, belying the raging torrents that had nearly killed David and the girl.

During that time, no one said a word. When David judged it safe enough, he slowly made his way back down into the bottom of the gorge, picking his way by the dim light of a crescent moon. Other people began to emerge, coming down from farther up the ravine where they had waited out the flashflood.

Eliam pushed his way forward, his eyes wide in relief and shock when he spotted his daughter next to David. With a cry, he fell down and gathered his daughter to him, crying tears of joy.

"Thank you, my lord!" he whispered to David, looking up over his daughter's muddy hair. "Thank you."

David smiled and knelt down next to father and daughter. "I am glad the LORD delivered us all from the waters. Give praise to Elohim, Eliam, son of Ahithophel. He is worthy."

Eliam nodded, tears still streaming down into his beard. "I will, my lord."

David turned to the girl. "What is your name, lass? I would know it."

She looked up at him with her green eyes and heart-shaped face. She was a beautiful girl, and she would clearly become a beautiful woman. She gave David a tentative smile. "I am Bathsheba," she said shyly. "Thank you for rescuing me, my lord."

David returned the smile and then looked around at the gathering men and women. "Mark who is missing," he said, knowing in his heart that some would have been lost to the flashflood. "We will seek them out, but for now we must find a safe haven."

The words seemed to soothe the fears of those who heard. David learned something then. Even when his own fears and cares threatened to overwhelm him, the people would always look to him for confidence. So, whether or not he had it, he needed to project it. He did so now, and the people rallied to him.

He turned to Abishai who had appeared at his elbow. "Let us find your brothers and let us be gone from this place."

A day later, they reached Engedi.

7

The waters lapped gently against the shore, giving leave to David's pensive and reflective mood. He stood alone upon the shore of the Salt Sea, looking far out across to the distant mountains of Moab. Somewhere over there his parents resided, protected by the king of Moab and giving David one less worry to bear.

He dug his toes into the salt-stained sand along the shore, feeling the warmth spread through the soles of his feet. Heaving a sigh, he marched out into the waters until he stood nearly knee deep in the salty water. He instantly felt the buoyancy the salt afforded the sea. If he flopped into the water, he would float with no effort at all. He dipped a finger in the water and licked it, shuddering at the intensity of the salty taste. The water was no good for drinking, but fortunately, the Engedi oasis had a spring at the top of a gorge that produced enough fresh water to sustain David's group of refugees hiding in various caves that pocked the limestone cliffs along the steep gorge that led down to the Salt Sea.

Ibex were in abundance, the desert goat-like animal grew large enough to feed an entire family for a few days. Shepherds that ranged down the seacoast often stopped at the oasis to water flocks, so barter could be made for sheep and other supplies to keep the people fed. However, it could not last. The oasis could not sustain a thousand people for long. They could wait until winter ended perhaps, at most, but then they would need to find another haven.

They had been ten days at the oasis, and already David was beginning to feel the strain of making their meager supplies last. Already murmurings of discontent had begun to spread about David's decision to cross the desert to Engedi. Four lives had been lost in the flashflood, and the strain of making their supplies last was already beginning to weigh on everyone. Doubtless, King Saul continued to hunt for them, and the constant fear of discovery ate away at everyone's resolve.

And worse, for David at least, was the pull on his heart, like the memory of a pleasant dream that lingered long after waking, of Ahinoam. The memory of the woman burned in his mind. He did not completely understand it. He had longed for other women, but not like this. Before, he had desired a woman because of what the union would bring—the benefits. Thus, it had been with first Merab and then Michal, King Saul's daughters.

Ahinoam was different. He could not shake the memory of her, and he felt compelled to do something about it. And he dared not wait long. A woman like that would not long remain unwed. The problem, of course, was Haroeh, her guardian. The elder of Ziph had to have been complicit in David's betrayal to King Saul. David had thought long and hard about this, and he could see no other possibility. Haroeh had betrayed David. There was no scenario where the elder would willingly give his ward to David to wife.

The betrayal awoke a deep abiding anger within David, and that along with sheer stubbornness would not allow him to barter for Ahinoam. He was trying to find the best way to simply claim her. He did not think Ahinoam would be against the union—not based on the look they had shared. Being David's wife was surely better than being Haroeh's ward—at least to his way of thinking. In truth, taking her away from Haroeh would be more of a rescue.

Still unsure what to do and needing the comfort of his God, David waded back to shore and picked up a borrowed harp. Sitting upon a flat rock and listening to the water lapping gently against the shore, he began to sing: "Be merciful unto me, O God, be merciful unto me: for my soul trusteth in Thee: yea, in the shadow of Thy wings will I make my refuge, until these calamities be overpast. I will cry unto God most high; unto God that performeth all things for me. He shall send from heaven, and save me from the reproach of him that would swallow me up. Selah. God shall send forth His mercy and his truth. My soul is among lions: and I lie even among them that are set on fire, even the sons of men, whose teeth are spears and arrows, and their tongue a sharp sword. Be Thou exalted, O God, above the heavens; let Thy glory be above all the earth."[1]

David paused, overcome with emotion and finding strength and resolve in the praise and worship. It always amazed David how such acts invariably calmed his fears, soothed the aches in his heart, and gave him direction. He sang some more, ending with: "Be Thou exalted, O God, above the heavens: let Thy glory be above all the earth."[2]

He let the music of the final chords drift off over the water. Resolved once again, he stood to his feet. He would send for Ahinoam. He would not go himself. He could not. He must remain at Engedi with the bulk of his men, but he could send someone to fetch her. But who? He ran through a list of the men he could trust with this task, weighing their abilities against Haroeh's possible resistance. One man stood out, one man who could be intimidating without being intimidating. One man who would complete the task without bloodshed, without doing any further damage to David's already marred reputation. David grinned and went in search of his new ambassador.

Haroeh, his long halug tucked between his legs to allow him to run, lumbered heavily toward the city gate, inwardly cursing everyone and everything. When he arrived at the open ground before the gate, he saw he was already too late. Most of the other elders had

---

[1] Psalm 57:1-5 (written when David fled to the cave...though which cave, the one at Adullam or the one at Engedi is debated by Bible scholars).
[2] Psalm 57:11.

arrived before him, the last few straggling in as he had, faces flushed, and fear clearly seared into their eyes.

Three warriors stood just inside the city gate, the one in the middle leaning casually against a well-worn spear. They had appeared as if springing up from the very ground. The watchmen had not seen their approach until they were already at the gate, and that fact alone had shaken Haroeh.

He needed to regain control of the situation immediately. Taking a deep breath to calm his heavy breathing, he let his halug fall around his ankles, adjusted his wide leather belt, and then sat down without so much as a word of greeting—a breech in decorum that the three warriors would not fail to notice. But if he didn't do something, things would quickly be taken out of his hands. The other elders stared at him in shock, hesitated briefly, and then joined him by sitting in a half circle facing the three warriors.

Whatever relief he felt by their compliance was short-lived. Unconsciously, he began pulling at his long nose in irritation. King Saul had failed to destroy David, and the consequences were coming home to roost. His mind worked furiously, and his feet twitched with the desire to move, to pace. He thought better when in motion. Sitting still was not conducive to clear thinking.

The three men standing before the elders possessed the hardness and ruggedness of violent men, warriors, who had seen battle. Two of them were missing fingers, and all bore the scars of their trade—though the one leading looked as if he couldn't be bothered to lift the spear he carried unless forced to it. Haroeh had never seen such a man. The man had to be the thinnest human Haroeh had ever beheld, which, given his own bulk, made Haroeh instantly dislike the fellow. The warrior's arms and legs stuck out like twigs and even his beard seemed long and narrow. He chewed on something as he waited to be addressed, pausing to spit out the shell of some nut, before leaning even more casually against his spear.

No one, however, could possibly mistake the man. Rumors and legends had sprung up around him. This man was Adino, known as the Spear. It was said he had singlehandedly stood up against eight-hundred men and had killed them all to the last man.[3] Exaggerated or not, this man was a one-man army. There was not even near eight-hundred men in all of Ziph.

Haroeh's worst nightmare had come true. Worse for him was the fact that his decision to betray David was made unilaterally. The other elders had not been informed or consulted until it was far too late to do anything about it. They would likely want to hang the entire mess squarely around Haroeh's neck.

The rugged, thin man's eyes looked sleepy as he waited, appearing like a willow tree in a storm. Haroeh did nothing, determined to wait out the warrior, to try to get him to speak first, but the whip-thin warrior seemed unbothered by the situation, his long jaw moving with exaggerated motion as he chewed on his nuts. He seemed perfectly content to stay like that indefinitely.

Haroeh shifted uncomfortably. He could deal with anger, even threats, but this blatant unconcern unnerved him. So, despite his resolve not to speak first, he burst out, "What business have you here, Adino who is called the Spear?"

He winced and cursed himself for a fool. He should not have revealed that information. Murmuring sprang up from the ranks of the townsfolk who had come out to watch. They knew this man's reputation, and with David's absence, Adino began to look more like an executioner than an ambassador. It had not failed to impress upon Haroeh and the other elders the ease by which these three men had infiltered their defenses.

A shifting among the people behind the elders caught Haroeh's attention. His wife and Ahinoam arrived to stand nearby. He pulled harder at his nose, uncertainty building like a river behind a new dam. His wife, her hair already graying, stayed protectively by Ahinoam's side. The younger woman, whom he hoped to marry one day and raise up a son, stood with obvious interest in the proceedings.

But it was the elders' low, outraged muttering that finally captured Haroeh's full attention. He turned back and gave Adino his

---

[3] 2 Samuel 23:8. See also *Valiant* for a further description of the mighty deed.

sternest stare. If Adino seemed perturbed at all, he hid it well. His laconic stance didn't so much as stiffen a hair. If anything, he seemed more disinterested than before. Most men would have been insulted at the lack of hospitality, and indeed, the two men who had accompanied the Spear were glaring at the elders in barely disguised anger, but the Spear treated the whole affair as if such behavior was perfectly normal.

After a long moment where Adino simply stood there, looking half asleep, he said, "You are the one called Haroeh?"

Haroeh nodded impatiently.

"Then it is you I have somewhat to say."

The elder shivered as fear sent cold chills down his spine. David knew. He had to know. "I am here," he managed to reply in a steady voice. "What would you have of me?"

Adino slowly leaned over to spit out the shell of the nut he was chewing. When he straightened, he fastened his eyes on Haroeh, and the elder stiffened in alarm. A fire burned behind those orbs—a sullen smoldering flame that could easily be kindled into a roaring blaze that consumed everyone around him. Haroeh swallowed, and Adino gave the barest of smiles in reply. The warrior understood Haroeh's fear. "I come to speak of the past and of the future," the Spear began, somehow addressing everyone and no one at the same time. "The son of Jesse has sent me to say this to you: *betrayal*. The Ziphites have betrayed the son of Jesse to deliver him into the hands of his enemy, to see the lives of those pledged to him wasted, their blood spilt, their wives and children destitute. This is what the Ziphites have done, and for it, they are all worthy of death."

Silence greeted this announcement. Eyes narrowed and the few guards who stood behind the elders tightened hands on spear hafts. Adino didn't seem to notice. He had eyes only for Haroeh. A coldness that had nothing to do with the fading light settled in the pit of Haroeh's stomach just by looking into the depths of the warrior's eyes. He saw before him a man who had clasped hands with death and was at ease with it.

Haroeh cleared his throat, preparing to rebuff the accusation, to defend his actions, to do something. Everyone in Ziph knew the truth of the charge. One of their number had already paid the price. Haroeh had personally sent the scouts that were to lead Saul's army against David. And one of those scouts had been killed— undoubtably by one of David's men. Perhaps even by the man who stood before them now.

But before he could speak, Adino continued, his laconic voice belying the gravity of his words, "Yet that is the past. The son of Jesse understands why you did this, why the voices of weak men prevailed upon your fears. The son of Jesse recognizes that the might of King Saul would stagger your hearts. It is no small thing to set Hebrew against Hebrew, to shed the blood of kinsmen. And this, elders of Ziph, is the present." He lapsed into silence again, looking at the elders expectantly.

The elders, for their part, held their peace, waiting for Haroeh to speak. The elder, for his part, struggled to keep his calm. He disliked the barb clearly directed at him about being weak. He wanted nothing more than to make the thin man eat those words, but he needed to be wise here. One misstep could doom them all to oblivion, either at the hands of King Saul or at the hands of the son of Jesse. Based on what had happened to their scout, he held no illusions as to what would happen if his words were displeasing to Adino.

He needed to buy more time to think this through to find some sort of advantage or at least parity in negotiations. He cleared his throat. "You spoke of the past and present, but what of the future?"

Adino's smile turned predatory. "The son of Jesse claims kinship with the Ziphites as he is also a son of Judah. He would not have you as enemies and would seek a peaceful resolution to the dispute that now exists between you. The son of Jesse proposes a union to settle the matter once and for all."

Suspicion bloomed in Haroeh's heart. "What union do you speak of?"

"A simple one. The oldest one of them all. Give to the son of Jesse a woman to be his wife from among you. Such a union will lay to rest any evil between you."

Haroeh's nose twitched uncontrollably. A wife? Such a simple request. The names of a dozen young women immediately sprang to mind, but before he could name them or seek further clarification, Adino's eyes shifted beyond Haroeh and fastened upon someone behind him.

"The son of Jesse has already made his choice," Adino continued, moving forward a few steps. "Good woman, daughter of Ishiah, will you be David's wife?"

Stunned, Haroeh glanced over his shoulder at Ahinoam, his ward. The girl didn't notice his look, her eyes above her veil were fastened on the legendary warrior. One of her slim hands had lifted to her mouth, giving her a helpless look that some men found endearing.

The elder surged to his feet, breaking their eye contact. "This is not possible, Adino, called the Spear! Ahinoam is under my care. She is my ward. She will do as I say."

Adino's eyes slowly worked their way back to Haroeh's face. Nothing in those eyes promised acceptance of the elder's words. Nothing there promised anything except death. Haroeh swallowed, but he would not back down. Not from this. He had come to covet Ahinoam as his own.

Adino's voice was flat and unemotional. "I think not, elder of Ziph. This is the son of Jesse's recompense for your betrayal. Look to your fellow elders, Haroeh. See the truth in their eyes."

Haroeh did so, though he wished for the rest of his life that he had not. He found no allies among the other elders. To them, the dangerous situation before them was all his fault. Why should he not be the one to pay the price? One by one, the elders looked away from him, silently stating their position on the matter.

"I will not give her," he growled anyway.

Adino shrugged ever so slightly. "I am to ask the woman if she would be wife to the son of Jesse. If she agrees to go, the matter is settled. I will *take* her to David." Fire sprang to life in the warrior's eyes. "No man here will prevent it."

Haroeh swallowed and unconsciously backed up a step. "This is not right," he muttered like a man seeing the inevitable collapse all around him.

Adino ignored him, moving forward. His presence was like a battering ram, and Haroeh gave way, sweat breaking out all along his long nose and forehead. Adino came to stand before Ahinoam and gave her a formal bow. "I am instructed to ask your leave, Ahinoam, daughter of Ishiah. If you are willing, David would have you to wife. What say you?"

Cowed into silence, Haroeh could only watch, silently praying that the girl would not take leave of her senses and agree to this absurdity. Why would she? Why would she want to be wife to a homeless vagabond? An outcast? A rebel?

Yet when her eyes lifted to meet those of Adino, he saw conviction in her look where meekness had always ruled before. She nodded. "I will come, my lord, most gladly."

Adino's smile did wonders for his thin, rugged face. "Then we are agreed." He turned to the elders. "This then settles the debt between you and the son of Jesse. We will stay for an hour while the maid gathers her things." He fixed Haroeh with a steely look. "For surely her present lord will forbid her nothing that she may need. Is that not so, Elder Haroeh?"

Haroeh, feeling as if the entire earth had shifted underneath him, could only nod.

Two hours later, Haroeh was pacing rapidly across the lower floor of his house. His rage knew no bounds. His wife, already the beneficiary of that rage, had retired to nurse a bruised cheek, leaving him alone to try and figure out how the situation had so rapidly gotten out of control. He regretted striking her, but never before had he been so misused...so robbed!

Ahinoam had left with David's warriors a half hour ago, likely passing out of his life forever. He fumed. The woman had belonged to him. David had no right!

And the other elders should never have agreed to or sanctioned such thievery! Yet they had repeatedly pointed out that he had put the city in danger by betraying the son of Jesse to King Saul, so it was only right that he bear the burden of appeasing the son of Jesse.[4] Could he not see that Jehovah God favored the son of Jesse? Could he not understand the danger his actions had called down upon the city? If one woman was the price of safety and security, then he should be grateful for coming away with such a cheap price.

The door to his house opened and his cousin, Nabal, stepped in, carefully closing the door behind him. Nabal had been in the city for the last two days negotiating a new trade agreement to export his wine, thanks to a favorable harvest of grapes.

"Have you heard?" Haroeh demanded, dispensing with the normal courtesies.

Nabal licked his bulging lower lip, his small eyes narrowing even further. "I was there. I saw. I heard."

The elder stopped his pacing and confronted his cousin. "Then what say you? What advice do you offer?"

Nabal found a stool and sank down upon it with an audible sigh. He began rubbing his feet. They looked purple, swollen. "My advice is as it was before. This son of Jesse is dangerous, but the king of Israel is more dangerous. Allowing this David to remain in the region will be bad for all of us. He is merely a thief, nothing more, and with the Amalekites raiding freely, we need King Saul as an ally."

"You propose that I find where David has hidden himself and betray him to the king yet again?"

"I am," Nabal said simply. "Cruel chance allowed David to escape the first time. The Philistines' raid turned aside the king. It

---

[4] The biblical text does not make it clear which one, Abigail or Ahinoam, David married first, just that he married them at roughly the same time (1 Samuel 25:43). I chose Ahinoam first because David's firstborn son was of her (2 Samuel 3:2), and she is mentioned first in every other instance (1 Samuel 27:3, 30:5, 2 Samuel 2:2).

won't happen again. The king wishes David dead. He will not stop once he knows where he has fled to. Send men to follow the son of Jesse's ambassadors. They will be burdened down with the woman and her things. Discover his haunts and whereabouts and then send messengers to the king. Leave the rest to him."

"What if David escapes yet again?"

"He will not. As I said, the first time was ill chance that pulled the king away from the hunt. That alone." Nabal leaned forward on his stool, his eyes intent. "We need King Saul to secure the region. Trade has all but come to a halt what with the Amalekites and this David preying on the good people of Ziph. What happened here today is clear evidence of David's greed. He is nothing but a rebel. We need the favor of King Saul or all of us, you and me, will suffer."

It came as no surprise to Haroeh that Nabal's first and primary concern was for his wealth, but his cousin did raise many good points. Rumors circulated of this Haman, the new leader and son of the former Amalekite king. The old king, Agag, had been killed by the Great Seer Samuel after Saul's return from the slaughter of the Amalekite people.[5] Thus his son harbored a great hatred for the Hebrews, murdering every Hebrew he caught, men, women, and children, without regard. Then there was this son of Jesse who thought to prey upon the people, demanding provisions and finally stealing away Ahinoam. It all had to stop.

Haroeh fixed Nabal with a hard stare. "So be it. I will discover where David hides and send word to the king."

Nabal nodded, satisfied. "It is well decided then."

Haroeh could only hope this was so. In his heart, doubt fed his insecurities, but his desire to see David hurt or, better yet, dead, overruled any caution he might have otherwise held to.

---

[5] 1 Samuel 15:33.

8

"David!" The voice penetrated David's brain from afar, like the distant cry of a bird of prey. "David!" Instantly, David came awake, his hand reaching instinctively for his sword. His eyes snapped open, but in the nearly impenetrable darkness he could see little. Only the faint glow coming from the cavern entrance cast any illumination, and the person crouched over him appeared as nothing more than a black shape silhouetted against it.

"Who speaks?" David asked, recognizing the urgency in the voice.

"Abishai, my lord. Joab sent me to fetch you."

David hauled himself upright, already dressed. He slept in his tunic these days, knowing that at any moment they could be attacked. He quickly struggled into his armor, leaving his shield untouched. If the enemy was upon them, Abishai would not have woken him alone.

"What is amiss?" he asked as he strapped on his sword.

"The watchmen report fires, my lord, in the desert. Many of them."

Which meant an army was camped out there, and the only army David could think of that would be so foolish as to camp in the desert was one that hunted. "King Saul?" David asked, following his young nephew toward the cavern entrance.

"I know not, my lord. I was bid to fetch you so that you may see."

They passed a side cavern, one where many of the women and children slept, including Ahinoam. She had agreed to be his wife, a fact that had thrilled David's heart. They would wait for a time to satisfy tradition and then he would wed her. To seal the betrothal, he had given her a golden bracelet that one of the men had sold him for extra rations for his family. David had made the bargain gladly, willing to go without his own share if need be.

Ahinoam had remained shy around David, rarely meeting his eyes, but he thought he detected a satisfied glow about her. He sensed more than knew that she had been glad to be away from the Ziph elder who had taken her into his home. He had gotten the feeling that Haroeh had meant to wed the girl himself and that she was not displeased to be away from him.

Whatever the reasons, she had agreed to marry him and that was all that mattered. He was surprised at the strength of his feelings for her, having only met her that one time when he had bargained for provisions with the Ziph elders. She was different to him than Michal, and he had yet to sort through what that meant. Regardless, she was here and safe—and his. That would do for the moment.

He followed his nephew out into the darkness beyond, pausing only to quench his thirst. David glanced at the stars, noting their position and determining that there yet remained four hours before sunrise. The cookfires would have been detected as soon as the sun had set, but it would have taken time to bring him word.

A steep, but navigable trail wound its way to the top of the canyon where a freshwater spring emerged from the rocks, sending water trickling down the gorge toward the Salt Sea. Most of the springs in the area were too salty. This one here at Engedi was only one of two freshwater sources that David knew of.

The two warriors climbed the trail carefully. A misstep here could send them rolling down into the gorge and to their deaths. Abishai carried a torch taken from a sentry based just outside the cavern where the majority of David's troop slept. The large cave system was the result of years of waterflow that carved winding caverns into the limestone. It was a perfect place to hide.

Until now. When they reached the top of the bluff, David and Abishai trotted along a predetermined route to where Joab, Uriah, and Eleazar awaited him. The three men had been tasked with this week's rotation of guard duty.

"My lord," Eleazar greeted David. "Ill tidings, I fear."

"What do you know?" David asked.

In the flickering torchlight, the expert swordsman grimaced. "I know that coming here was a mistake. I know we are trapped here. I know that yon army cannot fail to discover us."

"You think it is King Saul."

Eleazar nodded shortly. "I do."

"But we do not know for sure," Joab protested. "It could be shepherds driving goats across the desert. It has been done before. They use the sheepcote caves that lie between us and them."[1]

"With that many campfires, it must be an army of shepherds," Eleazar shot back. "They come directly here."

Which could mean anything. Fresh water was scarce this side of the Salt Sea. There were only a few places to go, and likely whoever was camped out on the desert knew this. Where else could they go? He chewed it over, trying to decide. Finally, he gestured to Joab. "I must see for myself. Lead on."

The five men moved out under the starlight, making their way through the ravines by torchlight, careful not to expose themselves or the light from their torches. They wound their way deeper into the desert until they came to the top of a ravine riddled with caves— the sheepcotes that shepherds had found shelter within from the earliest days of David's ancestors.

The extensive cavern system would take days to search thoroughly, a hope David counted much upon if Saul truly had found them. Perhaps it would give them enough time to escape.

---

[1] 1 Samuel 24:3.

Snuffing out their torches, they crept to the top of the ravine and peered over. Beyond them, the broken landscape faded away into more ravines, sand, and rock. But on an unbroken island between ravines, like brilliant stars, a scattering of campfires told of a large body of men. Occasionally, a few dark forms moved among the fires, the light casting eerie shadows against tents pitched atop the plateau.

"See," Eleazar whispered, "did I not tell you? Those are no shepherds camped there."

David agreed. He studied the camp for some time, not saying anything. From the number of fires, he estimated upward of three thousand men had come against him.[2] The other four men waited with the patience born from much hardship, giving him time to observe and think. They trusted him. Relied upon him. It was a heavy burden.

The army beyond had but one purpose: to kill him. He thought then of part of the song he had recently composed. One line stood out sharply in his mind: "My soul is among lions: and I lie even among them that are set on fire, even the sons of men, whose teeth are spears and arrows, and their tongue a sharp sword."[3]

David knew then that Saul would not be deterred. The king's burning hatred had set him afire with the need to kill David. He and all those he held dear were in danger of being swallowed up by it. Swallowing bile, David calmed his racing heart as best he could. Turning slightly, he looked at Uriah. "Hasten back to the encampment and take word to Shammah and Adino. Have them prepare the troop to flee. It will take time for yon army to search the sheepcotes thoroughly, but our people must be ready to flee on my word."[4]

"Aye, my lord." The young man hesitated. "What of you, my lord?"

---

[2] 1 Samuel 24:2.
[3] Psalm 57:4.
[4] 1 Samuel 24:3.

"I will keep watch over King Saul. I would know his search patterns and plans. There may yet be a way to escape without bloodshed. If so, I would know of it. Go. Make haste. Prepare the men. For on my word they must flee toward the south. I hear there is a mountain fortress we may resort to called Masada."

Actually, Masada was nothing more than a huge isolated mountain, rocky, barren of life, and with but a treacherous ibex trail that led to the top. If David was caught there, he would be trapped. He idly wondered what it would take to build water reservoirs atop the mountain fortress. If someone could do that, then Masada would be an ideal place to hide. A few could hold it against thousands— tens of thousands. He shook his head. Right now, Masada was a death trap. But he didn't know where else to go.

Uriah said nothing further. He backed up until he could stand upright without being lined against the starry sky and disappeared back down the ravine.

"This is an ill-conceived plan, my lord," Eleazar protested. "We should not stay."

David reached out to place a hand on the other's shoulder. "Fear not, my friend. We are in God's hands. I would know the speed and plans of our enemies. Perhaps in such knowledge the LORD will make an escape for us."

"I like it not," the swordsman grumbled under his breath. But he did not so much as move a muscle to retreat down the ravine. He would stay by David's side no matter what.

Joab and Abishai waited silently, content to follow David's lead. They took turns that night watching the distant campfires, while trying to sleep on the rocky ground. But they did not find much rest. When dawn rose, four more of David's men arrived to join them atop the crest of the gorge. Among them was Shammah and Uriah.

"We prepare to flee," Shammah rumbled, his scalp shining in the early morning sun. He had woven the bones of a rat into his beard, a habit he did whenever he thought he might be entering into battle. "The women and children already make their way down to the Salt Sea. They will follow the shore south as you command."

David could sense something more in the big man's unease. "What else?" David demanded.

"It is naught," the bald man replied, eyes shifting away. "I took care of it afore we left."

"What is this you speak of? Tell me."

Shammah sighed, running his hand through the bones entwined in his thick beard. "It is the man called Shobal. He bestirs the people's fears. He has gained ears among the people. I fear he will cause trouble."

"What did you do?"

The big man shrugged. "Mayhap I broke his arm."

"You did what?"

"He needed something else to consider than stirring up the people. As I said, I took care of it."

David struggled to suppress a grin. Shammah's ultimate solution to nearly everything involved breaking something. Still, the news worried David. Shobal had long been a thorn in David's side. He would need to put the man in his place, but that was a problem for another time.

Joab slid down the path from where he had been keeping watch over the enemy army beyond. "They break camp," he hissed. "Forward scouts are heading this way."

Eleazar cursed. "More ill luck."

Shammah flexed his muscles, brandishing his warclub. "Let them come. We will teach them a thing or two."

David thought fast. "How long before they reach here?"

"It will be yet several hours, I think. They have to follow a twisting route to reach here, but they come quickly."

"There be sheepcotes near to the king, yes?" David asked, wanting confirmation.

Shammah nodded. "I know of them having spent my youth nearby."

"Then the king will spend much time searching each cave. This gives us time."

"What of the forward scouts?" Joab asked. "They come quickly. Mayhap they are sent to search farther ahead?"

True. "Return and keep an eye on them. Bring word when they are close."

Joab went back up the ravine, and Uriah went with him. David walked off by himself to be alone, his insides in turmoil. How had the king discovered him yet again? How had he come so quickly? He mused the possibilities, turning them over and allowing conspiracies to grow larger in his mind.

His thoughts were interrupted about two hours later when Joab and Uriah returned. "They will be here soon," his nephew reported.

"Into the caves then," David ordered. "We will let the scouts pass us by and see where the king goes. Perhaps these merely flank their route, and the king searches a different way."

It was wishful thinking, but David wanted to keep a close eye on Saul's progress. They scrambled down the ravine, picking at random one of the caves with a narrow opening and ducking inside. The cave opened into a round bowl-like cavern with ledges and water-carved alcoves in the sides. David had the men scatter to the back while he and Joab watched from the mouth. The moment they spotted the four scouts trotting down the ravine path, they ducked into their own hiding spots.

Light from the cave mouth cast a pool of brilliance partway into the cavern. Blackness surrounded it, seemingly darker than normal. David held his breath. The rocky ground outside obscured footprints, though the scouts undoubtably could tell that someone had walked the path recently. Still, shepherds were known to travel these parts, so that in itself should not seem unusual.

One after the other, Saul's scouts trotted by the cave opening, not bothering to even glance inside. When they disappeared, the seven men gathered in the pool of light before the cave mouth.

"They did not look within," Uriah murmured, surprised. "It's a miracle."

"Nay," David disagreed. "The king will send other men to search the caves. These four have a different task." Everyone looked at him, but Shammah and Eleazar already knew. "The king does not know where we hide, only that we do. These four will travel farther on and scout out the way to see if they can discover us farther on. Notice how they travel spread out. If one falls, the others have a good chance of escaping and reporting the incident. It is clever."

Abishai looked troubled. "Then we are trapped. The scouts behind us and the king before us."

"The scouts are not the problem," David explained. "Doubtless they knew some of our spies are hidden within these caves if not the balance of our forces. They will expect it. No, they seek to startle us into action and thereby reveal our location."

"Like hunting the boar," Joab said. "They beat the brush to get us to reveal ourselves."

"It is so," David agreed. "We must trust that Adino and the others know what to do, that the women and children have already been sent beyond sight." Taking a deep breath, David let it out slowly, knowing that his next words would taste vile on his tongue. "Or we must prevent them from bringing word back to the king."

The others considered this with strangely mixed reactions. Finally, Eleazar nodded. "What would you have us do, my lord?"

"We will keep an eye on the king's progress and watch for the return of Saul's spies. If we must, we will prevent them from bringing word."

"An army that size will take time getting here and even longer searching each cave," Shammah said. "They will not reach the Salt Sea this day."

"Unless the spies bring word," Eleazar disagreed.

"Aye," David answered, uncomfortable. "This is why we must remain here and watch. We will need to trust in the LORD God of Israel. He will be our strength, our fortress. Let us keep watch and see how the LORD will deliver us."

The others nodded, their resolve strengthening. Together, they left the cave and proceeded back up the ravine until they could peer over it. Saul's army was strung out on the other side of the ravine. They were clearly searching every cave for sign of recent occupation. David worried. There were other paths, other routes that would lead to Engedi, but the one Saul followed offered the quickest and most direct route to where David's men were hidden nearer the Salt Sea. How could the king know this was the correct way? *We are betrayed!* David shivered. It was the only explanation.[5]

Abruptly, a hundred men of Saul's army appeared below them, moving rapidly toward the crest of the ravine. Eleazar let out a hissing curse, and David's heart skipped a beat. "Back!" he whispered urgently. "Back before they discover us!"

They slid down the ravine path, moving as rapidly as they dared until they reached the cave they had hidden in previously. David ducked inside with the other six men, and they quickly melted into the darkness beyond the pool of light. This time David went in farther with his men and immediately his throat began to constrict. Despite having lived in caves now for some time, he had yet to shake the feeling that the entire mountain was preparing to crash down upon him. He hated enclosed spaces.

But he had no more time to dwell on it. The hundred men approached rapidly, their footfalls and the rattle of armor and weapons echoing down the steep gorge. They moved past, one or two pausing long enough to peer inside briefly. Soon they were all gone. David kept still, waiting. He did this for perhaps half an hour before slowly edging his way to the cave entrance and peering out. At the bottom of the ravine, the company of a hundred men had taken up position to guard the exit out. Eleazar had crept up beside him, and he muttered an oath, "By Abraham's beard, we are truly trapped!"

David seethed inside. He should have seen this coming. He should have kept going, not stopped in the cave...of course Saul would seek to secure both ends of the ravine before commencing his search. If David and his men were indeed hiding in the caves

---

[5] 1 Samuel 24:1.

nearby, such a tactic would guarantee that they would be trapped or delayed long enough for Saul to bring the bulk of his force to bear.

Joab took a quick look. When he pulled back, his face was troubled. "What do we do now?"

David didn't know. He had no answers. There were only two ways out of the ravine, and both were now blocked by Saul's men. They had no chance of breaking through a hundred men, not unless the Spirit of the LORD infused them, but that would mean slaughtering a hundred Hebrews—something that despite his predicament, he determined not to do. Not like that. Not that way.

He met each man's eye and held it, letting them see that he had no fear—which was not true, but he had pushed it far down beyond where they could see or sense. "We will endure," he said. "If it be the LORD's will, we will be delivered. Have faith in Elohim, and He will see us through."

That was all he could give them. He prayed it would be enough. He did instruct each man to aid in erasing all signs of their passing within the cave. He didn't want any footprints to give them away. Then they settled down to wait.

They waited for hours and slowly the light without began to fade. While they waited, David noticed a peculiar thing. A spider had begun to spin a web across the entrance. It was faint at first, but the sunlight would glisten off the web when it moved in a breeze. David, hiding next to Uriah pointed. "Do you see thus?"

Uriah grunted a soft affirmative, adding, "I have never seen a spider act in such a manner. It is most peculiar."

Men often passed by, some peering inside, but no one breaking the spider's web to come fully into the cave. The sound of more men moving down the gorge became louder. And still the spider spun its web as if mad. David agreed with Uriah. He had never seen anything like it before.

The spider, no bigger than a coin, moved rapidly along its web, spinning more and more strands across the entrance until the whole of the cave mouth was spun over. Fascinated, David stared, momentarily forgetting about the danger that lurked beyond the cave.

And then King Saul stood beyond, appearing before the entrance to the cave as if materializing out of thin air. Deep shadows lay across the ravine, obscuring the features of the king, but David would know him anywhere. He stood head and shoulders taller than everyone else.[6] Another man moved to stand next to the king.

"It grows late," the second man said, peering into the sky. The cave acted like a natural funnel to hear the conversation without. David recognized that voice: Ishui, Saul's second oldest son, and brother to Jonathan.

"We will take rest in the caves," Saul replied.

"But we have not yet searched them all," Ishui protested. "It is not safe."

Saul snorted in disgust. "Keep searching. Word is that the son of Jesse is closer to the Salt Sea, but I take your meaning. Search every cave." The king looked over then at the cave mouth where David hid, and David instinctively crouched back into the darkness, worried that the king's gaze would somehow penetrate the gloom and see him. "You and I will take our rest in this cave," he said, gesturing to the cave mouth.

David's mouth went dry.

"We have yet to search this cave," Ishui argued.

Saul extended his hand and swiped through the spider web. He regarded the thick web attached to his hand and laughed softly. "This web took days to build, my son. No one is within."

Ishui shrugged. "Perhaps so, but I think the rest of these caves should be searched. I would not wish for the son of Jesse to escape us."

"Nor do I, my son."

In the faint light, David studied his king's face. Saul looked worn and weary, like an old hide left out too long in the sun. The evil spirit continued to plague the king, David saw, stealing his

---

[6] 1 Samuel 10:23.

strength, nibbling away at his mind. King Saul once possessed a presence that filled any room, but now he seemed somehow...diminished. That was the only word David could think of to explain what he saw. The hollow eyes, the sunken cheeks, the yellowish skin all spoke of a prolonged illness, but the king had not been sick in body, merely ill in spirit.

The sight was enough to make David weep, though a part of him rejoiced at seeing his enemy so smitten.

Saul sent Ishui to deliver his orders and walked alone into the cave. He stood in the diming pool of light, eyes staring into the blackness, unseeing. By some twist of chance, Saul stared directly at the place where David hid. David froze, holding his breath. He knew consciously that the king could not see him, but it did not lessen the fear he felt.

Ishui returned, finding his father standing just within the cave entrance. "My lord, we search the rest of the caves, but I do not think David is nearby. Surely he is encamped near the springs at Engedi as you say."

Saul shook himself, coming out of his reverie. "I agree, but too often the son of Jesse has escaped me. No more. We will not take the chance. Ensure that the caves are searched."

"It is being done as we speak."

"Then it is well." Saul heaved a sigh. "I wish to sleep here, and I would not be disturbed. Make your bed at the entrance, my son. Let no one bother me this night."

"It will be done as you command, my lord." Ishui disappeared again to search out the blankets they would use to make their beds.

The king continued to stand in the fading light, eyes staring off into the distance, a prisoner of his own thoughts. David, however, could hardly credit his ears. Saul would sleep but a score of cubits from where he now hid in the darkness. He knew what this meant. He knew that such an opportunity had been afforded him, one he dared not pass up.

David's men lined the cavern walls, hidden in niches, ledges and a few of the larger side passages. They remained quiet, their training doing them credit. No one said a word or moved. Eventually, Ishui returned with blankets and food, and Saul turned away, breaking his stare into the darkness where David hid. David couldn't help himself; a sigh of relief so soft it went undetected slipped his lips. The sun disappeared, and a full moon took its place; the pale light cast a dimmer pool of light just inside the entrance.

Alternating tensing his muscles and relaxing them to keep from growing stiff, he still felt the strain of staying so still. But he did so, doing it well enough that some small insect, bug or spider thought nothing of running across his hand. The moment he felt the touch, he nearly jumped out of his skin. He swallowed his heart and clamped down on his breathing lest he give himself away.

With his heart thumping wildly, he watched as Saul and Ishui spread their blankets on the sandy floor of the cave within the pool of light cast by the moon. Saul removed his sandals and then covered his feet[7] with one of the wool blankets, lying back on the sandy soil. Soon, the heavy breathing of father and son told him they were soundly asleep. Ishui had spread his blankets within the entrance to the cave, leaving the king closer to David and the men hidden within.

David stared at the king, realizing something miraculous had just happened. The spider's frantic efforts to spin a web across the cave entrance had saved them all from discovery. And now the king lay within a few cubits of David's sword. His hand trembled.

And then Joab appeared next to him, moving surely and swiftly from his place of concealment. David couldn't see his nephew's face in the dim light, but he clearly heard his whisper. "My lord, this is the day of which the LORD spoke, saying that He would surely deliver your enemy into your hand so that you may do to him as it seems good to you.[8] Rise up, my lord, and slay the son of Kish. Deliver yourself and us from his hand and fulfill the LORD'S promise when the Great Seer anointed you to be the next king of Israel."

---

[7] 1 Samuel 24:3. Some feel Saul went into the cave to relieve himself, but it hardly seems credible that he would not have noticed someone cutting off part of his skirt if he had been wide awake. Covering his feet in sleep seems the more plausible explanation for how David was able to do what he did undetected.

[8] 1 Samuel 24:4.

The urgency of those words slammed into David's heart like arrows. This was his chance to end his exile, to reclaim his name, to be at peace…to be reunited with Jonathan and Michal. All the fear, doubts, and misgivings could be undone with a single stroke of the sword.

Could there be any doubt that the LORD God had finally delivered Saul into his hand? There was not. Without a reply to his nephew, he gripped his sword tightly and slipped as silently as a hunting wolf toward his prey.

9

S tanding over the sleeping king was a surreal moment for David. The moonlight perfectly captured Saul's face, and in sleep, the anger, rage, and hatred David had so often witnessed were absent. The Hebrew king looked tired, his skin wrinkled, his beard streaked with gray, and his cheeks hollow. The last years had not been kind to King Saul.

David's hand tightened on the hilt of his sword, his cheek muscles twitching. One stab, and it would all be over. But he knew, standing over Saul, he could not do it. Despite everything that had happened, he still loved the king.

But he needed to do something. Bending swiftly, he drew an iron knife and cut off the skirt of Saul's robe that had escaped from the blanket.[1] Returning to his hiding place next to Joab, he slid down against the rock wall, breathing heavily.

Joab leaned close. "Is he dead? Did you slay him? I could not see."

David shook his head, a wasted gesture in the darkness. "I did not. He is the LORD's anointed." As soon as the words left his mouth, the realization of what he had done—what he had nearly done—struck him like a battering ram. His hands began to tremble, and he clenched them tightly to himself.

---

[1] 1 Samuel 24:4.

His nephew squatted down beside him, and David could sense more than see the puzzlement on the other warrior's face. "I understand this not. Why did you not slay him?"

The conversation drew some of the other men who crept over to listen. David knew he needed to give a better explanation of why he hadn't killed Saul. And he needed to regain control of himself. His hands still shook. He had come too close to killing the king, an act he would never have been able to live with. "The LORD forbid that I should do this thing unto my master, the LORD'S anointed." He cast his voice low so as not to disturb the two sleeping men lying less than twenty cubits away. "I dare not stretch forth mine hand against him, seeing he is the anointed of the LORD. I would not be blameless in this."[2]

Silence greeted his statement, and he sensed that the majority of those who had heard disagreed with him. But how could he explain this to them in ways they would understand? True, Saul was the LORD'S anointed, but it went deeper than that. He loved the king and loved his son, Jonathan. How could he ever face his friend knowing he had killed Jonathan's father. More to the point, God had put Saul in power. It was not David's place to undo that.

"Hold," he said softly. "No harm will befall the king this night."[3]

His men said nothing. It would have to do.

They settled in to wait out the rest of the night. It passed slowly, like an indecisive turtle making its way across the sands, but the moonlight faded and eventually plunged the entire cave into utter darkness, and then slowly, light began filling up the entrance as the sun rose into the morning sky.

Saul stirred first, coming awake with the dawn. He rose, shook himself, and nudged his second oldest son with a bare foot. "Rise, Ishui. Today is the day we find the son of Jesse." The thin warrior startled awake suddenly, snorting even as his hand grasped for his

---

[2] 1 Samuel 24:6.
[3] 1 Samuel 24:7.

spear. Saul looked on disapprovingly. "What is this? Did you sleep through the night and set no watch?"

Ishui yawned and abruptly forced his jaw closed as he rose to his feet. He looked around. "Forgive me, my lord. I meant to keep a watch, but weariness overcame me."

Saul grunted. "I have little to worry about anyhow, seeing as we are surrounded by our most trusted warriors." He looked about him, his jaw clenching tightly. "Come. We must continue the search. I like this cave little. Such dreams I had…" He trailed off, then abruptly he turned and strode from the cave.[4]

Ishui hastily gathered up all the blankets and foodstuff and followed his father out. A collective sigh of relief sounded from everyone hiding in the cave. The night had been hard on the nerves. David stood and took a few steps forward, his men moving out from their hiding places to stand nearby. David stared at the cave entrance, trying to decide what to do next.

Impulsively, he started for the entrance. "Abide here," he called over his shoulder. "Do not come forth, no matter what may happen."

"David!" Joab hissed in astonishment, following despite David's command. "What are you about?"

David turned on his nephew. "Abide here, Joab. Do not let yourself be seen."

Satisfied that Joab would obey, David turned and walked into the pool of light before the entrance and then out into the morning light beyond. Not far below him, the king and his son were making their way down the ravine floor to where the bulk of his army waited. David moved a few steps down in the same direction and then called to the king, "My lord the king!"[5]

Saul froze as if suddenly realizing asps surrounded him. Ishui, however, whirled around, dropping the bedding and bringing his spear to a ready position. The prince might have charged David right then, but one of Saul's hands reached out and gripped his son firmly

---

[4] 1 Samuel 24:7.
[5] 1 Samuel 24:8.

on the arm, either to prevent his son from a foolish attack, alone against David, or seeking support. Slowly, the king turned to face his greatest adversary, and the moment he did so, David bowed deeply.[6]

David straightened and called, "Why have you listened to men's words, claiming that I seek your hurt?[7] Behold, my lord, see what is in my hand!" With that he lifted the cut cloth of Saul's skirt. The cloth caught in a stiff breeze and flared out like a flag. The early morning sun shone directly on David, causing the cloth to glow. There was no mistaking it.

David continued, "This day, the LORD delivered you into my hand in the cave. Some bade me to slay you, but I could not. I said that I will not raise my hand against my lord, for he is the LORD's anointed."[8] So far, Saul had not moved to take David or called to his men gathering farther down the ravine. All stood as if frozen, looking back at the confrontation. Taking another deep breath, David waved the cloth, unmistakably cut from Saul's skirt. "See, my father, the skirt of your robe in my hand? I cut it off and killed you not. Know then, my lord, and see that there is neither evil nor transgression in my hand. I have not sinned against you, yet you hunt my soul to take it away.[9] The LORD judge between me and you, and the LORD avenge me of you, but my own hand will not be upon you!"[10]

Saul waited, knowing David had not yet finished. Ishui fumed at the king's side, the spear tip trembling in the grip of his rage and frustration. He knew he had failed his father. That David could sneak close enough to cut off the skirt of Saul's robe while he slept was a stark failure on his part. But his father's grasp on his arm remained rock solid, holding him in place.

Sucking in air, David made his case, "As the proverb of the ancients teach us, wickedness proceeds from the wicked." David paused here, struggling with his own words, knowing that the

---

[6] 1 Samuel 24:8.
[7] 1 Samuel 24:9.
[8] 1 Samuel 24:10.
[9] 1 Samuel 24:11.
[10] 1 Samuel 24:12.

implied insult could set heavily upon the king. But that was not his intention. He wanted to explain that if he was evil, then he would have killed the king without thought. But he was committed now, so he continued, "But my hand will not be upon you, my king.[11] Look upon me, my father, and know that there is no wickedness in my heart. After whom does the king of Israel seek? After whom do you pursue? I will tell you, O King, whom you seek. You seek after a dead dog, a flea.[12] The LORD be our judge, and judge between me and you. To Him will I plead my case, O King, and He will deliver me out of your hand."[13]

There, he had said it. With those words, he attempted to both make himself a nonthreat and hint that no matter what the king did, the God of Israel would continue to deliver him from the hand of the king. Bold, perhaps even rash, but David could think of nothing else to do. He could not lift his hand against the king, and neither did he want to die by the king's hand. Something had to prevail upon the king to let David go.

Saul stared up at David and shockingly, tears filled the king's eyes. In a quivering voice, Saul asked, "Is this truly your voice, my son David?"[14] Pushing Ishui behind him, the king took three heavy steps toward David and then stood with tears unabashedly running into his graying beard.

"Aye, it is, my king."

Saul wept then, a bitter weeping accompanied by a hoarse cry that echoed through the narrow ravine.[15] David flinched from the power of it, from the strength of the emotions that poured forth from the king.

"You are more righteous than I," Saul said, his voice raw and filled with such a mixture of pain and longing that it stunned David. "You have rewarded me good for all the evil I have shown you.[16]

---

[11] 1 Samuel 24:13.
[12] 1 Samuel 24:14.
[13] 1 Samuel 24:15.
[14] 1 Samuel 24:16.
[15] 1 Samuel 24:16.
[16] 1 Samuel 24:17.

You have shown me this day your true heart, dealing with such kindness, for when the LORD had delivered me into your hand, you slew me not."[17] Saul shook his head in wonder, his tears continuing to darken his beard. "For if a man find his enemy, will he let him go?" He locked eyes with David, straightening to his full height. "The LORD reward you good for what you have done this day, my son.[18] And now I know that you will surely be king one day and that the kingdom of Israel will be established in your hand. Swear unto me before the LORD that you will not cut off my seed after me, and that you will not destroy my name out of my father's house. Swear to me, my son David, and I will let you go."

David fell to his knees and bowed his face to the rocky floor of the ravine. "I swear it, my king, before the LORD God of Israel. I will not destroy your name nor cut off your seed after you."[19]

"Then depart in peace, my son," Saul said heavily, all vitality seemingly torn from him.

David couldn't imagine what the king was feeling at that moment, having hunted David throughout the land of Israel, finally catching up to him, and then allowing him to depart.

Ishui, however, did not bother to hide how he felt. "My lord, no!" He tried to push past his father, but Saul flung out an arm, thrusting him back.

"Hold your tongue," the king snapped. "I have spoken, and I will not go back on my word. He and his men are free to depart in peace." He gave Ishui a glare. "The LORD delivered me into his hand, my son, and he harmed me not. This should not be unrewarded." He shook his head as if wondering at his own words. "Gather the men. We march for home." He spared a single glance at David and in that look, David read much. "Go, my son," Saul said. "It would be well if you were well away—and quickly."

David couldn't agree more. He rose to his feet and beckoned to those still hiding in the cave. When the other men appeared, he

---

[17] 1 Samuel 24:18.
[18] 1 Samuel 24:19.
[19] 1 Samuel 24:20-22.

motioned them up the ravine. They would have to circle around to return to Engedi, but he dared not try to walk through Saul's main army, lest some fool took it into his head to try and save his king some future hassle by relieving David of his head.

Saul watched in silence, and Ishui seethed behind him, casting such hateful looks that David was forced to mark it. One day, he believed, that one would leave him no choice but to kill him. Killing Saul, the LORD'S anointed, was something David was unwilling to do, but if he ever met up with Ishui again, it would likely end badly for the son of the king.

Together, David and his men backed up the ravine until they could hasten away, leaving Saul standing below, looking up, locked in an internal battle of his own that David could scarcely imagine. But he dared hope that the king would cease this hunt, would seek him no more. Perhaps David's days as a fugitive were no more.

By now, he and his men knew the country well enough to know of several other routes back to the camp at Engedi. The circular trails took several hours longer to walk, but they arrived back at the camp to find Adino in the process of moving the people south. Several times along the journey back, one of David's men sought to speak, but each time David gave him such a look that he fell instantly silent. David did not want to talk about what had passed between him and Saul—not yet anyway. Not right away. He needed time to process his feelings, to work through what the king might or might not do next.

Adino showed little reaction to being told that Saul had turned back, other than to lean more casually against his spear. "I will send word to the women and children that they may return," he said to David.

David nodded. "I would see Ahinoam."

"Aye, my lord. She was among the first to leave. I will send Asahel. He is truly fleet of foot."

Again, David nodded, not sure what else to say. The wait was intolerable for David. He longed to lay eyes on his betrothed, to speak to her. He could not explain how this woman had so easily snatched his heart, but it was so. When she finally arrived with the other women, children, and elderly, she did not, however, come with good news."

"My lord," she greeted him, her face lined with sadness. "Ill tidings have reached our ears."

David's shoulders bowed. He could hardly claim surprise. Such news was the bane of his life, a never-ending cycle that would likely persist for the rest of his life. "Say on," he said, stiffening to receive whatever blow was coming his way, but what she said was something David could not have prepared himself for in anywise.

"A shepherd met us along the way, tasked with spreading the news." Her eyes filled with tears. "My lord, the Great Seer, Samuel, is dead."[20]

And just like that, David's entire world crashed down around his head.

---

[20] 1 Samuel 25:1.

10

Two men merged with the flow of mourners on their way to lament and then bury the Great Seer, Samuel, at Ramah.[1] David, dressed as a simple shepherd, a role he could still play, walked as casually as he could beside Gad, the prophet. The solemn progression of mourners kept a steady pace, and here and there a woman lifted up her voice and wept, her lament both a praise and prayer to Jehovah for the loss of Samuel.

The Great Seer's death had hit David hard. As long as Samuel had been alive, David had a connection to Elohim through the seer. Samuel had been more than a mentor, more than a friend. He had been a rock of stability for David in an otherwise turbulent life. It had been Samuel who had anointed him to be the next king of Israel when he had been but a lad.[2] David had never truly believed the old man would ever die, at least not until the anointing had been fulfilled and David sat upon the throne of Israel.

Samuel represented an end of an era. For centuries men and even a few women had been divinely chosen by God to judge Israel. They were deliverers sent by God to overthrow their oppressors and judge the people. Truly, this process had started with Moses, but Samuel had been the last. His sons had tried to take up the mantel of judges, but the people had rejected them when it became clear

---

[1] 1 Samuel 25:1.
[2] 1 Samuel 16:13.

that Samuel's sons did not walk in the way of their father.[3] So the people had demanded a king, and Samuel had given them one—against his better judgment.[4]

But it was now done. Israel had a king like all the nations around them, and Saul was the first, anointed as was David, by the Great Seer to rule and judge the people. Samuel was the kingmaker, David's single greatest light in an otherwise dark journey to the throne of Israel. But now that light had been extinguished forever.

Gad, the ever-smiling prophet, nudged him. "Be ready, my lord. The gates of Ramah are not far."

David nodded, saying nothing. Samuel was to be buried this evening in a tomb near his own house.[5] Many of the wealthier members of society not only owned a house, but also a garden next to their house in which a family tomb would be carved out of solid rock. So it was with Samuel, having in fact, inherited the land and house from his father Elkanah as the eldest son of his favored wife Hannah.[6] It was for this event that all Israel,[7] it seemed, was gathering to lament the man who had served them so faithfully all his life.

This included King Saul and much of Saul's army. David, from under the cowl of his shepherd's cloak, eyed the armed soldiers lining the roadway and scrutinizing the mourners as they gathered in and around the city. Trying to remain inconspicuous, he and Gad walked among the other mourners, not hurrying and not trying to do anything that would call attention to themselves.

"They look for you," Gad offered quietly. "The king must know you would surely come." The seer seemed so sure.

"Did the word of the LORD come to you?"

---

[3] 1 Samuel 8:1-3.
[4] 1 Samuel 8:4-6.
[5] 1 Samuel 25:1. It is unlikely that Samuel would have been buried under his own dwelling place, seeing as the Hebrews consider the dead to be unclean. Likely the tomb would be part of a garden or field near Samuel's house.
[6] 1 Samuel 1:1, 19.
[7] 1 Samuel 25:1.

Gad flashed him his signature grin. "Nay, my lord, it is but an observation."

And likely a keen one too. "Surely, they yet believe I am at Engedi."

"Perhaps word has come of your company returning to Judah. Perhaps Saul knows you are near."

David hoped not. His decision to leave his small army and come to Ramah was born out of a need to honor the man who had anointed him, and truth be told, because he harbored a small hope that he could salvage his relationship with King Saul. The king's abandonment of his hunt for David had revived that belief and was the spark that caused him to order his army back into southern Judah to settle in the wilderness of Paran near the cities of Carmel and Maon.[8] He wanted to avoid Ziph if possible. His experiences with the elders there had so far not been pleasant.

"We must be careful," he said at last.

Gad's eyebrows rose. "Surely you are a mountain of wisdom."

David ignored the prophet. He was committed. Turning to walk away while everyone else continued to gather would mark him as surely as Goliath's sword had in Gath. Ahead, the crowd thickened as they neared Samuel's house. The streets were thick with people and more had crowded the rooftop of the houses to see.

As gently as he could, he and Gad pushed their way through the crowd, approaching as close as they dared. Then spying a rooftop that seemed less crowded, David veered toward the house and called up, "May we enter and join you atop your house?"

A man from the watchers above turned and peered down at the two men. "Who goes there?" he inquired. "Can you not see that we have little room?"

Gad pulled back the hood of his robe and grinned at the man above. "Caleb, you old mule, let us up. What hospitality is this you give? Surely the LORD has blessed you with a dull tongue and a slow wit!"

---

[8] 1 Samuel 25:1.

Caleb leaned over the parapet. "Gad, is that you? Where have you been? Up to little good, if you ask me. And what do you? True men do not lurk about in the shadows. Get you up here!"

Grinning even wider, Gad led David around the house, through another small garden, and into the house. They found a ladder leading up and took it. Once atop the roof, Gad met his friend and embraced him. "It is well to see you, my friend."

Caleb was a medium-sized man with balding hair and a crooked smile. He laughed and then caught himself, looking around in embarrassment. "I forget myself," he apologized. "This is no time for mirth."

Gad sobered instantly. "Aye, it is not. We mourn a great man."

Caleb nodded and looked inquiringly at David. Gad shrugged. "A lost soul whom I have undertaken to instruct in the ways of the LORD. He is slow to learn."

Caleb smiled crookedly, dismissing David. "We surely miss you around here. The Great Seer's passing has created much uncertainty. Come look."

They followed the homeowner to the edge of the roof, squeezing between his family members. David stood next to Gad and peered over the crowd. He instantly found what he was looking for. Saul stood in Samuel's garden before an open hole that led down into the rocky earth. A wooden table upon which a shrouded body lay was visible before the entrance to the tomb. Jonathan stood beside his father, and at the edges of the crowd amid the soldiers placed there, women wailed their sorrow to the heavens.

It tore at David's heart to see Samuel's body so still, so lifeless. He knew in his heart that his mentor, his friend was no longer there, but that he awaited the redemption of Israel in paradise, one day to be reunited with Jehovah. Unlike the Egyptians who embalmed their dead and buried them in sarcophagi or other cultures that cremated their dead, the Hebrews had very simple burial practices. One similar aspect, likely borrowed from their time in Egypt, was the wrapping of the body from head to toe in cloth.

Samuel's death had come but two days ago, and his body had been anointed with oils, wrapped in cloth, and kept cool to delay decomposition. So, he would be taken into his tomb, placed on a stone slab, and buried this day. Perhaps a year later, one of his sons or grandsons would reenter the tomb and gather the bones that were left, placing them reverently in one of the side alcoves of the family tomb. This process was known as being gathered to one's fathers,[9] and Samuel would have his place near his father and mother.

King Saul stood before the shrouded body, looking upon it without moving. This far away, David couldn't read anything in his expression or posture, but the king did not strike David as being well. David turned his attention to Jonathan, and a longing sprang forth in his heart and soul. One day, he hoped, he would be reunited with his friend. Jonathan stood slightly apart from his father, also gazing upon the body of the dead prophet. David would have given much to know what he was thinking.

Samuel's sons and grandchildren stood near the house entrance, separate from the king and surrounded by the laments of the women nearby. They had made the journey north from Beersheba and were dressed in traditional sackcloth, having their robes rent. David didn't see any of the prophets that David had met while visiting Samuel's school—except one: Nathan. Standing at the forefront of the crowd, the young prophet was instantly recognizable by his white, blind eye. He had grown since David had last seen him, no longer a lad, but a young man with widening shoulders. The prophet watched the proceedings with an unreadable expression, but David knew what must be going through his mind. With Samuel dead, what would become of the school of prophets? The fact that David only saw the one prophet among the mourners below was revealing—and troubling. The prophets would likely be dispersed since they represented a power in Israel that Saul would not abide. It was probable that the dispersal had already begun.

---

[9] Genesis 49:29; Judges 2:10; 2 Chronicles 34:28.

But then David looked back upon the shrouded body, and memories flooded his mind as he did so. He saw again the aged, but powerful seer standing before him, a horn of olive oil lifted high to anointed him. He remembered his awe and fear of that moment, his confusion and uncertainty. He saw again the Great Seer standing before a company of prophets, leading them in praise and worship of the Most High God. He recalled how the song had swept him up into a spirit of comfort, erasing his fears, settling his mind, and giving him direction.

But looking back on that moment, David could clearly see the weariness in the aged seer's eyes and the stooped shoulders. Samuel had served his generation, but he was gone now. Who would serve David's generation? Who would stand forth as a beacon of light to keep the people from turning to the false gods of the heathen people around them? Gad perhaps…Nathan, maybe. David firmed his resolve. *I will.* David's love for Jehovah had only grown in the years of his exile, and he knew that if the Hebrew people were to survive, they would need to put their trust in their God. He determined to serve his generation—to point the people to Jehovah.[10]

Not a prophet himself, David nevertheless felt as if he had assumed the mantle that the Great Seer had vacated. Silently, his lips moving, he vowed to the memory of Samuel, "When I am king, I will continue your work. I will not let our people fall away unto false gods. I will be the beacon of judgment unto the LORD God."

Unable to hear him, Gad nevertheless knew that something profound had happened to his companion. He looked at David speculatively. David noticed and offered the prophet a tight smile. Together they turned their attention back to the proceedings before Samuel's house.

The king had turned to address the people. He stood with his hands clasped behind him, looking out at the crowd of mourners. David had a feeling that he was looking for him. At length, the king lifted up his voice and spoke to the people, "Hear now, O Israel, the

---

[10] Acts 13:36.

Great Seer, the last judge, is dead. Lament. Lift up your voice and weep for the man of God has fallen asleep to await the redemption of Israel." He paused to gauge the reaction of the crowd. "But know, O Israel, that your sorrow shall be turned to joy, for the Great Seer has not left us without a judge. On a day long ago, the people requested of Samuel a king, and the LORD directed him to anoint me as the first king of Israel, me and my house. His work is not in vain. Remember him, therefore, remember his labor and the great work on behalf of the Hebrew people." He turned then to look upon the body of the Great Seer. "Let him be taken to rest with his fathers to await the redemption of Israel."

Two young men stepped forward and together they lifted their faces to the heavens and began to sing. David recognized them. Asaph and Heman, the latter being a grandson of Samuel.[11] Their voices rose into the sky with such majesty and power that the crowd fell silent to listen. The song was of praise to Elohim: "Unto Thee, O God, do we give thanks, unto Thee do we give thanks: for that Thy name is near Thy wondrous works declare. When I shall receive the congregation, I will judge uprightly. The earth and all the inhabitants thereof are dissolved: I bear up the pillars of it. Selah."[12] And with that word, they fell silent, their eyes still raised to the heavens, giving everyone a chance to meditate on their words.

Then after a time, they continued their song, "I said unto the fools, 'Deal not foolishly,' and to the wicked, 'Lift not up the horn. Lift not up your horn on high. Speak not with a stiff neck.' For promotion cometh neither from the east, nor from the west, nor from the south. But God is the judge! He putteth down one, and setteth up another!"[13]

David was startled. That sounded like a rebuke aimed at King Saul! David thought about the horn Samuel had used to anoint him—perhaps the same horn used to anoint Saul. The king's words would have seemingly been an attempt to promote his anointing, to

---

[11] 1 Chronicles 6:33.
[12] Psalm 75:1-3.
[13] Psalm 75:4-7.

place himself as judge of the people in Samuel's place. Were the young men predicting that God had replaced Saul? David swallowed. He couldn't see Saul's face, but the king stood rock still, not moving a muscle.

The song continued and David strained to hear, "For in the hand of the LORD there is a cup, and the wine is red; it is full of mixture; and He poureth out of the same: but the dregs thereof, all the wicked of the earth shall wring them out, and drink them. But I will declare forever; I will sing praises to the God of Jacob. All the horns of the wicked also will I cut off; but the horns of the righteous shall be exalted."[14]

Finished, the two young men paused while the rest of Samuel's sons and grandsons came forward to take up the body. The family reverently gathered up the body and solemnly bore it into the darkened tomb.

David let his breath out explosively, though the sound was drowned out by the resumption of the weeping and wailing of the people. The words of the song lingered in his mind like thorns clinging to cloth. The king still stood rigidly, though Jonathan was shifting as if uncomfortable, refusing to look at his father. The song verged on a rebuke as well as praise to Jehovah. But it certainly reflected Samuel's life. If anyone had been used by God to judge and to promote, it would be the Great Seer.

The thought of Samuel struck a despondent note within David. He knew that Samuel had been old and knew that this day was inevitable, but David couldn't shake the feeling he had somehow been abandoned at the same time.

Still, he had vowed to carry on, so carry on he would. He squared his shoulders and turned to Gad. "Come, let us depart. We have done all we can here."

For once, Gad's ever-present grin was swallowed up in a deep frown. "Asaph and Heman walk a dangerous path. They had best beware of the king," Gad said softly. David could only agree. The

---

[14] Psalm 75:8-10.

prophet shook himself as if coming out of a trance. "Nay, son of Jesse, I cannot yet leave." He was staring out over the slowly dispersing crowd. "The seers of the LORD are scattered. I must see to them and find young Nathan."

David flinched as if bitten. "This is of the LORD?"

"Aye."

"But I have need of you. I will need your guidance in the days ahead."

"Fear not, son of Jesse. You will not be left without the word of the LORD. Does not Abiathar yet reside with your company? Let him stand in his father's stead and wear the ephod. Seek the LORD through him."

David nodded, accepting the inevitable. Yet he liked it not. The difference was that the word of the LORD did not come to the priest unbidden. But a prophet could, at any moment, hear the LORD's voice. David had relied upon that spontaneity since Gad had joined his company. Well, he would simply need to seek the LORD first. All would be well.

He clasped the prophet's arm. "Go with God and find peace, my friend."

Gad grinned suddenly. "This parting is but for a moment. We will cross paths yet again. The LORD has shown me this."

That made David feel much better. He matched the other's grin. "Then go in peace."

David gave Gad a head start, making a slow count to a hundred, and then he left the rooftop, pausing only long enough to give his thanks to Caleb, the owner of the house. Back on the street, he struck out directly for the edge of town, merging once again with the flow of departing mourners. It was cool enough in the evening breeze to justify keeping his hood pulled low over his face, but even so, he was understandably on edge. Saul's soldiers were everywhere, Benjamites who scrutinized everyone with a rude intensity that caused no small amount of muttering and black looks.

Unfortunately, David did not go unnoticed. One of the soldiers pointed at him. "You there! Stand and be known!"

The warrior and two companions stood at a junction of the road inside the short wall of the city. The spokesman wielded a long spear, and he took a menacing step toward David when the latter hesitated.

Deciding on a course of action, David veered toward the three soldiers, keeping his hands visible and unthreatening. The leader stopped when he saw David's obedience to his command. Keeping his head down and low, David effected a slight limp that hopefully would make him seem even less unthreatening. But when he neared the three, he lost all pretense and suddenly and smoothly stepped into their midst.

So abruptly did he move that the three warriors didn't even register the potential danger before David punched the nearest as hard as he could in the pit of the stomach. The man doubled over, gaging and emptying all the contents of his stomach, but David was already launching a heavy backhanded swing that sent another flying. The third man registered the attack and tried to bring his spear to bear, but David caught the spear and jerked the man close, headbutting him hard in the nose. The poor man's eyes crossed, and he sat down heavily in the dusty road, groaning softly, his reason gone.

David glanced around. His fight had not gone unnoticed, but most people, accustomed to violence, paid little attention, but it would not be long before more soldiers arrived to investigate. Turning, he leapt up and caught the top of the outer wall of the city, and pulling himself up and over, he landed heavily on the other side. People were streaming out of Ramah, many into camps pitched without the city gates. A small city of tents had been erected, for the mourning of Samuel was not yet complete.

Many would spend the next several days mourning. More songs would be sung, some as often as three times a day. David would have loved to stay, to join in the time of proper mourning of a great man, but he could not. Taking a deep breath, he plunged into the city of tents and was quickly lost to any eyes who would seek him out.

11

Ahinoam shivered, and David stepped closer to put his arm around his wife as they walked, trying to offer what heat he could in the wintery chill. Clouds hung low in the sky, threatening to rain. It was truly a miserable day. Only the presence of the thickly wooded hilltop broke the biting wind, but the temperature had dropped sufficiently to bring unseasonably cold weather.

Together, they moved through the trees until they came to a large tent set up in a small clearing, representing David's headquarters in the wilderness of Paran. A large fire burned before the tent warming the soldiers gathered around it. David nodded to them and escorted his wife inside.

Within, a smaller fire burned in the center, providing warmth to David's lieutenants and Abiathar, the priest, huddling near the blaze. Moving to an empty spot, David sat with his new wife.

Shammah, his bald head shining in the firelight, bowed. "We are all here, my lord."

David returned the bow. "I thank you. You have heard the tidings brought by our scouts. My wife has knowledge in this. I have asked her to lend us her wisdom and knowledge."

Though it was unusual to include a woman in a council of war, the men, with the possible exception of Joab, seemed content. They trusted David and his judgment. Adino, seemingly roused from sleep, yawned and fixed Ahinoam with sleepy eyes. "What know you of this Amalekite bandit, the one calling himself Haman, this son of Agag?"

Ahinoam flushed deeply under the scrutiny, and her eyes remained fixed upon the fire before her. David had learned more about his wife over the last few months. Her shyness and willingness to please him was in stark contrast to Michal's forceful and dutybound personality. David found himself liking her more and more. He fervently wished he could give her a proper house to be mistress of, but she never complained, never so much as hinted of dissatisfaction. He touched her hand. "Speak, my wife. Fear not."

She shivered at his touch, and her eyes slid to him gratefully. "What I know is what I have overheard while in the household of Haroeh," she said softly, her voice like silk. The men leaned forward to hear better. "He is the son of Agag, the Amalekite king whom Samuel slew when King Saul would not.[1] Haman was not yet a man when his father was captured, having fled into the wilderness with others to escape King Saul. Now his heart is black with vengeance and cold with hatred to all Hebrews. He seeks recompense for his father's death and the slaughter of his people."

Eleazar took up the story, his plain features glowing in the firelight. "King Saul's campaign against the Amalekites left them scattered throughout Amalek. The cities were burned and razed. Their fields sowed with salt. Their herds butchered or taken. The remnant are nomads, following small herds of desert animals." The swordsman leaned back. "Agag is not a name, but the hereditary title of the Amalekite kings. That this Haman has not yet taken this name to himself is revealing. It is likely that he does not yet feel he can—not until vengeance has been achieved and their cities rebuilt."

"Thus, he raids Hebrew cities," Joab muttered harshly. "This dog is worthy of death."

No one disagreed. David turned to Asahel, his chief scout. "Nephew, share your tidings of this bandit."

---

[1] 1 Samuel 15:9-33. It is thought that the Haman of Esther's time was a direct descendant of Agag as he is called an Agagite (Esther 3:1). I borrowed the name to show the possible relationship.

Asahel's long legs looked like plucked bird wings as he sat cross-legged before the fire. He squirmed as attention fell upon him. "He has attacked Beersheba in southern Judah," he squeaked out. He flushed with embarrassment and cleared his throat. His stretched face took on a look of intense concentration as he continued in a more normal tone of voice, "The city has been partially burned. The inhabitants only just able to repel his surprise attack. The Amalekites stole much of the flocks and herds and left a score of men dead. Word has come that he is coming in this direction."

"Beersheba is not a small city," David said. "Why would he be so audacious as to attack it?"

Ahinoam shifted beside him, and David looked at her. "You have ought to say?"

She nodded.

"Say on."

Keeping her eyes fixed on the fire, she said, "Perhaps it is because Samuel's sons reside in Beersheba. Haman surely blames the Great Seer for his father's death. Now that the Seer himself has been gathered to his fathers, perhaps he seeks vengeance upon the sons."

Her logic made sense. But apparently the attack had failed. No word had come that Samuel's sons had been killed or even injured.

"How many men does he command?" Shammah rumbled, the beads in his beard knocking as he swung his head about to address Asahel.

The young man shrugged. "I know not."

Several of the men glanced at Ahinoam. David noticed. "My wife, know you of Haman's numbers?"

"Only rumors, my lord," she whispered. "He is said to command above a thousand men. Perhaps two thousand."

Adino shrugged. "Nothing of consequence then."

For once, Eleazar agreed. "Rumor always boasts of greater numbers than the truth of the matter."

David pulled at his beard, thinking. His brother, Abinadab, spoke up in the resulting silence, "If this Amalekite dog is indeed on his way here, it would behoove us to ally with the cities hereabouts—

including Ziph. They may have need of our protection, and we have need of their supplies."

David stiffened. "I would not do business with those betrayers."

Abinadab's chiseled features hardened. "Be not hasty, my brother. They are not all false men. Only one has betrayed you. But Haroeh may yet be prevailed upon to aid us." He looked at David's wife. "You know Haroeh. Can he be reasoned with?"

Ahinoam nodded slowly. "If he can see that intreating with you instead of the king is in his best interests, he will deal truly. He is, my lords, a greedy man who fears the loss of wealth and position above all else."

David's brother nodded. "Then we must give this elder of Ziph reason to intreat with us as true men. Food runs scarce in the camp, and unless we be as the Amalekite bandits, we must barter for our sustenance."

"Is there no one else we may barter with?" David persisted.

"There is this fellow, Nabal, a descendant of Caleb," Joab put in. "His flocks and shepherds abide with us around Carmel. The shepherds have dealt kindly with us thus far, and we have brought no harm to them or their flocks."

David considered. He knew little of Nabal, except perhaps that he was the richest man in the region. But from all David knew, Nabal took little interest in local politics. This might make him easy to approach, to barter with. But David was unsure. By all reports, this Nabal was a hard man who saw little worth in anything except his own riches. Such a man would look for the better of a bargain, and David was in no position to grant it. Haroeh, on the other hand, was in a more precarious position. The elder was responsible for the security of the region, and people looked to him for leadership and protection. David could give him both. He had nothing to give this Nabal—not yet anyway.

Yet, David's anger over the betrayal by the elders of Ziph—particularly by Haroeh—was not something he could easily set aside. His instincts were to simply march on the city and take it. His hands itched to put a rope around the hairy neck of that treacherous elder. Perhaps the only thing that really stayed his hand was the fact that the Ziphites were of the tribe of Judah as was he.

Something in his face must have warned the priest Abiathar, for he spoke up, "Let not my lord's anger wax great. Heed my words for I have read the book of the law."

That arrested David's attention. He had only ever seen a single copy of the Law of Moses, and though he could read some, he had never been privileged enough to actually read the sacred words. Only the scribes could read and write fluently, so much of what he knew was recited and learned by repetition. "Say on."

Abiathar's spotless robe gleamed in the firelight as he gathered the cloth around him, sitting with a dignity that everyone else lacked. "It is written and commanded that we forget not what Amalek did to our ancestors at Rephidim,[2] how they came upon us from behind and slew the weakest among us, our wives, our children, our elderly. Moreover, it is written that Moses held up his arms and so the victory was secured. For so it was, that when his arms grew heavy and lowered, the tide of battle moved against Israel. But Aaron and Hur strengthened Moses and held his arms high until the battle was won.[3] What Amalek did was never to be forgotten. It was because of this that God commanded Saul to destroy Amalek, and because of this we must unify against these Amalekite bandits.[4] The LORD's will is to blot Amalek out from under heaven. This is a weightier cause than vengeance upon those who betrayed you. I beseech you, my lord David, ally with the Ziphites if you must, but drive these Amalekite raiders back into the desert from whence they have crawled."

The argument was compelling. David struggled with his anger, but the word of the LORD had spoken. He must heed it. With a sigh, he looked around the fire at his lieutenants, glad for their wisdom and presence. "We will intreat again with the elder of Ziph. Perhaps he will deal truly this time."

---

[2] Deuteronomy 25:17.
[3] Exodus 17:12.
[4] 1 Samuel 15:2-3.

"Once a snake, always a snake," Eleazar muttered in a dire tone of voice. "We must take care."

David smiled. "We will be in the LORD'S hands. Make ready. For on the morrow, I will go to Ziph and deal with the elders." He glanced at his wife as a thought struck him. "You will come with me, my wife. Surely, you know Haroeh better than I and might see something I do not."

Ahinoam shuddered and looked pleadingly at David. "Please, my lord, I would not return to Ziph. I can be of little use."

David raised his eyebrows in surprise. This was the first time his wife had ever resisted his desires, let alone a command. Her fear must be great for her to do so, he decided. He put his arm around her and pulled her close. "Fear not. I have but need of your eyes. You will not have to deal with Haroeh. That unpleasant task is mine alone."

She was still shaking, her eyes wide and frightened, but she bowed low. "As my lord wills."

Content, David dismissed his men. Not knowing the Amalekite army's current location could prove disastrous, but David could do only so much at one time. He needed to secure supplies first—and allies. Only then could he set out to utterly destroy the Amalekite raiders.

David studied the interior of the house as he waited. His arrival, unannounced and alone, had certainly driven a spike of fear into Haroeh's household. Ahinoam knew where Haroeh lived and had led him straight to the elder's house the moment they entered the city. David had chosen not to identify himself until he stood before the key elder's house. He had worn an outer cloak to conceal his armor and weapons but had put it aside the moment they reached the elder's door. And without her virgin's veil, Ahinoam had gone largely unrecognized by those who had seen them.

The elder's wife, pale and shaken, had admitted them while a servant ran to fetch the elder from some business elsewhere in the city. While they waited, Haroeh's wife had stood before the couple, shifting uncomfortably and wringing her hands indecisively, her eyes latched on to the sword strapped to David's side, so finally, David had gestured to his wife to take the other woman elsewhere and to reassure her. At the moment, they were busy in a whispered conversation in the kitchen just out of earshot.

The door burst open, and two men stumbled in. The first was the bulky chief elder and the second was a middle-aged man with thinning hair, narrow eyes, and a bulging lower lip. David caught a brief glimpse of a dozen aging warriors crowding the door from outside.

David turned the full force of his armed presence upon the two men. "Close the door and stay your men without."

The hairy elder held a rusty iron knife gripped tightly in both hands as he stood before the fully arrayed warrior in his house. David didn't move or twitch. He could have his sword out and through the elder's gut before the large man took one full step forward.

The two men shrank back from David, eyes wide and beads of sweat forming across both men's brow. The second man, the unfamiliar one to David, began edging toward the door as if to flee. David stopped him with a single implacable glance that took in both men. "Do as I say, Elder Haroeh, and no harm will befall you."

The elder's mouth worked until he finally blurted out, "What do you want?"

"For you to close the door." David glanced dismissively at the dozen warriors crowding close to the entranceway. Not one of them held his spear properly, and all had more wrinkles and gray hair than skill. "No one needs come to harm this day."

Moving slowly, the elder motioned for his guards to back away. He closed the door but did not latch it. David smothered a smile, carefully keeping his features impassive, knowing that this would be more intimidating. He had little love for the elder of Ziph and did not care to put the man at ease.

The second man watched this with eyes that clearly regretted his decision to burst in on David. He obviously wished to be anywhere else than standing in a house with an angry warrior whose skill and prowess were nearly legendary.

Haroeh looked around. "My wife?"

David gestured. "There."

At that moment, Ahinoam and the man's wife stepped into view from the open kitchen. The moment Haroeh saw Ahinoam, he flinched, causing David to wonder. Turning back, the elder set his wide bulk and pulled at his long nose. "What do you want, son of Jesse?"

A knock on the door interrupted David's response. He glowered dangerously at the door. Haroeh cleared his throat. "Who goes there?"

A woman's voice floated back through. "It is I, Abigail, wife to Nabal."

The second man's eyes narrowed in anger, nearly a match to David's. "Begone woman!" the man shouted.

David held up his hand. "Allow her entrance. But no other."

Both the second man and Haroeh hesitated until David took a step toward the door himself. Then the second man leapt to the door and jerked it open. The woman had remained standing without, her face calm and serene.

David was instantly captivated. She was much younger than he'd assumed, little more than a girl but incredibly beautiful. The thin-haired man grabbed her by the arm and jerked her inside. She came compliantly enough, but David caught the quick considering glance she cast at David as she passed before him. Her eyes showed neither fear nor anger. Without being told, she kept right on going until she joined the other two women, where she instantly took charge and ushered them farther away, back into the kitchen.

All the better as far as David was concerned. He had no time to deal with the women, and it helped that they were out of the way.

He turned back to the two men as the second man, presumably the one named Nabal, closed the door again. David wondered if this was the same Nabal who lived in Maon and was a descendant of Caleb.

Giving a mental shrug, David dismissed him and fixed cold eyes on Haroeh. "You betrayed me," he said, "and delivered me into the hands of my enemies. Twice was this done. As the LORD lives, you are surely worthy of death." The other attempted to speak, but David held up a hand to forestall him. "Heed me, elder of Ziph, and know my anger. Know that should I so desire, your life is forfeit. But I am not come for vengeance. The LORD God of Israel will require it at your hands if He so wills. I am come to barter, to deliver you from the hands of an approaching enemy." He paused to gauge the effect of his speech. Satisfied that both men were cowed, he continued. "I require supplies for those in my company. In return, I will safeguard your borders, your flocks, and your herds from all harm."

This was an echo of his first offer made to all the elders of Ziph. Only this time, the danger was more real than any in Ziph truly knew.

Haroeh grimaced as if having bitten into a rotten apple. "What makes you believe we need such protection?"

"You know of the bandit Haman, the son of Agag?"

"I know of him."

"Then you must know that he attacked Beersheba not three days ago. The city is partially burned, and many of the inhabitants were slain. My scouts believe he will come here as he has done so in the past." He took a step forward, hand coming to rest on his sword. "His army has grown since he last raided your flocks. Some say he has two thousand men under his command." Much to David's satisfaction, Haroeh paled at hearing that number. "Haman knows you are weak and alone. For King Saul has turned his attention to other matters, and you have only old men who no longer retain the strength of arm to be of any threat to this Haman. You need my army. You need my warriors."

"You leave me little choice," Haroeh muttered.

"None," David agreed. "You will provide meat, hides for coats and tents, water and wine to drink, and such else as we require."

"You will beggar our city."

"Nay. We will give good recompense. What will you lose if Haman the son of Agag lays waste to your city? Will he be content this time to take a few sheep?" David took a step closer, crowding the other two men back against the wall. "This offer is gracious, for in my wrath, I would have taken what I need. Seek not to betray me again, Haroeh, for in the day I learn of it, you will surely die."

The large man licked his dry lips and nodded. "Then so be it. I will send the first of the supplies on the morrow."

David's cold smile was a match for the outside frost. "Today, Haroeh. You will send them today."

The other flinched, nodding. "As you say. Where may I find you?"

"We encamp near Carmel."

The man called Nabal had yet to add to the conversation, but at this news of where David's men were encamped something in the man's eyes shifted. It was subtle, and David couldn't be sure he'd seen it.

Haroeh nodded yet again. "It will be done."

David looked long into the man's eyes, letting his anger sweep over the man, letting him feel the strength of his wrath, and making it clear what would happen should the elder fail or betray him yet again. Finally, he turned away, calling for his wife. Ahinoam came instantly. She refused to look at Haroeh, coming to stand beside David with her eyes downcast. David hoped she had paid attention to the conversation. It would be interesting to know her thoughts on the matter, to hear what she may have divined from it all.

He turned to the door and left. He saluted the aging warriors still waiting without, showing the respect due them. They relaxed and returned his salute. Moments later, he and his wife were gone.

Back inside the house, Haroeh collapsed onto a stool, his legs finally giving out. That had been the most terrifying experience of his life. Like most Hebrews, he lived with the threat of death and war, but never had such danger entered his home before. He fully believed the son of Jesse capable of murdering him, his household, and laying waste to the entire city if provoked enough.

Nabal hadn't yet taken his eyes off the closed door of the house as if he could still see David. "So, it is true then," Nabal murmured, "he has taken Ahinoam to wife."

"Did I not tell you so?" Haroeh replied bitterly.

"He is little more than a brigand."

Haroeh completely agreed but saying so seemed pointless. "What am I to do?"

Nabal finally ripped his eyes away from the door and began rubbing his left arm, a faint grimace sliding across his features. "Send for the king. Let King Saul deal with the son of Jesse."

Haroeh's eyes bulged. "You would have me risk my life—our lives!"

Snorting, Nabal winked insultingly. "You are a fool, cousin. What will you have left if the son of Jesse is allowed to continue in the region? Do you truly think he intends to ward us against the Amalekites? Nay, he seeks only to pillage us of our wealth. Any defense he provides will be in his own self-interest, mark my words." He leaned back against the wall as Abigail returned to the room. "This is what comes of a servant who rebels against his master. Such men lack all honor and will not keep their word. Call for the king. Let the king slay them all."

So saying, Nabal gestured sharply to his young, pretty wife. Obediently, she followed her husband out the door. Haroeh felt a moment of pity for the woman, knowing that Nabal would likely take out any frustration he had on her. Nabal had been disturbed that David and his army were encamped where many of his flocks wintered near Carmel. He all but owned the small town, but David's army would put a severe strain on the resources of the entire region—which meant Nabal's own wealth would be impacted.

Haroeh sat in silence for a long time, struggling to reach a decision. Nabal was right, of course. He would need to let Saul know that David had returned to the area, but he would need to do it in a way that the son of Jesse would not suspect. He could hardly credit the situation. And only his belief that David would kill him eventually anyway gave him the courage to consider the betrayal yet a third time. He listened idly to his wife working in the kitchen while sorting through problems in his mind and trying to determine the best course of action.

Undecided, he settled for simply waiting. If his cousin was right, then there would come a time when David would break their bargain, and he would be fully justified in sending for King Saul. And if an opportunity arose where he could get word to Saul without David knowing, then all the better. His life was about to change forever—regardless of the outcome. A shiver ran up his spine, feeding his doubt and fear.

12

---

ce gathered at the pool's edges, the crisp winter morning a harbinger of trouble that tickled David's senses and set him to looking about uneasily. He shivered, pulling his heavy wool coat closer about his body as he moved closer to the water and the bleating sheep milling around the edges. Several shepherds stood in attendance, watching David warily.

"Ho," David called in greeting, lifting a hand to show he meant no harm. "I would have words."

One of the shepherds cut through the sheep and came to a stop before him, bowing low. "You are my lord, David, the son of Jesse, are you not?"

"I am."

"I am Naam, the son of Zanoah, of the tribe of Judah."

David clasped the man's forearm. "Then we are kin, for I am of Judah as well."

The shepherd grinned, his young face brightening. "This I well know. All know of you, my lord."

David considered the young man before him. "How is it, Naam, that you have avoided the king's call to arms? I thought all young men hereabouts have been taken by the king to serve in the army."

Naam squirmed uncomfortably. "I am the only son of my father. We live in Carmel, but our lot is poor, and we are servants to Nabal, a very rich man who resides there at times."

David again wondered if this Nabal was the same one he had met in Ziph. "And this Nabal did not let you go to the king?"

Naam looked around at the few other shepherds, all young men, all of fighting age. "Aye. This is so. When the king's men came, we were hidden away. Truly, Nabal loves his comfort and would have us at hand to watch his flocks." He shrugged. "I would rather fight the LORD's enemies."

David smiled. "As you should. But Elohim knows that there is yet a need for shepherds. Do not fret over much on this."

The shepherd bowed again. "As you say." He shifted his thick coat and then leaned against his crook in a familiar stance of shepherds that suddenly made David homesick. Naam gestured to the women and girls moving through the sheep to the pool's edge, bearing pots needing to be filled. "You have a large company, my lord."

David glanced at his men's wives and daughters. Farther away, a scattering of David's men stood guard around the pool and up the slope of the hill. David's army had encamped nearby, taking over possession of the pool of water and the surrounding countryside, but he had given orders that the shepherds and flocks were not to be disturbed and that they were to be allowed to move freely into and out of the area.

"This is true," he finally said to the young man, giving nothing away. "Have you been treated well by us?"

The shepherd nodded. "We have, and I thank you for the courtesies."

"And does your master know?"

The young face turned troubled. "He knows, for we have told him. But he likes you little and would that you and your men were elsewhere."

David's face darkened. "And does he know that we are a buffer to you? That we have protected you from harm?"

"There have been no attacks, my lord. He does not believe you are responsible for our safety."

David's anger spiked, and he found himself gripping his sword hilt tightly. It was true that the Amalekites had not yet attacked. His spies had been sure they were coming, but that had been months ago. Since then, they'd lost track of Haman and his raiders. Supplies from Ziph had continued to trickle in, only just keeping David's company this side of hunger. But as of yet, David had little to do to keep his side of the bargain. Murmuring and grumbling coming from the cities in the region had reached his ears. It didn't matter that, in all likelihood, David's presence was what had turned back the Amalekites. It didn't matter that his army had brought stability to the region, reducing crime, and providing security to the shepherds and herdsmen to range farther away from their typical safe pastures. No, the elders of the region only knew that their winter stores were being consumed by David and his men. It frustrated David that people could be so blind—worse, be so intentionally ignorant. The only ones who seemed to understand were the shepherds and herdsmen themselves.

Naam noticed David's darkening features. "But, my lord, we are grateful." He gestured to his fellow shepherds standing some distance off. "We know you have made it safe for us."

A horn sounded, cutting off David's response. He whirled around instantly, facing the direction the sound had come from. His sword appeared in his hand as if conjured. "Start your flocks up the hill," he said to the shepherd.

The young man looked confused. "My lord?"

"Go. Now!" David glared at the shepherd. "Raiders come." David turned to the women and children, but they were already in motion, knowing what the horn signified. They knew what to do.

The clash of arms shattered the wintery stillness. From among the trees at the base of the hill, David spotted ragged-looking men, dressed in a hodgepodge of mismatched armor sprinting toward the sheep and pool of water. The sounds, yells, and screams unnerved the sheep so that they instantly scattered, bleating in distress, and rushing away from the threat in compact flocks.

The shepherd cursed, starting to follow, but David grabbed him. "Nay, get you up the hill. There will be more raiders where the sheep flee."

"But—"

David shoved him. "Argue not. We will see to the safety of your flocks!"

The man swallowed, motioned to his fellow shepherds and began scrambling up the hill and away from the ensuing battle. A score of David's men rushed to take the shepherd's place at their leader's side, David's three nephews among them. Instinctively, he knew there would be at least two bands of raiders. Those here were the distraction, meant to stampede the flocks into the waiting arms of others.

"Amalekites, my lord!" Joab spat.

David nodded. He had already come to that conclusion. *How did they get so close?* Putting that problem aside for the moment, he began barking orders. "Eleazar, take half. Follow the sheep and slay the Amalekites that would steal them. Let not one sheep fall prey to the dogs!"

"Aye, my lord!" the expert swordsman replied with a salute. He motioned, and ten men trotted after him in the wake of the sheep.

David motioned for the rest of his men to follow as he rushed to the aid of his hard-pressed scouts, guessing he faced upward of fifty raiders. The Amalekites had likely expected some resistance from the shepherds and perhaps a few guards, but they were woefully unprepared for David's seasoned veterans. David and his small force spread out and began a trotting advance through the trees, weapons at the ready. The beleaguered scouts continued a running retreat, pushed back by the greater numbers, but the moment they came even with David's line, they stopped, sliding into place seamlessly with their comrades and presenting a unified and dangerous front to the enemy.

The Amalekites hesitated, pulling back, clearly not expecting such a daunting response from what they must have assumed were mere shepherds. One of the warriors impatiently thrust himself to the forefront of his men. He was a large man, missing two fingers on his left hand and sporting several scars and burns on his face. His dark eyes scanned David's men dismissively. He ordered something in the Amalek tongue and the raiders, nearly fifty of them, rushed upon David's much smaller force.

The first Amalekite to reach David died with a single thrust to the throat. The man's nearly decapitated body flopped to the ground, the pooling blood creating a stark contrast of color against the brown earth and crusty leaves.

Two other Amalekites fell to David's warriors before the enemy pulled back in shocked dismay. Disciplined to keep rank no matter what, the Hebrews set themselves with a cold, dispassionate intensity that veterans of warfare often adopted. There was no nervous shifting of the feet, no trembling hands, no twitching eyes. Indeed, the Hebrew warriors welcomed the fight. After months of stagnation, the Amalekites would face the full pent-up wrath of David's men.

David barked an order and his men stepped forward in perfect unison, spearmen thrusting forward while the swordsmen protected them. Two more Amalekites fell, twitching as their life's blood seeped into the cold earth, the Amalekites retreated several steps, bunching together and milling about in an uncoordinated fashion.

Then the big Amalekite shoved his way forward again. He wielded a heavy sword and with a roar swung a mighty blow that shattered two of the Hebrew spears. The spearmen fell back, and David and one other stepped forward to face the enraged enemy. The Amalekite screamed something in his foreign tongue and launched an attack of his own. David's companion took the brunt of the blow on his shield, but such was the force that it cracked the wood and sent the Hebrew to his knees with a broken arm and a scream of pain.

As if the scream were a signal, the rest of the Amalekites attacked, and David found himself fending off two men with crazed faces and eyes too bright. David parried and dodged, dragging his wounded comrade back with him. The injured Hebrew tried to find his feet, but a sword thrust caught him a glancing blow to the shoulder, sending him face down into the bloody earth. David leaped to stand over him, driving the Amalekites back with a furious display of swordsmanship.

Surrounded, David's men formed a circle, fighting as ferociously as he'd ever seen them. David's sword locked with one of the enemy's, and they shoved against each other, trying to throw the other back with pure strength alone. David growled low in his throat, and with a violent heave, sent his opponent flying back to crash into two others. They went down in a tangled heap. David would have gone after all of them, but the empty space before him filled abruptly with the Amalekite leader. The big man swung a massive overhand blow at David.

David didn't have his shield, so he attempted to parry the massive blade with his own. Such was the force of the blow that it tore David's sword from his hands. Yelling in triumph, the large Amalekite prepared for another overhand swing to finish David off. Weaponless didn't mean helpless, however. David jumped forward and punched the other in the face as hard as he could. A crack penetrated the cold air, vibrating all around the combatants. The Amalekite's head snapped back, his nose crushed under David's blow, and he reeled away, his arms windmilling and his sword sent flying as he tried to regain his balance.

Something inside David gave way in that moment. His sense of balance was smothered by a towering rage that consumed him. He scooped up his sword and stabbed one of the other Amalekites pressing one of David's men to his left. Then, like the angel of death from Moses' day, he began chopping into the enemy with a ferocity that stunned even his own men.

He gave himself over completely to his rage, finding a perverse type of freedom that allowed him to lay about him with abandon, cutting, and slicing, and reveling in the shed blood. It became a craving, a need to slay all around him. He became a butcher, hacking away at meat, not people.

Before such ferocity, the Amalekites had no answer. Panic set in, and soon they fell back, their dead littering the clearing around the pool of water. Literally covered in blood, David found himself standing alone, his own men having pulled back too, lest they be caught up in the enraged storm that had become David. He blinked, coming back to himself. It was like hauling himself out of a river after having tried to swim frantically against the current for long minutes.

He took a shuddering breath, his face flushing with embarrassment as he saw the confusion and fear in the eyes of his own men. Never had he gone berserk, lost all control. He had seen other men do it, seen the battle rage take over so completely that they lost all sense of friend or foe and attacked anything that moved. But it had never before happened to him. He turned away from his men to hide his face and watched as the remaining Amalekites fled the battlefield.

Only one remained, standing three score cubits away, his chest heaving and his eyes gleaming with a hatred that seemed to radiate its own force—the Amalekite leader. He wiped the blood away from his crushed nose, smearing his beard red. He pointed his sword at David and in Hebrew said, "I know you now, son of Jesse. You are a devil, the offspring of Mot. And I will see you dead!" He turned then and disappeared among the trees, and David lacked the strength to pursue.

He simply stood there looking at the trees, trying to make sense of what had just happened to him. This was different than when the Spirit of the LORD had come upon him. In a way, he did feel as if some devil had taken control of him. He knew that to be impossible, for he was Jehovah's chosen vessel, but as surely as the LORD lived, it had not been Jehovah who had filled him. A frenzy had consumed him from within.

Joab and Abishai moved up to him. "Are you well, my lord?" the latter asked.

David offered a curt nod, not trusting himself to speak yet. Joab filled the resulting silence. "What did the dog speak of? Who is Mot?"

Struggling with his own emotions, David nevertheless cringed at the question. He took another deep breath before responding. "Mot is the god of death. The mortal enemy of Baal. The Canaanites believe that once every seven years the god Baal and the god Mot do battle. If Baal is victorious, there would be seven years of abundance and fertility. But if Mot won..." He trailed off.

"There would be seven years of famine and death," Joab finished for him.

David nodded, unable to keep his eyes from the dead Amalekites heaped around him. Most had been killed by his hand.

"Heed not that dog," Abishai said. "Let not his words linger in your mind, my lord. Jehovah has wrought a great victory here."

David wasn't so sure. This had not been by the Spirit of the LORD. This had been born of his own anger—an anger that had more and more come to dominate his life. And he didn't know how to deal with it. He shook himself, forcing his mind to other things. "What of the cities? Were they attacked?"

Asahel, Joab's youngest brother, stepped forward. "We know not. Word has not come."

"The bulk of the Amalekites are yet elsewhere. What happened here was a raid of opportunity only. Take men and find out where the rest are. We will not rest until the enemy is driven from our lands."

Joab saluted and ran off, his eyes gleaming with eagerness. Truly, his nephew loved battle. Joab's two brothers followed in his wake, and soon the clearing was empty save for him and the dead. David stood there among the slain as a sort of self-inflicted penance, as if the dead and dying was the world in which he belonged. One day, he vowed silently, he would build something, not destroy something. One day, he would honor Elohim with something other than war and battle.

He felt the familiar sensation of blood drying on his skin, and he clenched his jaw against the sudden urge to empty his stomach. No stranger to the carnage of battle, he was nevertheless dismayed by what he had done here. So much blood. So much death. He knew in his heart he would never be clean of it.[1]

"My lord?"

The voice shattered his musings, and he turned to find several of the shepherds returning, edging toward him tentatively, eyes fixed on the dead heaped around the pool.

"My lord, is it safe yet?"

David nodded. "Aye. We have driven away the marauders. Your flocks are safe." He gestured toward where the sheep had taken flight. "They are that way. Doubtless, my men have secured them." He hesitated, thinking of his promise to build something one day. "If any are missing, we will give just recompense."

The shepherds bowed as one. The one called Naam said, "You are most gracious, my lord. Our master will be grateful."

David silently hoped so. He would need the goodwill of the people if he intended to remain in the area. Thus far, King Saul had seemed content to let him be, though it was possible that the king did not yet know he had returned to southern Judah. Regardless, David's men would continue to need supplies and rich men such as Nabal would need to provide it.

One of David's scouts raced up to him. "My lord! Maon is besieged!"

David forgot the shepherds, pulling his scout close. "How many men?"

"At least a thousand Amalekites, my lord. Adino requests your guidance on what to do. We are gathering beyond them, but if we do not hasten, the city will fall."

"Then be a man of action and of few words," David snapped. "Lead on." David ran after the scout, his mind already turning to what must be done to deliver Maon from the Amalekites.

---

[1] 2 Samuel 16:7-8; 1 Chronicles 22:8.

13

A bigail peered over the wall at the Amalekites preparing to breech the main city gates. She unconsciously chewed on a lock of her hair, a nervous and unconscious habit. The raiders had appeared abruptly, emerging from a low hanging fog born from a cold morning. They came like spirits of the dead returned, ominous and frightening.

Sounds of battle had carried through the air in warning, providing the inhabitants of Maon the chance to fortify themselves, closing the gates and manning the stone walls with aged men and boys hardly able to wield the spear thrust into their slack hands. But with most of the able-bodied fighting men taken by King Saul, they weren't left with a lot of options when it came to defending themselves against just such a raid as was now taking place.

She knew David had six hundred warriors out there, scattered over the countryside between Maon, Carmel, and Ziph, and it had likely been his men clashing with the raiders that had alerted the city to the danger.

Abigail did a quick tally in her mind and determined that close to a thousand men had surrounded Maon. This then was likely the bulk of the Amalekite raiding force. Why they had gathered here, she could not say.

One of her husband's servants stood next to her, fidgeting from foot to foot, his face creased with worry. "My lady, is it wise to be up here?"

She removed the lock of hair from her teeth long enough to reply, "I want to see what is happening."

"If they start shooting arrows, we will be in peril."

"It looks as if they intend to assault the main gate."

The man, a long-time servant in Nabal's household, breathed a sigh of relief. "Then we are safe."

And that was the crux of the problem, Abigail knew. Nearly an entire quarter of the city was composed of Nabal's houses, barns, and sheep pens. To be more precise, the large compound of Nabal's fathers had been here before the city of Maon had even existed. The city had grown up around the compound over the centuries since Caleb had first settled in the region. Nabal had inherited the large compound, fields, flocks, and wealth from his father. From what Abigail understood, Nabal's father had taken more interest in the city, even governing it to an extent, but when he died and his son had taken over, Nabal had more or less ignored the city's needs except for when it could bring him more wealth.

Nabal's possession bordered one large section of the outer wall of the city. They had their own outer gates, their own inner wall, and their own fighting force. The only young men in the region—outside of David's men—worked for Nabal, and he wouldn't let them help with the defenses of the larger city. They were all tasked with defending Nabal's possessions, forbidden to leave. Nearly every family that had a son working for Nabal was in significant debt to Abigail's husband.

Many of Nabal's servants had long ago served their required six years and had been left with little choice but to continue their service.[1] When a servant was to be set free, Nabal always provided a day's rations, but nothing else—contrary to the law—nothing that would absolve the servant of all debt. But he did give them a choice to continue their service. Few had any other choice. So, most of the servants sported the pierced ear of their lifetime of servitude. Truly, Nabal was a cunning and devious man.

---

[1] Deuteronomy 15:12-17.

Looking at the young men lining the walls of the compound, Abigail thought Nabal's resistance to lending aid to the city was a profound mistake. If the Amalekites sacked the city, they would set it on fire—their signature depredation—and such a fire would likely consume Nabal's entire compound. She thought it best if Nabal would give the young men to defending the entire city. But Nabal would not hear of it. When she had broached the subject, he had struck her across the face. The bruise was only now beginning to show. Clearly, he hoped the Amalekites' lust for plunder would be sated on the outer city, sparing him and his own goods.

"They are truly a cursed people," Abigail observed to the servant while staring at the Amalekites gathering before Maon's main gate. "See how they are arrayed? They maintain no discipline and possess little coordination, relying on rage and numbers to carry the day."

"As you say, my lady," the servant agreed. "I still think we should resort to a safer place. Perhaps with your husband, my lady?"

Abigail gave the man a patient look. She had no intention of going to where her husband had barricaded himself in the main house and had surrounded himself with the most capable of his servants. "We are quite safe here for the moment. The main gates are the weakest point. See?" She pointed to the Amalekites. "They know this and are preparing for the assault."

The milling enemy warriors had lit torches, clearly preparing to set the gate on fire. Someone had cut down a tree and formed a crude battering ram that would be used to knock the gate down when the fire had weakened it enough. Abigail saw that the Hebrew defenders were ill-prepared to resist such an assault. They should be soaking the dry wood of the gates with water to help rebuff the flames. What archers there were should be gathering to try and pick off those carrying the battering ram. She could think of half a dozen other things that should be done as well, but the citizens of Maon were doing none of it.

The men called upon to defend the walls weren't truly warriors. They were aged shepherds, smiths, and farmers—traders, woodsmen, and carpenters—or wide-eyed boys hardly able to lift spear or sword. They stood little chance against the enraged enemy before them. Abigail fumed, itching to help, to take command and set things right. She knew it wouldn't take much. The Amalekites were more of a mob than an army. Any coordinated defense should succeed in repelling them.

But nothing was being done, and her husband refused to help. She was trapped here. She could only watch.

Just before the Amalekites could launch their assault, a flight of arrows stabbed out at them, seemingly coming from nowhere. Abigail gasped in surprise as a score of the Amalekites crumbled under the unexpected assault. She scanned the terrain, searching. Hills, the tops covered with trees, the troughs barren except for tall, brown grass and low shrubs dominated what she could see. *Where had those arrows come from?*

Then another volley sliced through the air, raining death down upon the enemy. Abigail still hadn't seen where they had come from. Then with a roar, Hebrew warriors charged the Amalekites, seemingly to have sprung up from the very earth itself. She watched in amazement as the Hebrews smashed into the confused Amalekites, slicing their way deep into the enemy ranks.

She saw a giant of a man, bald but for a massive beard laying about him with a war club. Something tangled in his beard flashed white in the dying fog of the early morning. Another man, thin as a rail, whirled about with a spear, delivering death wherever he appeared. And still a third man, heavily muscled and striking in appearance, walked along behind the Hebrews, shouting orders, and coordinating the attack against the enemy.

Abigail recognized the third man instantly. "David," she breathed. The son of Jesse had come to the city's rescue.

"That be David?" the servant next to her asked, peering into the haze of dust beginning to rise above the battlefield.

"Aye," she responded. "The son of Jesse has come to our succor."

She studied the mighty warrior, comparing him to the one other time she'd seen him at Haroeh's house. His light-brown hair looked closely trimmed, and his skin gleamed golden in the afternoon sun. But it was more than his appearance that struck Abigail. The son of Jesse brought a powerful presence onto the battlefield. No one would doubt who commanded, and no one could doubt that he was the most lethal man to stride into battle that day. His bloodstained armor bore testament to an earlier battle, but here he did not join the fight directly, instead holding himself back and directing his troops in a flanking maneuver that rolled up the Amalekite ranks like a rug.

It was over in minutes. Not prepared to meet such well-trained resistance, the Amalekites fled the field in panic, leaving behind much of their equipment, their wounded, and their dead. The last enemy warrior to flee the field of battle was a big man missing fingers on one hand. Abigail knew him, having heard his description gossiped about among the women. This was Haman, the son of Agag, the Amalekite leader.

She turned to her servant. "Make haste. Take two asses and send wool and bread to the son of Jesse. Let us give him thanks for his timely rescue."

The servant frowned. "My lady, your husband, my master, will not like this."

"Take wool from the women's house and bread from the kitchen. They are mine and thus mine to give."

The servant bowed. "As you say, my lady."

Abigail watched as the servant scurried off. He was right. Nabal would likely be furious when he found out, but if there was one thing Abigail knew, it was that a generous gesture here would go a long way to securing an alliance with David. Like it or not, the son of Jesse was the dominant power in the region. If her husband wanted to continue his trade unmolested, he would need to show some generosity.

She turned back to the battlefield and froze. David was looking right at her. The intensity of his gaze carried to her even from such a great distance. She could feel the force of it, and she felt suddenly vulnerable, as if he could see straight into her soul. But she refused to look away, holding his eyes with her own. He broke the shared look first, turning away as his men surrounded him.

Abigail left then, feeling satisfied. She had helped secure Nabal's good standing with David, and he would profit from it. Perhaps, when he found out, he would not beat her too badly.

David wondered at the woman who had watched him from the wall. It was odd to see a woman where guards and warriors normally took up position. Something about her was familiar, but he couldn't place his finger on it. Young though, he decided. Very young. But married. She did not wear a veil. Still, most men would have moved their young wives to a safer place than the wall of a city about to be attacked.

Shaking his head, he turned his attention to the reports now trickling in. He had lost a dozen men, and another two score would need treatment for their wounds. He grimaced, already hearing the lamenting that would take place in the camp later that night. Every death weighed upon him, but after so many years of battle and blood, he had learned to set it aside, to focus on the living. He felt nothing but satisfaction, however, when he looked upon the enemy dead. They were enemies of the LORD. Their end was justified.

He deliberately refused to think about his loss of control back by the pool near Carmel—of going berserk—or of the Amalekite's words.

Eleazar strolled up, bloody sword resting comfortably over one shoulder. "The Amalekites flee, my lord. Should we give chase?"

"Nay," David replied. "Let them return to their desert holes. We must tend to our dead and wounded."

The swordsman nodded and gestured with his bearded chin. "Already the women come."

Turning, David saw the women of his camp making their way onto the field of battle. They carried pitchers of water and wine. They would clean the wounds, bandaging them up as best they could. Listening to the groaning and hisses of pain from some of his men, he would need to send for Abiathar to pray for the wounded. Few men practiced the art of healing, and none of them lived in the region.

The first wail of a stricken woman discovering that her husband was dead rose up to lash at the sky. David bowed his head, muttering, "This too is for the good."

An unfamiliar servant trudged up to David leading two asses laden with wool, bread, and wine. "My lord, my master, Nabal sends greetings and our thanks for delivering us from the hands of the Amalekites. Accept these tokens, my lord, for we are truly grateful." He bowed deeply.

David nodded to the old servant, hope blossoming in his breast. Perhaps now a true alliance could be struck with the people of Ziph, Maon, and Carmel. If so, maybe, just maybe, he and his men would have a home and find true safety from King Saul. "Tell your master that we are most grateful." He gestured and the women converged on the asses, quickly removing the goods there. Much of it would find immediate use for the wounded. "Also tell your master that I would be honored to meet with him and to intreat with him about our future to the betterment of us all."

The servant bowed again, revealing a small bald spot in the center of his head. "As you will, my lord." He hesitated, eyes shifting back to the walls of the city and then returning to fix on David. "You have more than my master's thanks. I too am most grateful."

David grinned. "Then it is well."

The servant turned his beasts around and began a slow walk back toward one of the smaller city gates. David watched him go speculatively, his heart warmed with hope. A small seed of doubt, however, raised walls around itself to keep the hope at bay. Something about the situation in Maon bothered David. From the slight rise he stood upon, he could see an inner wall that sectioned off an entire quarter of the city. This, he had learned, was Nabal's house. He supposed the inner wall might have been there before the larger city had been built, but something about the disposition of the men atop the walls bothered David. Wouldn't it have been better to send all the men to the outer walls?

Shrugging, he turned back to the task at hand when a lad of no more than twelve years ran up. "My lord," he cried in a shrill voice, "I bear a message!"

David regarded him gravely. "Then say on," he said, hiding a grin.

"The elder Haroeh sends greetings and thanks. He begs you to return to Ziph there to confer with him more about this matter."

David's hope surged, overwhelming the seed of doubt and crushing it. He was frankly amazed that the lad had reached him so quickly. To do so, he had to leave Ziph before David had even routed the Amalekites. He wondered about that and what it meant. Fixing the lad with a kind smile, he said, "Return then and tell your master that I come." He bent over and whispered. "You did well, lad. You will surely grow to be a mighty warrior one day."

Pleased, the boy grinned from ear to ear. "Thank you, my lord. I will bear your answer back with haste."

"This I know. Thank you."

The boy bowed low, turned and darted back across the brown grass in the direction of Ziph. David watched him go fondly, remembering his own youth and enthusiasm. He then began to arrange for his departure. He did not want to wait long. He wanted to meet with Haroeh while the taste of victory was still fresh.

The blow sent Abigail reeling into the rock wall of the house. She hit hard, her teeth rattling and her head swimming. Tears sprang into her eyes causing everything to lose focus in her vision. Nabal stood before her, red with rage and clutching at his left arm. "You will learn your place, woman!"

Knowing better than to stand against him, she slumped down to her knees and bowed, worried that her jaw might be broken. Despite being in late middle age and not being a healthy man, Nabal packed a mighty blow when his anger consumed him. Her head still rang from the strike.

"I beg your forgiveness, my lord!"

He ignored her plea, his bulging lower lip turning a sickly dark purple. "By what right do you give away what is mine? Answer me this, woman!"

Abigail swallowed, deliberately retaining her bowed position. It would be harder to hit her like that. "The son of Jesse delivered us from the hands of the Amalekites, my lord. He is a powerful man, and I believed an alliance would be profitable for my lord. I would not presume to set the terms of such an agreement, but I believed that gifts would allow you to find favorable terms when you speak with him."

Nabal sneered. "You presume too much, woman. The son of Jesse delivered us not. We would have withstood the Amalekites and delivered ourselves. I will not intreat with any man who has fled his master. There can be no trust with such a one. You have given him gifts without cause."

Abigail could not agree less, but she dared not speak her mind. Her husband could not see beyond his own greed and stubbornness. Frankly, his blindness amazed her. "I beg forgiveness, my husband. I sought only to lift you up in the son of Jesse's eyes."

Nabal rubbed his left arm, grimacing. "What do I care for this son of Jesse? He is an oath breaker. I will have naught to do with him."

"As you say," Abigail agreed, silently wondering if one day her husband would have no choice but to deal with David.

Nabal regarded her, frowning, eyes narrowed, and his wispy, graying hair standing on end. "You need a further lesson, woman. The servant you sent to deliver my goods will be flogged, and you will watch, wife, every stripe. You will show no compassion and no remorse, or the flogging will continue. Do you understand?"

Abigail's heart turned to cold stone. Her husband knew exactly what to do to cause her the most pain. She would rather be flogged ten times over than watch the older servant be flogged once because of her misdeed. She desperately wanted to protest, but she knew any such sign of compassion would only increase the poor servant's misery. "As you command, my lord," she whispered instead.

Her two years of marriage to Nabal had done nothing to endear him to her or her to him. Her father had arranged the marriage, having negotiated a better than fair dowry for her. But her father could have never imagined the cunning of the man he had sold her to. Within a year of her marriage, Nabal had managed to indenture her father into six years of service as his debts continued to grow. Nabal had found it most satisfying and constantly reminded her that he had won back the price of her dowry twofold.

And no matter what she did, he resented it. Thrice, she had helped land trade contracts that brought her husband more wealth than he could have managed on his own, but instead of praising her, instead of rejoicing with her, he scorned her. He would not abide another rival to his own cunning, even if that rival was his own wife.

Nabal turned, gesturing to his young men to bring the old servant out into the middle of the courtyard for his flogging. Abigail tried to school her features into impassivity, but a single tear defied her efforts, and she hastily wiped it away lest her husband see.

The old servant, his eyes wide with fear and dread, looked over his shoulder at her pleadingly, begging with his eyes for her to intercede. Forcing herself to give him a cold, emotionless stare nearly broke her.

Her husband's coarse laugh flailed her like whips, causing more pain than any real scourge could ever do.

14

Adino spat out the shell of his Elah nut and leaned casually against the bark of a tree. He looked for all the world as if he fully intended to take a nap right then. David prodded him with a question. "What do you know, Adino?"

The spearman regarded David through slits in his eyelids, shadowed further by an overcast sky that threatened to sprinkle rain from a spring storm. "Many things, my lord. Many things. Most I suspect have been forgotten." He shrugged a single shoulder. "I know not."

"About our supplies!" David snapped. Just once, David wished the man would show more interest in something other than sleep.

"Ah. Aye, the supplies. We have little. What the elder of Ziph gave us for the winter is nearly exhausted."

"Do you think Haroeh would deliver more?"

The spearman looked doubtful. A single raindrop hit his forehead, going unheeded. "I think the elder did what he could. I think that if we press for more, we would cause hardships among the people. Spring has come, but food remains scarce. I think we need to be careful lest we push the elder into something all of us may regret."

Despite his rising irritation at his lieutenant's laconic manner, David knew he was right. His small army, numbering six hundred men with now an equal number of women and children required a lot of food. The sparsely populated region of the Maon wilderness could not continue to meet their needs. Since repelling the Amalekite raiders, the region had settled into an uneasy peace. David's meeting with Haroeh had gone well, resulting in more supplies, but that had been weeks ago. And now David needed more food.

"Can we barter with the elders of Hebron?" The larger city could likely spare more food.

"With what do we barter?" the lieutenant replied, stifling a yawn.

Tiny raindrops fell upon their heads, and David glared at the uncaring sky. He and his lieutenant stood in the midst of the camp that had been built near Carmel. Men and women bustled about them, intent on one chore or another. Cookfires sent lazy streams of smoke into the sky to lose themselves in the gray clouds and hissed angrily when raindrops fell among them. David had used the location as a base throughout the winter months. Food rationing had been in effect for some time, and grumblings continued to increase in equal proportion to the decrease in supplies.

The man Shobal had become the voice of the discontented and disgruntled. The talk rarely got out of hand for the stocky, pock-marked man walked a bit more carefully ever since Shammah had broken his arm back in Engedi. But murmurs and whispers had still reached David's ears. There had even been talk of stoning David, of all things.

Regardless, David needed to do something. "Do you have any suggestions on the matter?" he asked, not thinking the laconic man would.

But Adino surprised him. "What of this man Nabal? Did he not send us foodstuff after we rescued him from the Amalekites?" Adino shifted against the tree. "I hear he is a prosperous man, the most prosperous of all hereabouts. I hear also that he has personally come to Carmel to shear his sheep by the pool. It is said that he always throws a mighty feast after the sheep are sheared. Perhaps he has enough to share."

David considered. He could see no harm in making the request. The rich man had already proven his generosity, and David had protected the man's flocks and shepherds through the long winter. In a way, he was owed the food as wages for his service. Sheepshearing was a time of celebration, of rejoicing in the LORD's bounty and provision. Nabal would have food, drink, and other supplies brought for the shearers and shepherds. A similar feast would be thrown after the harvest. In both cases, generosity and food would be in abundance.

Looking around, he spotted Joab and Asahel not far off. Joab was seldom far from earshot. He beckoned his nephews over. "Joab, take your brother and eight other young men and go to the pool where the sheep are sheared and greet Nabal in my name."[1] He gave Joab his instructions and bid him to make haste.

His nephew saluted and then headed off to obey, his fleet brother restraining himself lest he overtake Joab. David watched them go in satisfaction. With all he had done for Nabal and based on what the man had already sent to David, he felt confident their food shortage would soon be over.

Later, he would regret not having spoken to his wife about Nabal first.

Turning, he moved toward his own tent. His fingers itched to play the harp. Words had come to mind early that morning, words that burned through his soul and sought release. He ached to sing them, to rejoice in his God. As he walked, he sang low, under his breath, "O God, Thou art my God; early will I seek Thee: my soul thirsteth for Thee, my flesh longeth for Thee in a dry and thirsty land, where no water is. To see Thy power and Thy glory, so as I have seen Thee in the sanctuary. Because Thy lovingkindness is better than life, my lips shall praise Thee."[2]

Joab and his companions found Nabal overseeing the shearing. Having done some shepherding and shearing himself, Joab was still

[1] 1 Samuel 25:4-5.
[2] Psalm 63:1-3.

impressed with the scope of the operation before him. He had heard that Nabal owned as much as three thousand sheep and at least another thousand goats.[3] Shearing that many sheep was a massive undertaking. The profits from the wool alone would likely keep Nabal's entire household and staff fed and clothed for years. Truly, the man lived in prosperity.[4]

The sheep were brought in by the flock, each lamb cut from the rest and delivered into the hands of the shearers. The sheepshearers sought to keep the fleece whole during the process, and the sheep-master applied a patterned dye to the back of the fleece as a mark of ownership. Nabal's fleeces were of the highest quality and would command the highest prices.

Nabal clearly knew his trade. The shepherds and shearers went about their tasks in an organized and proficient manner. There was a sense of haste, but not of recklessness. The bleating sheep, old hands at this, went to their shearing with the wide-eyed herd mentality inherent in their nature. Already, heaps of fleeces dotted the area around the pool, protected from the rain by blankets.

A smallish man with thin, wispy hair stood atop a white rock that overlooked the pool and the shearers. He seemed oblivious to the slight drizzle as his eyes darted everywhere, watching everything. He would occasionally snap an order that appeared to be unnecessary. To Joab's eye, the shearers knew their jobs and did them with skill. But the man standing upon the rock had to be Nabal. No other man commanded as much authority.

To be blunt, Joab instantly disliked Nabal. He did not like the way the rich man treated his servants, but he clamped down on any further judgment until after they had talked. If the man helped to provide the needed supplies for David's men, then he would gladly swallow his dislike. Still, he couldn't help but finger the hilt of Cutter, his sword. Not the most imaginative name, but Joab needed little imagination to be satisfied.

---

[3] 1 Samuel 25:2.
[4] 1 Samuel 25:6.

Bidding the other young men with him to stay near the tree line, he approached Nabal. Interestingly, Nabal stood nearly in the same place where David had stood when he had driven back the Amalekites those months back. Sights of that day were forever burned in Joab's mind. He could still see David, enraged beyond anything he had ever before witnessed, laying about him with his bloody sword, hacking indiscriminately at anything within reach. Twice, David had nearly attacked his own men—though Joab didn't have the heart to tell him this afterward. The incident had been stunning and disturbing on many levels.

Nabal had spotted Joab and Asahel's approach and turned to confront them. He looked mightily displeased to see strangers intruding on his labor.

"What do you here?" the man demanded in a high-pitched voice. "Strangers were to be turned back."

Joab bit back a hasty retort. Instead, he bowed deeply and in measured tones, said, "Forgive us, my lord. Your shepherds did stop us, but we are known to them, and we come on behalf of David, the son of Jesse, who sends this greeting: Peace be both to you, and peace be to your house and to all you have. I have heard of your shearing. Know, therefore, that your shepherds we hurt not, neither was there anything missing unto them all the while they were in Carmel. Ask your young men, and they will show you. Wherefore, let the young men sent to you find favor in your eyes, knowing we come in a good day of bounty. Give, I pray, whatsoever has come to your hand unto your servants and to your son David."[5]

Joab ceased talking and straightened to take Nabal's measure, to see the impact his words had caused. The rich man's bulging, purplish lower lip quivered and then curled into a cruel sneer. "Who is David? And who is the son of Jesse?" Nabal deliberately turned aside to spit onto the ground, causing Joab and Asahel to stiffen. "There be many servants in these days that break away from his master. Should *I* then take *my* bread, *my* water, and *my* meat that *I*

[5] 1 Samuel 25:6-8.

have killed for *my* shearers and give it unto men I know not what they are about?"

David's warriors were struck speechless. Asahel glanced sidelong at his brother, his face a mask of confusion and outrage. Joab felt the same way. He had known Nabal might refuse their request, but he had not expected insults. "Is this the word you wish for us to return to our master David?"

The persistent drizzle had plastered Nabal's hair to his scalp, making him look nearly bald, so when he nodded, not a hair moved. "Aye, I will not deal with traitors and masterless men."

Spinning around, Joab marched away, his back stiff, his hands trembling with the desire to slay the pompous fool where he stood. Asahel walked beside him, looking back over his shoulder at Nabal in confusion. "Why has he spoken thus?" he asked his older brother.

Joab lifted a hand as if to shoo a fly. "Speak not. Let us return to David."

When they rejoined their men at the tree line, one of the shepherds met them, carefully shielding his body behind trees so that Nabal couldn't see him. Joab recognized him as the one called Naam. The shepherd looked nervous when he spoke, "What will the son of Jesse do?" he asked in a whisper.

"Do?" Joab spat onto the ground. "The dog has insulted the LORD's anointed. He is surely worthy of death. Be gone from this place lest you share your master's fate."

Naam paled. "My master will not remain here. He will return to his house to begin the feast."

"Then return not with your master if you value your life." Joab shoved past the shepherd and gestured for the remaining young men to follow. He would repeat the fool's words to David, but knowing his uncle's state of mind recently, Joab fully expected to return to deal harshly with Nabal. He, for one, would be most pleased to end the rich man's miserable life.

The shepherd watched them go, and Joab didn't see him abruptly turn and dart into the trees in the direction of Maon.

Abigail dropped her bundle of wool when young Naam burst into the compound shouting her name as if the entire Amalek nation was about to descend upon them all. As startled as she was, she was still glad to see the young man. The two were about the same age, and she had always gotten on well with the shepherd.

"I am here," she called. "What ails you? What is wrong?"

Naam spun on one foot, hunting her by the sound of her voice. When he spotted her, he darted over, breathing hard from a long run. "David sent messengers out of the wilderness to salute our master, and he railed on them."

Abigail gasped, quickly divining the source of Naam's terror. But surely her husband would not have so abused David. "He did so?" she had to ask.

Naam nodded frantically. "Aye. He called them traitors and masterless men. But, my lady, the men were very good to us, and we were not hurt, neither missed we anything as long as we were with them in the fields. They were a wall unto us both by night and day all the while we were with them keeping the sheep."

Abagail clutched the front of her halug[6] tightly to her. She did not know David well, but she knew most men tolerated her husband's wicked tongue because they had no choice. David had a choice. He had a small army to deliver chastisement if he so desired.

Naam fell to his knees, his eyes betraying his panic. "What will we do, my lady? What will *you* do? Evil is determined against our master and against all his household, for Nabal is such a son of Belial that a man cannot speak to him."[7]

She saw it clearly then. If Naam was right, David would take the Amalekites' place in besieging Maon. She saw again the discipline and lethal ferocity with which David and his army had dispatched

---

[6] A tunic-like garment worn by both men and woman—the difference being in the cut, color, decoration, and other means to distinguish between the masculine and the feminine.

[7] 1 Samuel 25:14-17.

the enemy raiders. If turned against Maon, the city would not stand a chance. Even Nabal's small guard would be swept away like so much chaff. Worse, once in the compound and in a killing rage, no man would be safe. The women might be spared, but every man that stood with Nabal would likely perish. Looking into Naam's terrified eyes, she knew she couldn't allow such a tragedy to happen. She had to do something. She had to do it now.

"Naam, hasten to the storehouses and fetch whatever comes to hand." She turned and began shouting, "Abital, Japhia, Izrahiah! Lend aid to Naam. Fetch asses and be quick!"

Izrahiah, shuffled over, his eyes worried. "My lady, what is wrong?"

She studied the aged face of her servant, knowing he had not yet fully healed from the flogging her husband had given him. At his age, he might never fully recover. She could not—would not—let him die for her husband's folly. "Evil may descend upon us all if I cannot prevent it," she said. "Put your trust in me this once, I pray."

The servant smiled. "You are much like my daughter, my lady. I will do as you require."

"Then take all that is prepared for the feast and laden the asses. I must depart at once. When I am gone, dress other sheep so that my husband does not realize I have taken much of the feast food. Lay out wine so our master does see it first. Let him indulge in strong drink as is his want, and in the meantime, prepare other foodstuff for the feast. Act in haste. I know not how much time yet remains to us."

The older servant clearly didn't understand, but he trusted her. He bowed. "As you wish, my lady."

Abigail's eyes filled with tears. The servant knew his actions might result in another beating, but he didn't even hesitate to do her bidding this time. Such loyalty and love were rare, and she was grateful to find it in this house of pain.

A flurry of activity followed wherever Abigail went. In the two years she had been married to Nabal, the servants had come to love her even if her husband did not. Soon, she had managed to gather two hundred loaves of bread, two bottles of wine, five sheep ready dressed, and five measures of parched corn, a hundred clusters of raisins, and two hundred cakes of figs.[8] She hoped it would be enough to placate David, for surely it would not be enough to feed a thousand people.

Naam ran up, his face drained of blood. "My lady, your husband approaches!"

Abigail bit her lower lip and then unconsciously slipped a lock of her hair between her teeth and chewed on the ends. Her husband must have been shaken or bothered by David's request for him to return home so soon. A dozen asses brayed in the courtyard, laden down with the foodstuff. If her husband saw them, he would instantly know her intentions and would put a stop to it. As cunning as he was, he often acted without wisdom. He would risk his entire household to preserve his pride.

"Leave by the south gate," she said to Naam. Take three of your fellows and make haste."

"But what of you, my lady?" He was fairly hopping from foot to foot in his anxiety.

She smiled to calm him. "Go before me. I will come after you."[9] Looking over her shoulder at the north gate, she added, "I must be here to greet my husband."

Naam bowed and then ran over to the milling asses. He gathered up the lead ropes, and with two other servants helping to herd the stubborn beasts, he led them out the south gate into the city proper. They would circle around and head toward Carmel to intercept David. Hopefully, they would not be too late.

When the gate had closed behind Naam, she beckoned to two of her maidens that Nabal had chosen to serve her. "Bring me two more bottles of wine, a cluster of raisins, and begin roasting new meat over the fire." She clapped her hands when the women just stared at her causing them to jump. "Make haste. Our master comes, and we should greet him properly." The girls scurried away.

---

[8] 1 Samuel 25:18.
[9] 1 Samuel 25:19.

Nibbling on a loose strand of her hair, she tried to think as the last few drops of the passing storm struck her head. Nabal would be in surly mood after having rebuffed David's messengers. He would seek his wine, and she had no intentions of refusing him. Nabal was a mean drunk, and he would likely abuse his servants and her when in the grip of intoxication. But there was no help for it. She could not allow him to stop the supplies from reaching David. All their lives, including Nabal's, were at stake.

When Nabal rode in on another ass, he immediately began bellowing for wine. Anticipating such, she had a wooden cup in hand and offered it before his demands could fade away. He glared at her in surprise as he snatched the cup away from her. He sniffed at it, grunted, and then drained it. She held a second one up as he tossed the first aside. His lower lip bulged unnaturally as he squinted down at her. "Have you at last decided to be dutiful, my wife?"

She bowed her head. "I am ever dutiful, my husband."

He grunted doubtfully as he slid down off the ass, careful not to spill his second cup of wine. More and more servants entered, bearing the newly sheared fleeces. He watched as they marched by, heading to the storehouse where they would be further prepared for transport and sale. "That remains to be seen," he muttered.

"Has the shearing gone well, my lord?"

"It has. It will be a good bounty. Jehovah smiles yet upon me." He said the last so casually, so flippantly, that Abigail had to swallow a dozen retorts that sprung instantly to mind.

"The LORD is good," she whispered instead.

"Aye." He turned away from her, moving toward the main house of the compound. "This is a day of feasting, woman. What have you prepared?"

"Come and see," she replied, nearly running to precede him into the house where her maids were just finishing laying out bread, raisins, and more wine.

He stared at the food. "Where is the meat?"

"It is being cooked, my lord. It will be ready soon."

He casually backhanded her, catching her completely off guard. She reeled away, crashing heavily to the ground, the side of her face stinging as if a dozen bees had attacked her all at once. She stared up at her husband in shock, but he didn't even look at her, he was already reaching for more of the wine.

"Next time," he muttered, "have the meat ready against my coming. Get you gone from my sight, woman."

"As you command," she managed to say through her aching mouth. She rose and darted away, her heart thumping in her chest. Outside, Nabal's ass stood placidly in the yard, a blanket over its back. Izrahiah held the lead rope. She ran over.

"Will you follow Naam, my lady?" the servant asked.

"Aye. Words will need to be said to turn aside David's wrath."

He nodded, understanding finally dawning. His nervousness jumped by measures. "Then go with God, my lady." He looked around. "Does our master know?"

She shook her head. "I have not told him yet."[10]

"He will discover this, my lady."

"Aye. He will. I will tell him when I return. Izrahiah, make the feast great. Send word to the elders of Maon and invite them to the feast. My husband will enjoy their words of respect, and it will keep him from seeking me until I return."

"I will see to it."

She laid a hand on his arm affectionately. "You are a good man, Izrahiah. May Elohim smile upon you."

He smiled and helped her to mount the ass. Kicking the beast into motion, she rode out the north gate. If she hurried, she could catch up to Naam. They would need to act quickly. Too many things could go so wrong. If David came by an unexpected route, she could return to a house in ruins. If Nabal found out too soon, he would attempt to stop her. With a prayer to Elohim on her lips, she urged the ass on.

---

[10] 1 Samuel 25:19.

15

---

nmatched fury boiled through David's veins, consuming him absolutely and replacing the passing storm with a whirlwind that drove all other thoughts from his mind. It was all too much. The running, the hiding, the discontent whispers, the hunger—and now this.

David snagged Joab with his eyes, two smoldering orbs that lacked anything resembling mercy. "Choose two-hundred men to stay in the camp with the stuff. The rest—" He jerked around to address those who had stopped to listen. All knew of the men sent to barter with Nabal and to fetch badly needed supplies. They also knew the results. Now they watched to see what he would do. He would show them gladly. "Let every man gird on his sword and prepare for battle. No longer will we suffer at the hands of those who should be our allies! If they seek an enemy, they have found one! Surely in vain have I kept all that this fellow has in the wilderness so that nothing was missed of all that pertained unto him, and he has requited me evil for good!" His eyes swept across the men gathering around. They were growing excited, for they too felt the sting of the insults and the pang of hunger. "So and more also do God unto the enemies of David if I leave of all that pertain to him by the morning light any that pisses against the wall!"[1]

---

[1] 1 Samuel 25:21-22.

Nods and heavy whispering of agreement broke out among the men, only Adino and Eleazar regarded him doubtfully. Shammah fingered his beard, a sure sign of his growing excitement. "Do you mean to lay siege to Maon?" Adino asked.

David growled low in his throat. "We will do what we must and take what we must. If the inhabitants of Maon get in the way, then so be it. Their lives belong to us, seeing as we delivered them from the hands of the Amalekites. No longer will our women and children go hungry!"

That got everyone's attention. Growling bellies made for a good incentive. A ragged cheer erupted from the men, and suddenly they scattered to arm themselves and prepare for the march. Only Abiathar remained standing near. The young priest stood rooted in place with arms crossed and wearing a frown that disappeared into his well-trimmed beard. David didn't care. He already knew the LORD'S will in this matter. God had anointed *him* to be king. If men rose up against him, then they rose up against the LORD God of Israel also. Their deaths would be on their own heads!

David moved to the edge of the camp, his anger unspent and his body trembling with the need to do violence. He itched to kill Nabal personally, to hack his body into pieces. The rich man's insults had struck a nerve with David he hadn't realized was so sensitive. He knew he was out of control, but he had ceased to care. He felt much like he had when he had caught the Ziphite spy betraying him to King Saul. He had killed the man then, and he meant to kill again.

Every effort on his part to do things right had been met with suspicion, derision, and insults. No more. He would not put up with it one more moment. Someone would need to be made an example of, and Nabal would do. Once word spread of what he did to the rich fool, the elders of the cities would cease their prevarications and deal with him truly.

Soon enough, four hundred men stood ready to march. No one attempted to talk David out of his course of action. They all had suffered at the hands of suspicious and greedy men. They were more than ready to act and take a bit of revenge on those who had treated them so badly.

A scout sent by Joab had reported that the pool at Carmel had been abandoned, the shearing finished. Nabal would be in Maon, feasting in his house for the evening. David would not wait until morning. He would launch a surprise night assault. By morning, it would all be over.

They left the wilderness around Carmel and began traveling south. The three cities, Ziph, Carmel, and Maon, formed a straight north-south line to the southeast of Hebron. Carmel and Maon were the nearest neighbors with Ziph equidistant between Carmel and Hebron. David and his men would reach Maon in a couple of hours, just as the last of the light faded from the clearing sky. The feasting would consume Nabal's attention; his men would be lax. It would be all too easy. No one would know a hostile force was among them until it was too late. Even if someone did give alarm in time, Maon lacked the defenses to properly repel David's elite fighting force. Nabal and all he possessed were doomed, and that thought brought a satisfied smile to David's lips.

A cart path led between Carmel and Maon, winding around the hills. David's men proceeded at a quick walk. Scouts ran on ahead as a precaution. Even in his anger, David would not walk blindly onto a field of battle. He led the main body of men, however, refusing to remain in the background. But his mind and body edged toward that moment of no return, where, like by the pool in Carmel, he would go berserk. He knew this. He could feel it happening. And he cared not.

He was still shocked when an unexpected disturbance from the side of a darkened hill reached his ears. The clatter of hooves on rocks and displaced dirt caused him to whip out his sword and turn to face a line of beasts descending upon him, their shapes in the deepening shadows like something springing forth from his nightmares. He barked a command, and his men reacted instantly, spreading out to face this new threat.[2]

At the base of the hill, one of the beasts literally broke in two and a smaller shadow flung itself in his direction. He braced himself to meet the attack, but the shadow fell short, collapsing almost at his feet. His heart thumping wildly, he raised his sword to slaughter this nightmarish apparition, but then it spoke, freezing him in place.

"Let not my lord, I pray thee, regard this man of Belial, even Nabal: for as his name is, so is he; Nabal is his name, and folly is with him!"[3]

David sucked in his breath, sword raised above his head, quivering with the need to do violence. The shadow before him resolved itself into that of a woman, her face pressed tightly against the earth, ignoring the rocks and scratchy grass. She was breathing heavily, sucking in great amounts of air. David blinked and then looked beyond her. The line of nightmarish beasts loomed into view, transforming themselves into heavily laden asses. Two servants cringed among the nervous animals, holding lead ropes and trying their best not to be noticed.

The woman at his feet spoke again, "I, your handmaid, saw not the young men of my lord, whom you did send. Now therefore, my lord, as the LORD lives and as your soul lives, seeing the LORD has withheld you from coming to shed blood and from avenging yourself with your own hand, heed me I pray. Listen to my words, my lord!"

David's anger drained out of him all at once, leaving him exhausted. He lowered his sword and then reluctantly sheathed it. Bending down, he raised the woman easily to her feet. He recognized her then. This was Nabal's wife, Abigail. Intrigued now and wondering why she had come, he said, "Say on, my lady. I will hear your words."

She regarded David without fear, but neither did her eyes hold any disdain. She saw David as he truly was, a mighty captain. The

---

[2] 1 Samuel 25:20.
[3] 1 Samuel 25:25.

respect she held for him intrigued him. She bowed her head. "Then let your enemies, and they that seek evil to my lord, be as Nabal. His own folly be upon his head. But behold now this blessing which your handmaid has brought unto my lord, let it even be given unto the young men that follow my lord." She gestured, and her two servants pulled the burdened asses forward as an offering.

David glanced at them, noted the foodstuff, smelled the fresh meat—causing his stomach to rumble—but ignored them otherwise. He had thoughts only for the beautiful young woman in front of him. Unbidden, he wished she was unmarried, for then, he would surely take her to wife on the instant. He had never met such a combination of beauty and intelligence in a woman before. Michal was beautiful and cunning. Ahinoam was meek and loving. But Abigail was something altogether different. She lacked Michal's lust for power and position, while possessing courage and fortitude that surprised David. Here was a woman worthy of sitting next to him when the LORD turned the kingdom to him. His desire for her burst into life, burning away his remaining anger and resentment, and filling him with longing.

He refrained himself with effort. Abigail was a married woman, and he would honor her station—though, he reflected, it would not take much to make a widow of her. No, he would not dishonor the courage that had driven her to risk her life to save those of her husband and his household.

"Your words have merit," he said softly. "Say on."

Startled, she glanced up into his eyes and then swiftly looked away. Taking a breath, she continued, "I pray, forgive the trespass of your handmaid, for the LORD will certainly make my lord a sure house because my lord fights the battles of the LORD, and evil has not been found in you all your days." She took a deep breath. "Yet a man is risen to pursue you and to seek your soul, but the soul of my lord will be bound in the bundle of life with the LORD your God, and the souls of your enemies, them will He sling out, as out of the middle of a sling."

David was touched. The reference to how he had slain Goliath was well spoken. He could see that she had more to say, so he waited. There was a courtesy in hearing out a petitioner.

"One day, when the LORD will have done to my lord according to all the good that He has spoken concerning you and made you ruler over Israel, then what my husband has done will be of no grief to you or offence of heart. Indeed, your mind will be at ease, knowing you have not causelessly shed blood or avenged yourself."[4]

Her words rang in his ears and seeped into his soul. He understood in that moment what Abigail had divined instinctually. If he killed Nabal and his household, then his reign as king would be stained by the blood of his own people. He thought again to the Ziphite spy he had killed in rage. Multiply that by a hundred, and he would never be able to win the hearts of Israel. Regardless of the instant satisfaction he would receive from killing Nabal, he needed to take the longer view—a kingly view.

He bowed then to Abigail, showing her tremendous respect. Sudden murmuring from his men reached his ears, but the whispers sounded relieved, not angry. They had heard her words too and were equally moved. He looked into Abigail's brown eyes. "Blessed be the LORD God of Israel, which sent you this day to meet me. And blessed be your advice, and blessed be you, which has kept me this day from coming to shed blood and from avenging myself with mine own hand. Truly, as the LORD God of Israel lives, which has kept me back from hurting you, except you had come to meet me, surely I would have left not a single man alive unto Nabal by the morning."[5]

He gestured for his men to come forward and take the asses. They would not be enough to feed his entire company, but it was a good start. He would seek aid from Carmel and Ziph for the time being and let Nabal alone. "Go up in peace to your house. See? I have hearkened to your voice and have accepted your person."[6]

---

[4] 1 Samuel 25:28-31.
[5] 1 Samuel 25:32-34.
[6] 1 Samuel 25:35.

She smiled then, a smile so beautiful in aspect that his heart sang to behold it. "When the LORD has dealt well with my lord, then remember your handmaid."[7]

David started. That was a bold request, and he wondered what had possessed her to ask it. She was a married woman. He would surely remember her, but he could do nothing about it—not while Nabal lived. Nevertheless, he bowed his head in response. "As you will, my lady."

David stood there for a long time after Abigail had departed for her home. He ran her words over and over in his head, particularly those last words, an invitation to call upon her when circumstances would allow. He fairly shivered with excitement. He would absolutely call upon her when time and circumstances permitted. Nothing short of Elohim Himself would stop him.

Footfalls interrupted his musings. Turning, he was confronted by several of his lieutenants and warriors of his army. Among them, he noted, was Shobal. The stocky man was first to speak, his pock-marked face unable to hide his disappointment. "Are we truly turning back, my lord? Will you leave this insult unanswered?"

David pointed to the laden asses. "The man's wife has given us compensation, Shobal. Be at peace."

The stocky man scowled and looked around at his fellows seeking support. "This is hardly enough to feed our families, my lord. We should smite this wicked man and take what we need."

David met scowl with scowl. "Nay. Hold your peace. We will not spill Hebrew blood this day."

The pock-marked man quivered in rage and would have said more if Shammah hadn't crowded up to him, his face looking like a thundercloud. Shobal swallowed whatever he wanted to say and backed away. But David read defiance in those eyes. Something would eventually need to be done about the stocky man and his followers. They were all sons of Belial. Unfortunately, David

---

[7] 1 Samuel 25:31.

couldn't afford to dismiss them yet. He needed every man willing to fight.

Adino appeared, leaning against his spear as if he'd always been that way. "Perhaps additional advice would meet with your approval, my lord?"

Sighing, David gestured for the man to continue.

"Now that spring is here, it is not good for us to dwell so close to the cities. Rumors have spread, and ill feelings have sprung up. We occupy land that their shepherds and farmers traditionally use. I fear we are a thorn in their side, and they will be less likely to intreat with us fairly while we abide here."

David's brother agreed. "This is so, my brother. We would be better served if we made camp elsewhere."

Pulling at his beard, David tried to think. The young man, Uriah, bowed. "May I speak, my lord?"

"Say on," David replied, amused. He really liked the Hittite. He had rarely seen someone so loyal.

"The hill Hachilah where we encamped before is a likely spot. We know better how to defend it, and the inhabitants of the land are unlikely to begrudge us the use of it as it lies at the very edge of Jeshimon."

It was also close enough to continue to trade and help defend the region. David liked the suggestion. "This is well spoken. Let it be so. We will move to Hachilah."

As his men moved out to return to their camp and begin preparations for the move, David turned back to peer into the darkness where Abigail had disappeared. She had impressed him mightily, and he vowed then and there that when the time came, he would indeed remember her.

Abigail felt lighter than she had in years. She had prevented blood from being shed, saved her husband, and turned aside the wrath of arguably the most dangerous and powerful man on earth.

That the LORD God was with David was obvious to her, and if he had attacked Maon in his wrath, he would have easily been successful. Her decision to intercede had been the right one, her judgment of David's character correct. He could be persuaded to reason—unlike her own husband—and she knew deep down that one day the son of Jesse would be king, and the nation would be better off for it.

Perhaps that thought had been the genesis of her plea that David would remember her when the LORD God had delivered him from his enemies and installed him on the throne of Israel. Not that he would. He would be busy judging and defending a nation. Why would such a man remember her? But she had read sincerity in his eyes when he had agreed. There was weight to such a covenant, and the son of Jesse appeared to be a man of some integrity.

She sighed then, silently wishing that things had worked out differently for her. But she was a married woman, and even if she didn't love her much older husband, it mattered not. She would honor her vows and do whatever she could to protect her husband and her husband's possessions.

But Nabal would be furious when he learned of what she had done. Naam was right. Nabal was such a son of Belial that he would listen to no one once his mind was made up. She had spoken the truth to David regarding her husband's character, a truly un-wifely thing to do—though doing so was the only way she could see to save his life and the lives of his household. None of that would matter to Nabal. His own narrative of events would be the only thing he would believe.

Abigail and her two servants entered Maon long after darkness had fallen upon the land. They had to make their way carefully, for the overcast sky obscured the moon and stars, so only Naam's quick thinking of providing a torch had given them enough light to return by. The streets of the city were nearly deserted. Only a few guards stood atop the wall looking out, and they didn't even challenge Abigail and her two servants. Indeed, David would have had little trouble in overrunning the city.

Not overly large, Maon sprawled across the slope of a lofty, conical hill. A full quarter of the city enclosed Nabal's compound. She moved quickly through the familiar streets until coming to an inner gate that led to her husband's house. The gate stood open, and revelry could be heard from within. No one challenged her as she entered, and she found her quite drunk husband, his loud and boisterous voice leading her straight to him in the largest of the houses.

He sat at the head of a large table, his legs sprawled out beneath the wood, a gold cup curled in one hand. He was railing at the Maon elders, chiding them for imagined imperfections. The elders, four in total, sat stoically around the table and took it. They knew that Nabal's wealth and power outshone theirs put together. It would take little effort for Nabal to usurp what little authority they possessed and make paupers of them. So, they abided his drunken insults and raucous laughter without protest.

Nabal spotted her the instant she walked in the house. "Behold!" he bellowed. "My wife! Is she not beautiful to look upon?"

A chorus of murmured agreements followed.

Nabal glared around the table. "And which of you would take her?" Anger made his voice sound squeaky. "Which of you would dare?"

Silence greeted him.

Abigail hasted over to him. "My lord, speak not such words. I am yours. Have no fear."

He growled and slapped her. He was so drunk that the blow lacked much of the force he normally would have put into it, but it knocked her back on her heels anyway. "That," the drunken man proclaimed, "is the only way to keep a perverse woman in line. She thinks I see it not. Thinks I know not that she flaunts her beauty before any man with a lustful heart. My wife is a harlot, for so did she beguile me with her beauty." He spat on the floor. "Else why would I have taken her to wife?" He laughed then, finding his words humorous.

Abigail flushed, the words stinging. Nabal was too drunk to hear what she had done to save his life. She would need to wait until the morning to tell him.[8]

"Begone, woman!" he shouted at her.

With a bow, she complied.

Morning came swiftly, however. She rose from her bed, washed, and dressed quickly. She needed to tell Nabal what she had done before he could discover it on his own. She fully expected to be beaten, but perhaps the beating would be less if she confessed first instead of discovering it on his own.

She found her husband snoring beneath the table where she had left him. The elders of Maon had long since departed, and the servants had cleaned up the remnants of the feast. Nabal lay on several cushions situated around the table. His loud snores seemed to vibrate the polished cedar floor upon which he lay—one of the few non-dirt floors in the entire region. In his sleep, her wealthy husband seemed much less intimidating. The smell of him turned her stomach.

She knelt beside him and gently shook him awake. He sat up with a snort, his eyes blinking owlishly in the morning light. He squinted then as his head reminded him of how much wine he had consumed. With a groan, he turned away from the light and buried his head in his hands.

"Is my lord well?" she asked, trying to add as much sympathy as she could.

"Begone from me, woman!" he shouted, never looking up at her. "Leave me in peace."

"As you command, my lord, but there is a matter of import that I must confess. It concerns the son of Jesse. Will you listen to my words?"

Nabal lifted red-blurry eyes to look at her. His thin, gray hair stood on end about his head, giving him the appearance of a partially plucked bird. "What of the son of Jesse?"

---

[8] 1 Samuel 25:36.

Taking a deep breath and trying to keep her voice as even as she could, she said, "When the son of Jesse learned of your words to his messengers, he commanded four hundred men to march on Maon."

Nabal shuddered, shock rocking his body. "What is this you say?"

"David sought to slay you, my lord, you and your entire household. But fear not, I dissuaded him. But I must confess that to do so, I gave him supplies from your storehouses. It was the only way, and I beg forgiveness of my lord and husband." She bowed before him, tensing to accept the beating that surely was coming.

But it didn't come. Her husband was making strangled noises, and she finally looked up at him. Nabal's mouth worked soundlessly, and he clutched at his chest, his hands pushing as if against some internal pressure. She found his eyes then and saw pain and something else—something she couldn't identify. Abigail stared, unsure. He finally gurgled low in his throat, his eyes rolling up in his head, and then he fell over backward.

Abigail leaped to her feet with a cry. Rushing to Nabal's side, she knelt. Something had obviously stricken him. "I need aid!" she shouted.

Izrahiah and one of her handmaidens hurried into the room. The old servant took one look at Nabal, and his lips tightened into a straight thin line.

Abigail noticed. "What? What ails him?"

"It is his heart, my lady. I have seen it before."[9] The older servant moved to Nabal's head. "We must carry him to his bed. Hurry now."

Abigail and the handmaiden each grabbed a leg while Izrahiah picked up Nabal by the shoulders. Together they carted him to his bed. They made the rich master as comfortable as they could. Abigail hovered over her husband, unsure what to do. Her emotions tugged

---

[9] 1 Samuel 25:37.

at her heart in a jumble of confusion. "What can we do?" she asked the older servant.

Izrahiah bowed his head low. "We can but pray, my lady. He is in the LORD's hands now."

Abigail straightened. "It is because of his trespass against the son of Jesse."

The servant nodded. "As you say, my lady."

Something in his tone caused Abigail to snap her eyes up to meet his. She heard much that was unsaid. Nabal was a horrible master, given to greed, fits of rage, and indiscriminate beatings for the most trivial of matters. If the LORD indeed had stricken him, then there were many more trespasses to atone for than the one directed against David. In truth, few of Nabal's servants would shed a single tear if the LORD took him.

Indeed, Abigail would not grieve overmuch either. She wondered if this inclination reflected a flaw in her own character. She had been married to Nabal for only two years, and now she might be widowed before even reaching her twentieth year of life. In the nearly two years of marriage, she had not come close to loving Nabal. She had little respect for the man, but she had done her duty and, she determined, she would continue to do her duty.

"Fetch more pillows," she ordered. "Let us make our master as comfortable as we can."

Izrahiah gestured to the handmaiden, and the girl hurried off. The old servant turned troubled eyes on his mistress. He whispered so that Nabal could not hear, "My lady, what will become of us if the LORD smites him that he dies? He has no heir."

Abigail placed a lock of hair between her teeth. That was the crux of the problem for many in Nabal's household. The entire purpose of purchasing her as his wife was to produce an heir. Nabal had once been married before, but his first wife had died young. He had then been caught up in increasing his wealth, and only in middle age had he thought of producing an heir.

But Abigail had yet to conceive. There was no heir, and now it looked as if there would be no heir. According to law, the property and possessions would pass to the nearest kinsman able and willing to redeem them. Likely, that would be Nabal's cousin, Haroeh, the elder of Ziph. And if she wasn't careful, she would be given to the hairy elder along with the rest of Nabal's possessions. That troubled her more than Nabal's plight.

Somehow, she needed to avoid such an outcome at all costs. Unfortunately, she wasn't given a lot of time. Ten days later, Nabal died without ever having spoken another word.[10] He died hard, choking on his own blood. When it was over, Abigail sat by his side unmoving. She felt numb all over. Once word of Nabal's death spread, the vultures would begin to circle, each seeking a portion of his wealth. And now she was caught in the middle of it.

[10] 1 Samuel 25:38.

16

"Her husband is dead, and Abigail has returned to her father's house in Carmel," Joab said. "Nabal's house in Maon is kept by the servants, but already there are those who seek to lay claim to all that Nabal possessed."

The words "her husband is dead" rang in David's ears like trumpets of triumph. He barely registered the rest of the message. "Blessed be the LORD that has pled the cause of my reproach from the hand of Nabal. The LORD has kept His servant from evil and has returned the wickedness of Nabal upon his own head."[1]

Joab muttered the benediction for the dead, "Even this is for good."

David nodded, feeling as if a weight had been lifted from his shoulders. He felt no sympathy for Nabal. His death was a just reward for his insults and wickedness. And with that thought, he cast the rich man from his mind, turning it instead upon Abigail. "His wife has returned to her father's house?" he repeated.

"Aye. In Carmel."

"This requires considerable thought," David mused. He hardly noticed when his brother Abinadab and the priest Abiathar joined the discussion. They all stood at the edge of a rocky gorge, facing west toward Carmel. Behind them, the activity of camp lent comforting sounds to David's ears. Laughter and the buzz of

---

[1] 1 Samuel 25:39.

conversation gave a pleasant sound. It was good to hear the people happy. The hill at the edge of the desert was a good place to camp.

Joab, his squarish face furrowing in confusion at David's comment, asked, "How so?"

"I have never beheld such a woman as Abigail. She risked much to stop me from avenging myself with my own hand. Did you not see? I hear tell that Nabal was not a kind master or husband."

Joab shrugged. "She is as any other woman in my eyes."

"Nay, she is much more."

"Then send and take her to wife," Joab said. "You are anointed to be king over Israel. You can take whom you will. The LORD will not refuse you."

Abiathar's brow furrowed, the young priest clearly making his disagreement known. David noticed. "Have you ought to say, priest?"

"I would advise caution, my lord. You have two wives already, what need have you of a third?"

David scowled at the priest. "Is this of the LORD, priest?"

"Nay, it is but my advice. The law makes mention of this, nevertheless. It is written that kings should not multiply wives unto themselves."[2]

Abinadab nodded. "This is good advice, brother. Take heed of the priest's words."

"Three is hardly so many that I would be in violation of what is written," David protested. "And I am not yet king. And tell me, priest, what purpose lies behind this law?"

Abiathar's frown deepened. He did not like being challenged. "To diminish the influence of women not of our nation and who serve false gods and have no acceptance of the one true God of Israel. All men do know that kings take wives of foreign nations to seal alliances. It is likely for this concern that Moses wrote such words."

---

[2] Deuteronomy 17:14-20.

"Is Abigail then a strange woman from a strange land?" David asked. "Is she not a daughter of Israel? Why then do you resist me?"

Abinadab placed a hand on David's shoulder. "There are other reasons, brother. Who else among us has taken more than one wife? Will this not sow discord among the men?"

David irritably shrugged aside the reasoning. He had already made up his mind. He liked Joab's words best. Saul, upon becoming king, had taken whom he would for whatever purpose he desired. It was his right as king. No one could withstand him as long as the Spirit of the LORD was upon him. That Spirit had been transferred to David. So, it was his right.

He knew the law as well as anyone. Though he personally did not have a copy of the law as spoken by Moses, the elders of each city possessed a communal copy or scraps of copies. Reading and reciting from the law were common occurrences during feast days and even during meals. When he became king, he would be required to have his own personal copy.[3] He very much looked forward to that day. To have the law read to him whenever he wanted thrilled him. To David, and to much of Israel, the law of Moses, much like the ark of the covenant, represented a personal connection with Jehovah. To have a scribe read the law aloud was to stand in the presence of God.

Abiathar didn't back down from David. "The words be also a warning to the king," he said, eyes hard. "That his heart be not lifted up above his brethren."[4]

David sucked in his breath. The words stung. Was he truly defying the LORD God of Israel by seeking to take another wife? Was he lifting his heart above his brethren?

Joab interrupted his musings. "There may be another reason to take her to wife."

This earned a glare from Abinadab and a frown from Abiathar. Intrigued, David returned his full attention to his nephew. "Say on."

---

[3] Deuteronomy 17:19-20.
[4] Deuteronomy 17:20.

Joab squirmed, prone more to action than thought. "Word has come that Nabal had no heir. His wife retains his possessions and lands. Would not taking her to wife also bestow these riches upon you, my lord?"

Possibly. The land would be held in trust by Abigail until she married. The land would then be transferred to her new husband. However, the right of redemption was clearly given to the nearest kinsman—whoever that might be.[5] This would likely mean that Abigail would be given to this near kinsman to raise up seed unto Nabal.[6] But if David could reach her first, and she consented to marry him, then all the land and possessions would revert to him. He would not need to worry about raising up seed to Nabal as he was not a near kinsman. He would also have the means of feeding his small army. And they desperately needed the supplies.

The law favored near kinsmen, but there were exceptions. Fortunately, David was of the same tribe, Judah, himself. There was a precedent for land being transferred from one family to another— as long as the marriage occurred within the same tribe. The daughters of Zelophehad had won this concession from Moses, and it had become law.[7] It could work. Remembering Abigail, he desperately hoped it would work.

"As the LORD lives," he said to Joab, invoking one of the strongest binding oaths possible having made up his mind on the matter, "go to Carmel and find Abigail. Beseech her to come to me that I might take her to wife."[8]

Abiathar and Abinadab exchanged worried glances, but David chose to ignore them.

"And the days of her mourning?" Joab prompted.

"Blessed be you of the LORD," David said, impressed. In his excitement, he had forgotten this necessity. The days of mourning varied between seven and thirty days—mostly depending upon

---

[5] Ruth 3:12-13; Deuteronomy 25:5-10; Leviticus 25:25-26.
[6] Genesis 38:8; Ruth 4:13-17.
[7] Numbers 36:5-9.
[8] 1 Samuel 25:39.

circumstances. Joseph had mourned his father, Israel, for seven days,[9] and the entire nation of Hebrews had mourned Moses' death for thirty days.[10] "Let her mourn here, with us, if she is agreeable. When her days be past, we will be wed. Make this plain to her. I would not have another take her while I am elsewhere."

Joab bowed, his flat face expressionless. David doubted that his nephew much cared one way or another. The wealth and thus the ability to feed David's army was his main concern and priority. David appreciated that aspect of his nephew but wished the young man had a bit more foresight. "As you command, my lord," Joab said.

"Go then. I must have words with Ahinoam. She must prepare to receive a sister into our household."

Joab turned to go, and David turned to seek his tent and his wife, leaving his brother and the priest staring after him in a bubble of disapproval. Multiple wives were not uncommon in Israel, though usually only the wealthy could afford more than one wife. David would have three—counting Michal. Thinking of Michal caused anger to flash through his body, and his hand twitched to draw his sword. His first wife had been given to another man. David would need to rectify that one day. Regardless of what Saul said, Michal was still his wife, and he fully intended to claim her. Woe be to any man who stood in his way.

Putting Michal out of his mind for the moment, he went to inform Ahinoam of the new living arrangements. He hoped she would be agreeable. Sharing a man, he figured, would be hard for some to do. But knowing her, she would not make a fuss; she might even be happy with the arrangement.

"Men have come from the camp of David to have words with you, my daughter."

---

[9] Genesis 50:10.
[10] Deuteronomy 34:8.

Abigail looked up, surprised. Her father hovered over her, his face reflecting his worry. She understood his concern. Already a messenger from Nabal's cousin, Haroeh, had left word that he sought redemption rights. Knowing the Ziph elder as she had, she had rebuffed the messenger, sending him away without an answer, claiming that the days of her mourning had not yet expired. But she could only rebuff Haroeh so long. He had the right, but she did not care for the Ziph elder. He reminded her too much of her late husband.

To make matters worse, her father had urged her to accept Haroeh's offer, worried that until she was firmly inscrolled in another's household, he would be held responsible for the custody of Nabal's wealth. He was a simple shepherd and such responsibility weighed heavily upon him. He instinctively knew that the arrival of David's men would only complicate the matter beyond his ability to handle.

Abigail loved her father dearly, but she held no illusions as to his capabilities. She turned her thoughts to the son of Jesse. She had never known such a man as he. A true leader, and clearly the LORD God was with him. She had no doubt he would one day be king— and she could guess as to why these men had come. And it excited her.

"Allow them to come unto me, Father."

He looked at her sharply. "You would intreat with these men?"

"They are honorable, Father. I will—and gladly."

Her father studied her for a time, trying to think through his various course of actions, but in the end, he gave in. "As you will, Daughter."

The men who stepped into the small stone house were warriors true. They walked with the lethal stride of men who were trained to violence and were not afraid to face death. They were young, but already the scars of battle marked their features. One was missing the smallest of fingers, and at least two bore unhealed wounds. The leader was a flat-faced young man who, in some vague way, resembled David. Even his beard looked squarish.

"I am Abigail, wife of Nabal," she announced when they had gathered before her. She noted absently that they still wore their sandals. In his agitation, her father had not offered them water to wash their feet. "You would have words with me?"

"Well met," the flat-faced one replied, bowing. "I am Joab, kin to David, the son of Jesse, in whose name I am now come. He has bid me to ask you to return with us to his camp where you may fulfil the days of your mourning. Then, when you are agreeable, he would have you to wife." He paused to study her. "What say you?"

Excitement burned through her like a wildfire. She wanted this union now that the opportunity existed. Despite her words to David to remember her, she had not meant them for this purpose. She had been content to abide with Nabal, yet the words had come unbidden, and once said, she could not take them back. But now that her husband was dead, being wife to David would be all she could ask for. David was fully capable of handling the affairs of Nabal's wealth, and from all she had heard of the son of Jesse, he was an honorable man, one who loved the LORD God and Israel.

She found her hands shaking. "Is this truly the will of my lord, David? Does he not already have a wife?"

Joab nodded, trying to smile reassuringly. Someone should tell him that his smile looked more at home on a snake than on a man trying to reassure a maiden. But in truth, she didn't mind. She thought his smile glorious! "You know his wife already from what I am told. She too is agreeable. We now wait for your consent."

"Then I will come," she said, sounding giddy. To control herself, she bowed low before the young men and added, "Let thine handmaid be a servant to wash the feet of the servants of my lord."[11]

She rose without waiting for a reply and fetched the large clay jug of water, a wool rag, and a wooden basin. She knelt before each of the five men come before her and carefully washed their feet. They said nothing during this, but approval radiated off them in

---

[11] 1 Samuel 25:41.

waves. They liked her and that bode well when they vouched for her to David.

When she finished, she rose easily to her feet. "If my lord wills, we will tarry not. Let, I pray, five damsels of my household attend me during my days of mourning."[12]

Joab nodded. "This was foreseen. Bring them." He gestured to one of the other young men. "Uriah, prepare an ass for the journey. We will leave as soon as the women are ready."

She did not tarry. Bidding goodbye to her father and mother proved easier than she had expected. Being a widow gave her certain powers of her own, among them the right to accept a marriage proposal. Her father had sold her once and had profited by it, but he could not do so a second time. There would not be another dowry, and David had not offered one. Her mother looked happy, but her father's face warred with itself as conflicting emotions flickered across his features.

Soon enough, she and her maids were riding to meet David and her new life. She thanked Jehovah constantly that she did not have to deal with Haroeh. She believed in David's anointing and was glad that Nabal's wealth would fall into his hands rather than Haroeh's greedy ones.

"Leave me, woman!" Haroeh roared, his long nose quivering with rage that filled his veins like blood. His wife squeaked in fright and scuttled away. He wasn't like his cousin, Nabal, who found pleasure in striking women, but neither did he believe his wife had any part in his business. She would feel his anger if she tarried overlong.

Curse David! He began pacing, pulling at his nose in an effort to think, to try and come up with some solution to the problem. Word had just reached him that Abigail had accepted David as her husband

---

[12] 1 Samuel 25:42.

and had left to join him at his camp near Carmel. Along with her went Nabal's lands and wealth—*All of which should belong to me!*

He decided that the son of Jesse must have threatened Abigail to get her to agree so quickly. Haroeh's own messengers had been rebuffed. Everywhere he turned, David interfered. The winter and spring had been hard on Ziph, what with being forced to provide supplies for David's camp. This in turn had blown back on Haroeh. He was the one the other elders blamed for the suffering of the people. If he hadn't betrayed David to begin with, they said, none of this would have happened, they claimed. As if David would not still have demanded food, water, and tents.

Then David had stolen Ahinoam right from this very house, offering no dowry, no compensation, not even coming to deal with Haroeh face to face. All Haroeh had of David was threats. The man was a menace, a blight upon the land that consumed everything he touched. How he hated David!

And now this. Abigail and Nabal's wealth were rightly his as nearest kinsman to Nabal. But David had stolen her and all that Nabal possessed. Somehow the son of Jesse had murdered Nabal. Certain poisons could afflict Nabal's heart, killing him slowly over time, and all knew that David hated the man and was envious of his wealth and prosperity. Doubtless, David's envy had driven him to kill Nabal—how it was done remained a mystery—and steal Nabal's wife and wealth.

No more could the son of Jesse be tolerated to prey upon the people of Ziph. Something had to be done about him. How to be rid of David and lay claim to Abigail and Nabal's lands at the same time was the problem. A plan began to form in his cunning brain, a way to accomplish both objectives. Haroeh knew it would be chancy, but no one, not even the son of Jesse, had the right to steal from him. There were lines that should not be crossed, and David had crossed not a few of them.

He called for his servant. The middle-aged servant appeared and bowed. "What do you command, my lord?"

"Prepare for a journey, Omri. I must needs travel."

The servant bowed again. "How long will my master be gone?"

"Four days, perhaps five."

"Am I to accompany?"

"Aye. You and two other servants will go. The rest will remain to see to my wife's needs."

"As you command, my lord."

The servant left to do his master's bidding. It was well. Haroeh stopped his pacing and set his bulk down on a stool, smiling. His plan, as he saw it, could not fail. Soon he would finally be rid of David, and he would finally be rich—as was his due.

17

King Saul stood upon the wall of Gibeah, gazing south. He looked toward Jerusalem and Bethlehem, toward Hebron and the smaller cities of southern Judah—toward where, somewhere, David yet abode. The mountains rose tall, creating steep slopes and narrow valleys that ran down the spine of Israel. He couldn't see past the peaks to the cities in question, but he could picture them.

A wind bit into his face, but he didn't so much as blink as he stared over the mountainous terrain. His enemy yet lived, and he, Saul, had allowed it. Like he did every day, he replayed the moment when he had realized David had spared his life. Letting the son of Jesse go had been the honorable thing to do—but also terribly foolish.

Saul's oldest two sons stood beside him. They tolerated each other in his presence, but he knew of their animosity, their anger and hatred of the other. He wished otherwise, but such a gap would never be bridged while Jonathan yet loved David. It all came back to the son of Jesse. His sons barely tolerated each other, and Saul knew of at least one instance when their animosity had come to physical blows. Neither ever spoke of it, so Saul had not pursued the matter either.

Turning to his sons, he pointed over the wall at the mountains. "What do you see, my sons?"

Both turned to stare toward the south. Ishui shrugged immediately. "Land, my father." He squinted. "Perhaps a merchant comes?" He shrugged, his scarred face taking on a pinched look.

Jonathan, however, never took his eyes off the land. "Nay, there is much more. I see the people, my father, of all tribes. Our charge. Our care."

Jonathan's voice hinted at more, and Saul suspected it had to do with the son of Jesse. Nevertheless, his eldest son's response warmed him. "Aye, my son. As king, it is the people of the land that I rule. All tribes, all men, bow to me. Understand what this means?"

His Jonathan nodded. "Aye, father. To you and one day to your successor."

Saul waited, but his son said nothing further. Sudden anger contorted his face, and he shouted, "And to you, my son! You are my heir! You!"

Jonathan backed up a step. "As you say, my king."

Saul clenched his fists, fighting down the impulse to strike his son. He knew what lay in Jonathan's heart. He knew his son believed that the son of Jesse would be king after Saul and that he would be next to David. But his son was wrong. The moment David became king, the son of Jesse would slay all those who pertained to Saul. It was the way of kings.

Ishui glared at his brother, saying nothing. Saul glared at both his sons. The tension mounted when Abner arrived. He must have felt the friction, but his face gave nothing away. "Messengers have come, my lord." He eyed his cousin meaningfully. "From Ziph."

Saul pushed forward, his eyes alight with sudden excitement. "They bring word of the son of Jesse?"

"So I believe, my king."

"Where do they wait?"

"At your house, my lord."

Saul considered. He wanted badly to hear the news. Not hearing about David's whereabouts for so long had been concerning. He wished now he had simply slain David when he had the chance. He chastised himself for that oversight every day. He glanced sidelong at Jonathan. Should he allow his son to hear the tidings? He refocused on Abner. "Bid them come here, cousin. I will hear their words."

Abner bowed. "As you command."

Saul's general left, his pace neither hasty nor lacking. Fire could descend from heaven and Abner would likely not react any different than he did now. The king fixed his eyes on his oldest son. "Return to your house, Jonathan. Attend to your wife and son."

"Father—"

"Speak not," Saul cut in. "Your heart and mind are known when it comes to the son of Jesse. I will hear the words of the messengers from Ziph, but you will not." The king's eyes softened. "Turn your thoughts to your own household. You have a son now. Mephibosheth will need his father."

Jonathan couldn't resist. "And what of David, my king?"

"He is not your concern. Leave now. My mind is not settled as it pertains to the son of Jesse. Did I not spare him when the LORD delivered him into my hands? Leave now."

His eldest son stared long at his father before turning away, but not without sparing a scathing look for Ishui. Saul's younger son only grinned maliciously in response.

Saul turned to Ishui after his oldest son had departed. "You will not speak, my son. Your mind and heart are also known. You will listen only. Am I clear?"

Ishui bowed, his lips compressed tightly together.

Soon enough Abner returned with three men in tow. They ascended the stone steps to the parapet behind the outer wall until they stood arrayed before the king. Saul recognized the leader as the elder from Ziph who had once betrayed David's whereabouts. He couldn't recall the man's name. Not that it mattered.

The delegation bowed deeply to him, showing proper respect. "You have ought to say to your king?" Saul asked. "You have word of David?"

The hairy elder straightened. "We do, my king."

"Then say on."

"David seeks to make himself king, my lord. Even now he has slain Nabal of Maon of the house of Caleb, taken his wife as his own, and stolen the lands and herds of your faithful servant. All do fear the son of Jesse. He pillages the land, takes what he wills, and holds our women hostage."

Saul trembled. His worst nightmare had come true. David's actions had put the lie to his words. The son of Jesse was raising a rebellion against him. David's vow not to raise his hand against Saul was but smoke. By building an army in the wilderness, David was directly challenging Saul's authority. By seeking to rule over the people, David was directly challenging Saul's kingship. Rage swept through him, caught him up, and held him firm. "Where is the son of Jesse now?"

"Does not David hide himself in the hill of Hachilah, which is before Jeshimon?"[1]

It was the same place as before! "Blessed be you of the LORD for having mercy on me!" Saul cried to the elder. Whirling away from the Ziphites, he stabbed a finger at Abner and Ishui. "Gather the men, all the garrison of Gibeah, we march immediately. The son of Jesse shall not escape me again."[2]

Ishui bowed, a feral grin stamped across his scarred face. "As you command, O King!"

Abner's bow came slower. His face remained calm, unreadable. "We will be ready to march in two hours," he said.

But Saul didn't hear. Already he was calculating the time it would take to march to Hachilah east of Ziph. He knew the terrain, knew how David had sought to escape him once before. He could box in the son of Jesse this time, leaving him with no hope of escape. With Samuel dead, there would be no one to rescue David—not even the Philistines.

He gave thanks to Jehovah for delivering the son of Jesse into his hand. Clearly the LORD was with him yet. Perhaps Jonathan would yet rule after his father and Mephibosheth after Jonathan. Saul

---

[1] 1 Samuel 26:1.
[2] 1 Samuel 26:2.

smiled, his rage mixing with his confidence to create both hope and desire. David would die, and all would be well with the kingdom.

⎯⎯⎯⎯⎯⎯⎯⎯⎯⎯⎯⎯⎯⎯⎯⎯⎯⎯

David burst into his tent. Startled, Abigail and Ahinoam looked up from where they knelt preparing bread. It warmed David's heart to see his two wives getting along so well. He had known they knew each other, but he hadn't known they liked each other.

"Abigail, you had it aright," David said, kneeling before the two women so he could look them in the eyes. "My spies report that Haroeh has left Ziph, his home. No one knows where he has gone."

Abigail sat back on her heels. David could almost hear her sharp mind turning to the problem. "He has gone to the king to betray you, my lord," she said. "I know the man. He is likeminded with his cousin Nabal, and his messengers made clear he intended to redeem the land and me. He will not look favorably upon you for taking me to wife. He will betray you."

"You think he has already." It was not a question.

"Aye, my lord." She reached out to touch David's arm. "The king is doubtless coming. We need to leave this place."

David growled low in his throat. They had just settled in. He didn't want to leave. "But surely the king will forbear to come. He knows I should be king after him—he said so. He caused me to swear not to cut off his family after him. Why should he come now?"

Ahinoam bowed with her face to the ground. "My husband, heed your wives this once, I pray. I too know Haroeh, and the elder will not abide this perceived insult. He will have spoken words in the king's ear that will cause the king's fear and anger to swell within his heart. You have laid claim to all that Nabal possessed. Perhaps the king believes you seek to become king too soon. Trust in us, my lord; we are betrayed."

Leaning forward, he kissed both his wives on their cheeks. Then rising to his feet, he looked upon them with growing affection. "I have heard your words, and I thank you both." To Abigail, he said, "You were wise to suggest we keep watch over Haroeh. Your wisdom is of the LORD. Now, prepare yourselves. We depart immediately."

David left the tent and immediately began shouting orders to break camp. The hill became alive like a kicked ant den as each man, woman, and child began to prepare to march. Flocks of sheep and herds of goats that had once belonged to Nabal—and that Abigail had brought to David upon their marriage—began moving south, the shepherds leading the way. The flocks would go first, and the people would follow. No one wanted to risk their food source, not after going for so long with so little.

Then Shobal appeared from among the chaos, his pock-marked face and bristling beard streaked with dust and sweat. "This is madness!" the troublemaker shouted at David. Two of Shobal's lackeys flanked the large man, each wearing a scowl meant to support their chosen leader. "We have only arrived, and now you are requiring us to leave! Why must this be?"

"It is enough that I command it," David growled, looking away dismissively after the merest of glances at the men. "Prepare to march."

But Shobal wouldn't leave it alone. He grabbed David by the arm and pulled him around. "Nay," he spat, "our lives are endangered, and we would know why!"

Two things happened then that would trouble David much when he looked back upon it later. The first was a surge of uncontrollable rage that hijacked his mind and body. The second was what became of that rage.

He went berserk.

His thoughts ceased and battle lust, the desire to kill the men in front of him, took over. Not even conscious of his actions, he attacked all three men with such ferocity they never even had a chance to defend themselves. If he'd been wearing his sword, he would have drawn it, but all he had was his own body, and he used it as a weapon. He flung himself upon the three shocked men, striking indiscriminately with his heavy fists, kicking, and biting like an animal gone wild. He never felt the damage he did to his own fists until later. Red filled his vision and madness filled his heart. He pummeled the three men into a bloody mess, and then suddenly others began piling on top of him until he couldn't move, could barely breathe.

Voices began to register in his mind, shouts for him to be calm, to desist. That's when David felt the pain. His hands felt as if he'd broken them, and when he groaned, he tasted blood, likely not his own given the animalistic nature of his attack. His body went limp then, all the strength leaving him in a terrible rush that left him weary to the soul.

Slowly, men began to pull away until only Joab and Shammah remained, each holding down an arm. It didn't matter, he scarcely had the strength to raise them anyway. He blinked at their concerned looks, at the fear that stained their faces. *What have I done?* He groaned again and turned his head, shame filling him.

Shobal and his two lackies moaned feebly, trying to crawl away, leaving bloody stains upon the ground. David stared. Had he done that? The memory of the fight refused to come. He recalled nothing but hazy and blurry shadows that might or might not have been his victims.

Shammah's deep voice rumbled in David's ears. "Are you well, my lord?"

"Nay," David admitted. "I fear something is terribly wrong."

Joab cast a glare at Shobal who had collapsed not far away, groaning deeply in pain. His two friends were not much better off. "Would you that I slay them, my lord?"

Loyal Joab. His nephew didn't know what had happened, but he presumed that Shobal was at fault. If David gave the word, both Joab and Shammah would fall upon the helpless men and kill them quickly. But no. The fault lay within David—a madness akin to the evil spirit that often fell upon King Saul, but at the same time something more—and less. This was not an evil spirit. This was something inside David—a rage that, like a coiled rope, had begun to wind itself around his heart and mind. This had been building for years—a byproduct of the constant running, hiding, and fear that had become his entire world. It had exploded out of him when he'd caught the Ziph spy. It had consumed him near the pool of Carmel when he had engaged the Amalekites. It had burned through him upon hearing Nabal's insults. And now it had transformed him into something less than a man—a beast, an animal—at Shobal's touch.

David knew instinctively that if he didn't deal with this fault, he would fall prey to it again and again until it devoured his personality and replaced it with something bestial and feral. He had seen it before in other warriors who had seen too much battle, too much anger, rage, and fear.

"Nay, son of my sister," he said in a croaking voice. "Slay them not. The fault is mine."

Joab looked doubtful, but he sat back, releasing David's arm. Shammah, after a momentary pause to see if David would do anything rash, did likewise. Slowly, to try and mitigate the pain in his hands and the soreness in his entire body, he sat up. The entire camp had come to a halt, watching him.

Swallowing bile and blood, he rose shakily to his feet, using Joab's shoulder as a crutch. "I beg forgiveness," he said as loudly as he could. "This iniquity is upon me, and I must bear it." Fixing his eyes upon Shobal and his two followers, he hesitated. He didn't have time to deal with this mess as he should. "Lend them aid. Bind their wounds, but we must hasten to leave. King Saul comes, and we cannot be here when he arrives. Let every man, woman, and child labor in haste. We must go."

Activity started up again. Like a dam breaking, men and women began moving away and the bustle of activity rose. Three women appeared, wives of the wounded men, to attend to the injuries. They cast fearful glances at David as they worked. He sighed.

Joab moved to face him, his two brothers flanking him on either side. Asahel, the tallest, being long of leg and antsy, shifted from one foot to the other as if wishing to run. Abishai bore a strange mixture of Joab's squareness and Asahel's length. His lantern jaw was covered in a curly, thin beard that did little to hide his youthful face.

"Asahel," David said, trying to dispel the uncomfortable feeling that suddenly sprang up, "run to the west and north. See if the king is coming. Joab, Abishai, lead the people south."

"And what of you, my lord?" Joab asked.

David glanced again at the three injured men. He flexed his bruised hands and winced. Surely at least one finger was broken. Swallowing hard, he whispered, "I need to speak with Abiathar the priest."

Leaving the women to minister to the beaten men, David went in search of the priest, finding Abiathar leading an ass down the trail that led south. David pulled him aside, taking the lead rope from him and giving it to one of the boys who skipped along the trail. "He will keep your possessions safe," he told the priest. "I have need of you."

The priest's intelligent eyes took in David's ragged appearance, his bloody and bruised hands, and the young bullock that David had taken from the herd. The creature chewed contentedly on a mouthful of straw, oblivious to the purpose David intended for it. The priest knew instinctively what David wanted to do, and his smile of approval cut like a knife. David idly wondered if the young priest loved properness more than the reason behind the deeds. In truth, it didn't matter. David needed to offer a sin offering to the LORD, and Abiathar was the only priest to whom he could bring the offering.

Together they turned aside, walking deep into one of the gorges that cut toward the east. When they reached a place that satisfied the priest, he directed David to build an altar of stones. Each time David picked up a heavy stone, his fingers screamed at him, but he shunted aside the agony, thinking the pain a just reward for his trespass. Not wanting to do a half-rate job, he built the altar much higher and wider than necessary. The finicky priest watched, holding a lighted torch that revealed his approval or disapproval in turn at David's efforts.

Wood was harder to find in the desert, but David had foreseen this and had laid the wood on the bullock before finding the priest. He took the wood now and spread it thickly on top of the altar.

When David finished, he approached the priest, leading the sacrificial bullock. He knelt in the rocky ravine before the altar and bowed his head. "I must make confession," he began. "I have sinned before the LORD and trespassed—that in my wrath, I shed innocent blood. I bring this bullock as a sin offering to atone for my trespass."

Abiathar planted himself in front of David, a knife held firmly in his right hand, torch in the other. "And is atonement all you seek?" he asked.

David flinched. This was unexpected. He thought about the words, sifting them in his mind, trying to discover what more the priest sought. It came to him that it wasn't what the priest wanted that mattered. What more did David want from this offering? He knew instantly. "To be delivered from my anger for I fear it has much filled me of late."

Abiathar nodded. "Well said. You are the LORD'S anointed, and you must be guided by the Spirit of the LORD and not by your wrath. A king belongs as much to the people as the people do to a king. Stand." David stood. "Place the bullock atop the altar."

David did as instructed, grunting with the effort and the strain of keeping the animal from kicking itself off. Abiathar handed him the knife. The young bullock squirmed some, but David held it down by placing his hand on the animal's head.

"Slay it before the LORD," the priest ordered. "Let its blood atone for your sin."[3]

Swiftly and with practiced ease, David slit the animal's throat. Hot blood spilled over the stones of the altar. The priest moved close, pushing David back. He gave David the torch and then dipped his fingers in the blood. He turned away, putting his back to David and sprinkled the blood seven times in the direction of the tabernacle,[4] murmuring a prayer all the while. Lifting up his voice,

---

[3] Leviticus 4:4.
[4] Leviticus 4:5-6.

he said, "And with this shed blood there is remission of your sin. Let it be no more spoken or thought of."

David stood back, watching. The priest drained the carcass of blood, the majority running down the side to pool at the foot of the altar.[5] He then dressed the bullock, removing the kidneys and other organs. Then he cut the bullock into pieces, swiftly and surely, laying it all atop the altar. Then he looked upon David. "Your sin is atoned. Burn the carcass. Let the sacrifice be a sweet smell to the LORD God of Israel."

David lit the wood which caught immediately. Together, they watched as the bullock burned. Much of David's burden and guilt lifted and drifted off with the smoke. His relief was palpable. He knew he would still wrestle with his anger, but with the LORD's help, he did not intend to let it control him again. He turned his mind to the danger of King Saul. Some would argue he should not have taken the time to deal with his sin—not when danger lurked so close—but he felt differently. To deal with Saul in the right frame of mind meant first dealing with his own trespass. That done, he could now seek the LORD's deliverance with a clean conscience.

---

[5] Leviticus 4:7.

18

"The king has encamped on the hill Hachilah in the same place ours once lay,"[1] Asahel explained, gasping for breath. "The entire garrison of Gibeah does accompany him." David's nephew had run hard to bring this news. Apparently, David had ordered abandonment of the hill just in time. The king, unlike the last time he had attacked David on that hill, had charged straight in, hoping surprise and speed would catch David off guard.

A brilliant sunset cast deep shadows, outlined in golden hues, across the land. Within moments, the sun would disappear behind the Judean mountains. David's army followed a narrow track that cut west into the Maon wilderness. They would need to make their own camp soon. Doubtless, Saul had made camp early because his scouts had not yet found where David had fled to. That would change soon. It was hard enough to hide the tracks of over a thousand people, let alone the herds and flocks they had been forced to drive before them.

Fortunately, nightfall fast approached. He motioned to his lieutenants. "Keep everyone moving until two hours after true darkness. Then make camp as best you can."

Adino spat out one of his Elah shells. "And what of you, my lord?"

---

[1] 1 Samuel 26:3.

"Joab, choose you out scouts who are light of foot and quick of eye. We will return to Hachilah and see what we may do to delay the king."[2]

His nephew's eyes narrowed. "How may we do this?"

David grinned. "We are in the LORD's hands, son of my sister. He will deliver us from the king's hands. We but seek the opportunity He will provide. We will know it when we see it."

Joab's flat face looked unconvinced. "This is surely folly, my lord."

"Perhaps, but some action must be taken."

Shammah pushed closer. "Then let us take all the army. Attack while the king sleeps."

"Nay, we will not shed Hebrew blood."

No one said anything, but Shobal and his two friends, bloodied and broken, likely came to everyone's mind. David's hands continued to send stabs of pain to remind him. Besides, even if a fight did develop, David doubted he could hold a sword for very long.

"Choose your men," David said to Joab before addressing his other lieutenants. "Adino, Shammah, find Eleazar. Keep the people moving; let none fall behind." He fixed Shammah with a stern look. "All must reach safety, including the wounded." Including Shobal and his friends, but David didn't need to say that. All knew it.

"As you command," Adino said, saluting with his spear.

Disdaining to wait, David set out alone back up the trail that led to his former camp, now occupied by King Saul. He took his time, allowing Joab to gather his scouts and catch up. He had no wish to run afoul of Saul's army alone.

When Joab did catch up, he was accompanied by his two brothers and, strangely, two Hittites. The first, Uriah, David knew well, but the second David had only a passing knowledge of, a recent recruit named Ahimelech.

Joab saluted. "What is your will, my lord?"

---

[2] 1 Samuel 26:4.

David turned to Asahel. "Tell me more of the king's situation."

The lanky youth hopped from foot to foot as they walked, uncomfortable with the attention. "He encamps upon the hill," he said. "Before I left, he was building earthworks around the camp and setting up a watch. I fear we will not catch him alone as we did afore. He is well protected in the center of the camp."

David turned this information over in his mind. Saul clearly didn't intend to be taken by surprise again. "Is there a place we may observe without being seen?"

Asahel nodded. "Aye, my lord. A hilltop across the gorge to the east. The ravine is deep and difficult to navigate. If we are seen, we will have plenty of time to escape."

And, David thought with satisfaction, the king was unlikely to have set a watch on his eastern flank, depending upon the canyon to keep him safe. Likely, his scouts would have already reported that David had fled to the south. David motioned the lanky youth forward. "Lead on, Asahel. Take us to this outpost that we may see how the king is arrayed and thereby determine his intentions."

Deep shadows lay across the land when David finally reached a spot where he could observe Saul's camp without being seen. The sun had dipped behind the mountains, but there was enough light to see from their vantage point across a deep ravine to the east. Asahel was right. Saul was taking no chances this time. He had his men building rocky earthworks around a large section of the flat hilltop where David had once made his camp.[3]

Men stood guard along its perimeter, and more were pitching tents outside the entrenchment. A few wagons had been manhandled across the ravine and were used to help bolster the barricade. Cookfires had already sprung to life and from what David could see, roughly three thousand men had come out against him.[4]

As the six men watched, scouts came and went, most running in from the south to report. Following them with his eyes, David

---

[3] 1 Samuel 26:5.
[4] 1 Samuel 26:2.

found the king, standing tall among his men, his face obscured by the shadows of the fading sun. David also recognized the blocky figure and stance of the man standing next to him, Abner, the son of Ner, Saul's cousin and general.

They watched for nearly half an hour until the light faded completely and only a moon and the campfires shed any light to see by. Looking carefully, David thought he saw where Saul had bedded down for the night—right in the middle of the entrenchment.[5]

David looked at his oldest nephew. "Joab, take two men and move farther along the ridge. Ensure we will not be discovered."

The flat-faced young man gave David a peculiar look. David could just make it out in the growing darkness. "Is that wise, my lord?"

That was not the question he really wanted to ask. After the beating David had given Shobal and his two followers, Joab had to be wondering what was in his lord's mind.

"Go," David said softly. "Secure our position."

Joab took Asahel and Uriah to accompany him. David waited until he could neither see nor hear them. He then focused on the hill across the ravine, looking for the spot where he believed Saul had bedded down. Something in him stirred. Not the anger that had so recently come to dominate his life—but something else, something he hadn't felt in some time. The Spirit of the LORD was moving in his heart. It felt so good—so right—that he unconsciously released his breath in a long, deep sigh. Even with Saul having come out against him yet again, the reassuring presence of the LORD settled his heart, and a growing peace seeped into his mind.

Impulsively, he turned to Abishai and Ahimelech the Hittite. "Who will go down with me into the camp?"[6]

Both men stared at him, their faces in the dim light so astonished that David chuckled. "I am compelled," he told them. "Fear not. All will be well."

---

[5] 1 Samuel 26:5.
[6] 1 Samuel 26:6.

Abishai bowed his head. "I will go down with you, my lord."[7]

David nodded. "Ahimelech, secure our way back. Wait for us here."

The Hittite's face looked unusually white in the growing moonlight. "Nay, my lord, let me I pray, accompany you into the enemy camp."

"Abide here," David ordered as he stripped off his armor, leaving only a worn tunic to protect him if he had to make a stand and fight. "Two is risk enough, and we have need of someone to secure our way back."

Ahimelech bowed low while Abishai followed David's example and stripped himself of weapons and armor. "As you command, my lord."

Touching Abishai on the shoulder, David slipped out from the rock they hid behind, and on feet that hardly made a sound, he descended a winding animal trail toward the bottom of the ravine. Having spotted the path earlier in his reconnoiter of Saul's position, he had determined that the animal track would allow him to get close to Saul's camp without being seen.

He honestly didn't know what he expected to do or find. He only knew he must go. Careful not to dislodge any loose rocks, the pair edged down into the ravine, keeping to the deep shadows of the gorge.

It took a long time. Any unusual sounds would alert the guards posted around the camp, so in the darkness, they often had to feel their way along with hands as well as sandaled feet. When they reached the bottom, they paused, looking up. Firelight from campfires lit the hilltop like tiny islands of light. The sound of casual conversation and laughter drifted down to them.

"Any closer and we risk discovery," Abishai whispered in David's ear.

David didn't agree. He was compelled to continue—a recognizable compulsion, one in which the Spirit of the Lord had

---

[7] 1 Samuel 26:6.

come upon him and was directing his steps. The danger was nonetheless extremely real. If either he or Abishai were discovered, three thousand angry Benjamites would descend upon them in a moment.

"Be wary," David replied unnecessarily. "Watchmen stand at the crest of the path. We must not alert either."

Slowly, moving up the faint trail in handbreadths, the two warriors climbed the trail. Moonlight now illuminated the landscape, replacing the failing light of the sun. Still, enough shadows from large rocks and the face of the ravine provided David and his middle nephew with the needed cover. Like spirits, they wove silently along the ravine slope, climbing carefully until they reached a point less than fifty cubits from the crest. Two Benjamites stood there, talking quietly as they peered into the darkness beyond.

David knew if he and Abishai could sneak past the two guards and gain entrance to the camp proper, they could simply walk about as any two warriors who belonged in the camp. Being Hebrews themselves, they would only need to be wary of someone noticing they did not wear the distinctive armbands that marked them as Benjamites. Hebrew armies under Saul fought in regiments according to tribes, each wearing a distinguishing armband to identify them from the rest of the tribes.

"Wait," David whispered so softly that his nephew might not have heard the word. He placed a hand on Abishai's wrist and found the young man quivering with excitement.

They waited, gauging the habits of the two sentries and studying how their eyes moved, where they lingered. The guards appeared to be at ease, not expecting trouble. They were more interested in their conversation than in what might be happening beyond the firelight.

Lying flat against the rocky earth, David crawled forward. The effort caused no small amount of pain in his hands. He winced each time he put weight on his fingers, a subtle reminder of the price of allowing his anger to control him. Despite the pain, he kept at it, moving as a lion would, carefully, slowly, and low to the ground.

When he was within five cubits of the two guards, he slithered into the deep shadow cast by a boulder. Abishai joined him there, his breath barely audible to David's ears. Again, they waited. He could feel the tension in Abishai. His nephew struggled to hold himself still with danger so close.

David understood. Warriors were men of action, the need to be doing something paramount in their psyche. David laid a single hand on Abishai's arm to calm him. David took slow, shallow breaths, watching the two Benjamites as they continued their conversation. Something would happen to distract them or call them away. He sensed it. Believed it. So, he waited and watched.

Still, when the distraction came, it surprised David. Being this close to the guards, David could hear their words clearly. They were, of all things, arguing about him.

The bigger of the two turned and spat to the side. "You speak of treason," he hissed, turning a glare upon his companion.

The other, a slender man that reminded David of Adino, also spat to the side. "And you speak as a fool," he retorted. "You were not there the day the son of Jesse slew the giant. You were not there when he turned back the Philistine tide again and again. I was. How is it treason to fight against the enemies of the LORD?"

The bigger man looked his companion up and down. "You have ears, but you hear not. Eyes you have, but you see not. The son of Jesse seeks to lift his hand against the LORD's anointed. He seeks to supplant our rightful king. How is *that* not treason?"

The slender man snorted. "You have a brain, but you use it not!" The sentry looked out over the darkened landscape, his voice lowering. "I fear that the Spirit of the LORD is upon the son of Jesse—and no longer abides on our king."

"Treason!" the bigger man barked.

Giving his companion a withering look, the slender man turned and stalked off. "Keep watch alone," he snarled back over his shoulder. "I will seek the captain of the guard for another post!"

The bigger man followed his companion for a dozen cubits, his face a mask of rage in the firelight and his back to David. David saw his chance. Motioning for Abishai to follow, David got up and walked quickly into the camp. The two sentries never saw him or his nephew as they merged into the shadows within the camp.

When the bigger sentry turned back to man his post, there was nothing to see. David and Abishai had already slipped beyond his view walking casually among the many tents pitched atop the hill. They found a cache of weapons stacked neatly beside a group of tents. They each selected a spear and a shield, becoming just two more Benjamite warriors walking through the camp.

"Follow," David said to his nephew. "You may speak, but let your words be of finding food or other such camp talk."

"This is foolish," Abishai whispered. "We will be captured."

"Nay. We are but two warriors walking where we belong. Keep a slow, but steady pace. Do not look around overmuch. Speak in normal tones. If challenged, we reply that the captain of the guard has assigned us to watch the northwestern side of the camp."

His nephew nodded shortly, taking a deep breath to calm himself. Then they moved off, David setting an easy, casual pace that wound through the tents toward the center of the camp and the entrenchment erected by Saul's men. Keeping their voices low, but casual, they spoke of simple things, camp talk. The few men they encountered gave them barely a glance. Except for the sentries that watched the perimeter, most of the warriors had chosen to get some sleep, so only a few were up and about—the restless or those with unfinished tasks.

They reached the rocky entrenchment without challenge. Several of the wagons had been pulled in line at barrier's edge to provide the defenders with a safe place to launch arrows if attacked. It was a typical defensive structure of an army on the move, providing the men with a fallback position to defend themselves if attacked. In the middle of the entrenchment, the king's standard fluttered weakly in the cool breeze of the spring evening.

David glanced casually around, saw no one, and quickly scrambled over the rocky wall and slid into the shadows under one of the wagons. Abishai joined him. Together they jammed the shields against the wagon bed and ground to form a wall and placed their ungainly spears to the side. Laying side by side, they waited silently to see if an alarm sounded. Nothing happened. And since it was not unusual for warriors to bed down under the carts, saving them the effort of raising a tent, David didn't expect anyone to be concerned if they were spotted.

Together, they peered through their makeshift wall toward the king's standard, not fifty cubits away. Campfires burned at intervals around the perimeter of the trench, casting flickering light over the campgrounds. Tents had been erected here and there, but the king had disdained their use. He lay in the open, already asleep, with a spear stuck in the ground near the pillow under the king's head. A flask, likely filled with water for purification or refreshment, lay on the other side of the king's head. Abner and the king's elite guard lay around Saul, a maze of bodies that protected the king.[8] Beyond the king slept Ishui, Saul's second oldest son and brother to David's friend Jonathan.

David's heart leaped when he recognized the sleeping form of the king. Old memories, old desires plowed their way into his mind along with an old longing for Saul's love—for David yet loved his king. Tears came unbidden to his eyes as he studied the king's face in the faint glow of the campfires. How he wished things had turned out differently. How he wished he could yet be in Saul's household, to play the harp once again for his king.

He didn't know how long he stared at the king, but the sounds of the camp gradually began to die down as more and more of the king's men bedded down for the night. Then, sometime during the second watch of the night,[9] untended campfires burned low, casting deeper shadows and less light. Crickets began chirping to the accompaniment of snores and heavy breathing. Soon it became clear that the LORD had brought an unnaturally deep sleep among the

---

[8] 1 Samuel 26:7.
[9] Israel, in David's day, only had three watches of the night. It wasn't until Roman influence that Israel incorporated the more well-known four watches of the night.

king's men. There was little twitching or rolling over. Everyone lay as they were.

Abishai recognized the opportunity instantly. He reached out and griped David's wrist. "God has delivered your enemy into your hand this day!" he whispered fiercely. David turned in astonishment at the fervency of his nephew's voice. Abishai gestured toward Saul and the king's spear. "Let me smite him, I pray, with the spear even to the earth." He paused. "I will not smite him the second time.[10] The first blow will be sufficient. Then we can be away, and none will know."

David returned his nephew's grip, squeezing hard enough that the young man turned to look at David. "Destroy him not. Who can stretch forth his hand against the LORD's anointed and be guiltless? As the LORD lives, Jehovah will smite him, or his day will come to die, or he will descend into battle and perish." He fixed Abishai with an intense stare, lending his words the full weight of his countenance. "The LORD forbid that I should stretch forth mine hand against the LORD's anointed."[11]

He stared at his nephew without blinking. The fervency seeped out of Abishai's face to be replaced by surrender. He bowed his head, touching his forehead to the rocky ground. "As you command, my lord."

David let his breath out slowly in a grateful sigh. He turned his attention back to Saul, thinking. An idea came then. It wasn't as audacious as when he had cut Saul's garment in the cave near Engedi, and neither was it as disrespectful. Yet he would need proof that God had indeed delivered Saul into his hands. He would need leverage.

"Abishai, take the spear that is at his pillow and the flask of water, and let us go."[12]

The young warrior gave David an incredulous look. "My lord?"

---

[10] 1 Samuel 26:8.
[11] 1 Samuel 26:9-11.
[12] 1 Samuel 26:11.

"Do as I bid. Fear not. This is what the LORD has given us. As you have said, Jehovah has delivered him to us. Saul must know. Only then may he leave off this pursuit and return to Gibeah."

Abishai clearly didn't understand, but he slid forward, catlike, using his toes and fingertips to slither through the narrow opening between the two shields. Once out from under the wagon, he crouched, looking every which direction to assure himself that he remained unobserved. He needn't have bothered. David knew no one would wake. This sleep was of the LORD.[13]

The young warrior crept through the sleeping Benjamites until he came to the king. There he paused, looking back at David. When David made no move, he gathered the spear and flask and returned. David took the spear, examining it. Even in the faint light he could see he now carried the royal scepter. This was no traditional spear, but one carved with images and words. Two bands of gold encircled the shaft just behind the head and at the butt.

He gripped the spear tightly, feeling the smoothness of the wood and metal, worn that way by the king's hands. Saul would certainly miss it when he woke. Without taking his eyes off the spear, he said, "Come, let us go."

The pair had no problem leaving. When they reached the perimeter of the camp, the sentries there had fallen asleep so deeply that they didn't stir when David accidently kicked a small rock to clatter down the ravine edge. Abishai watched it all in stunned fascination. He kept giving David surreptitious glances filled with awe. The warrior had not been there when David had slain Goliath or faced the Philistine champions. To him they were only stories, but to witness Jehovah's direct intervention on David's behalf in this way filled him with wonder.

David knew exactly how he felt.

---

[13] 1 Samuel 26:12.

19

King Saul stirred, his mind struggling to rise out of a heavy sleep, the like of which he had not enjoyed in many years. It felt good to sleep so soundly. Still, a vague sense of uneasiness warned him to wake. He fought against the weight of it, like a submerged man trying to find the surface of a dark lake, unsure which way was up. He stirred again, stretching muscles and trying to force his eyes to open.

He sensed that morning had come, that he had lain too long in sleep. He needed to be up and about, to begin the hunt for David before the son of Jesse could escape him. His need for this fought against the sudden desire to simply lie back and enjoy the rest.

His left eye crept open, followed slowly by his right. Sunlight streamed in, nearly blinding him, forcing him to blink rapidly against the brilliance. Vaguely, he knew he should be shocked, disturbed that that so much of the day had already past while he slept. Where was Abner? Where were the rest of the men? Why had they not awakened him?

He yawned then, taking a deep breath of the cool morning air, and his body responded by coming awake in stages. He felt invigorated. He hadn't slept so well since he was a boy. He yawned again and sat up, continuing to blink.

Abner lay beside him, breathing deeply. Ishui lay on the other side, so soundly asleep that drool ran out of the corner of his mouth and into his beard. The rest of the men lay scattered about also sleeping soundly. Snores filled the air to the accompaniment of a few chirping birds. Saul frowned, thinking he should be angry. Time slipped away, and everyone slept. Shaking his head, he reached for the cruse of water he always kept at his side.

It was gone.

Frowning yet more, he searched briefly for it. Someone had taken it. Odd. He then realized his scepter was gone too, and that vague sense of uneasiness flared into something tangible, a recognizable fear that had always followed him around as of late. A cold shiver coursed down his spine. He jumped to his feet and scanned the entrenchment his men had built the evening before. He looked everywhere but could not see the scepter. Something was wrong.

"Awake!" he roared. "Awake ye men of Benjamin! Arouse yourselves!"

Abner came awake with a startled snort. He sat upright, his hand instinctively seeking the hilt of his sword. He found it and then leveraged himself to his feet, looking around for an enemy. "What is it, my king?" he demanded, bemused.

"We are undone!" Saul shouted even as Ishui rolled to his feet, snatching up a spear and brandishing it defensively. "Thieves have come in the night and taken away the scepter and water that lay at my head!"

More and more men came awake. Many of them had to claw their way to alertness to shake off the weight of the sleep that clung to them. Captains began shouting, demanding reports, demanding answers from the sentries tasked with guarding the camp. The camp erupted into an all-out uproar as the Benjamites realized that every last man in the camp had slept straight through the night!

Saul stood rock still in the midst of it all, a sinking feeling settling in the pit of his stomach. Instinctively, he knew what had happened, so when a voice, clear as a bell, and carried on the breeze cut through the other noise to draw his attention, he barely flinched.

Turning toward the east, he spotted the silhouette of a man standing atop a large boulder across the ravine. The sun shone brilliantly at the figure's back, masking his features. But Saul knew who called. Knew it in his bones.

"Why do you not answer, Abner?" the voice shouted.[1]

Abner heard and spun around, squinting into the early morning sun toward the man standing across the ravine. "Who are you that cries to the king?"[2] the general shouted back.

The figure stirred atop his rock, lifting high a spear and what might be a bottle or flask. "Are you not a valiant man?" the voice responded. "Who is like to you in Israel? Why then have you not kept your lord the king safe? For there came one into the camp to destroy the king, your lord, and you prevented it not. This thing is not good that you have done. As the LORD lives, you are worthy to die because you have not kept safe your master, the LORD'S anointed." Hefting yet again the spear and flask, the voice continued, "And now see where the king's spear is and the flask of water that was at his head!"[3]

Abner quivered in both rage and shame, showing unusual emotion for the normally taciturn general. Saul placed a hand on his cousin's arm to still him. He knew who stood beyond the ravine even if he couldn't see him clearly with the sun shining at the man's back. He also knew what had happened. Once again, Jehovah had delivered Saul into the son of Jesse's hand, and once again, David had spared his life.

Strong emotion filled him, and if the evil spirit yet rested upon him, it departed in that instant. For the first time in years, he felt at peace despite the shame and guilt that filled him. But such was the difference from the typical anger and fear that had ruled him for so long that even these new emotions brought relief. In truth, the pain felt healthy. Perhaps it was the sleep that the LORD had laid upon him. Perhaps it was the knowledge that if he continued this pursuit, he would die. Regardless, he knew of a certainty what he must do.

---

[1] 1 Samuel 26:13-14.
[2] 1 Samuel 26:14.
[3] 1 Samuel 26:15-16.

He took long strides away from Abner and closer to the gorge that separated David from him. "Is this your voice, my son David?"

"It is my voice, O King!"

Gasps and murmurs sprang up behind Saul. He raised a hand to still them.

David took a step closer and shouted, "Why does my lord pursue after his servant? What have I done? What evil is in mine hand? I pray, let my lord the king hear the words of his servant!"

Saul nodded. "Say on," he replied, his voice easily carrying across the ravine.

David bowed low. When he straightened, he said, "If the LORD has stirred you up against me, then let Him accept an offering, but if the children of men have stirred you against me, cursed be they before the LORD. They have driven me out this day from abiding in the inheritance of the LORD, saying that I should go and serve other gods. O my king, let not my blood fall to the earth before the face of the LORD. The king of Israel is come out to seek a flea—or as when one hunts a partridge in the mountains. There is no harm in me, O King!"[4]

Saul waited a moment to let the echoes die away. What he intended to say would seal his fate and the fate of the kingdom. He glanced back at Abner who watched with his face once again schooled into unreadability. Ishui had slipped away and was nowhere to be seen. Saul would deal with his son later. Turning back, he lifted up his voice. "I have sinned! Go in peace, my son David, for I will no more do you harm—because my soul was precious in your eyes this day. I have played the fool and have erred exceedingly! Go, for I will pursue you no more."[5]

Saul knew the son of Jesse was studying him, weighing the truth of his words in his mind. Finally, the mighty warrior brandished Saul's scepter yet again. "Behold the king's spear! Let one of the young men come over and fetch it."

---

[4] 1 Samuel 26:18-20.
[5] 1 Samuel 26:21.

Saul gestured and one of the warriors began the descent into the ravine. David watched him for a moment and then looked back at Saul. The king still couldn't make out David's eyes in the glare, but he heard his former armorbearer's words clearly enough. "The LORD render to every man his righteousness and his faithfulness. For the LORD delivered you into my hand this day, but I would not stretch forth my hand against the LORD'S anointed. As I set your life much in my eyes, so let my life be much set by in the eyes of the LORD, and let Him deliver me out of all tribulation."[6]

And so Jehovah had, Saul knew. And would continue to do so. The knowledge that if he pursued David any longer would mean his death at the hands of the LORD filled him with such certainty that he knew instinctively what would happen if he defied it. That David continued to love him despite all Saul had tried to do to him also weighed heavily upon the king's heart.

Saul did something then he had not done to another human being in a long time. He bowed before David and said, "May you be blessed, my son David. I know of a surety that you will both do great things and prevail."[7]

David returned the bow. Then placing the spear and flask gently atop the rock he stood upon, he turned and disappeared, leaving only the sun to shine where he had once stood.[8] King Saul turned his back, knowing in his heart he would never see David again. He resigned himself to what would come. Perhaps the LORD would be yet merciful. Perhaps.

He gestured to Abner. "Prepare to depart. We are returning to Gibeah."

Abner bowed. "As you command, my lord." His voice betrayed nothing, but Saul knew his cousin like he knew his own heart. His general was relieved to have this at an end. In a way, so was Saul.

The king looked around for Ishui. "Where is my son?"

---

[6] 1 Samuel 26:23-24.
[7] 1 Samuel 26:25.
[8] 1 Samuel 26:25.

Abner turned, casting his eyes over the men still watching the pair of warriors. The son of Saul was nowhere to be seen. "I know not, my lord."

When a count was made, it was determined that Ishui had disappeared along with a score of his personal guard. They had slipped away during the discourse with David.

"Find him," Saul ordered, knowing already what his son planned to do. "I would that he returns back to Gibeah with me. The kingdom must be renewed, and I would have my sons at my side. All my sons."

Abner bowed in reply and left to organize the search, but Saul doubted his second son would be found. Hatred resided in Ishui's heart—a mirror image of the same spirit that had so recently consumed Saul. The king feared for his son, knowing he was likely to do something rash. Much blood had been spilled in the hunt for David. Blood of his own family. Blood of Hebrews. Blood of the priests of the LORD. He shuddered. That last haunted Saul the most. He knew deep down he had not yet paid the price for what he had done to the priests. And a price would be paid. A blood price.

He prayed it would not begin with Ishui.

Haroeh paced the hardpacked dirt floor in agitated silence. He pulled hard at his nose, the pain a distraction from his fear. His beard stuck out haphazardly in all directions, a testament to his growing panic. Abruptly, he stopped and called for his servant. "Omri! Get you in here!"

Omri appeared. Of the same age as his master, the servant affected a looming appearance, unable to straighten his back completely. His lean body always made it seem as if he was perpetually in a partial bow. "My lord, I am here."

"We must depart on the instant. Gather food and whatever else will be needed for a long journey."

"Where do we go, my lord?"

Haroeh ran his hands through his beard, pulled on his long nose as he thought. "I know not. Gibeah perhaps. Maybe some other city in Benjamin." Maybe even as far north as Dan, he mused silently.

The servant's face cracked in concern. "Your wife is at market. Should I send for her?"

"Nay. She is not in danger. She may stay and tend the house while we are gone. But we must be away quickly. I have learned that the king has abandoned his pursuit of the son of Jesse. David yet lives!"

The servant paled. "Will he come here?"

"What think you? Did he not march against Nabal and slay him? Did he not lay claim to Nabal's wife and all that he possessed?" He flung his hands up. "Did he not threaten to slay me if he was yet betrayed again!" Haroeh resumed his nervous pacing. "We must be well away afore he comes. For come he will. Mark my words."

The servant had begun to fidget. If David sought vengeance against the Ziph elder, then everyone in the household was at risk. "I will do as you command, my lord." The servant fairly ran from the room.

Haroeh hesitated, but such was his anxiety that he could not wait for the servant to do the job alone. He took three steps toward the storeroom to help when a voice hailed him from outside. He froze. His heart pounded in his chest and his bushy eyebrows attempted to climb right off the top of his head. He didn't recognize the voice, which bode ill. He had no other way out of the house except through the front door.

Omri appeared from the storeroom, his throat swallowing dryly. They exchanged a long glance. Maybe if they said nothing, the stranger would go away. But it was not to be. Another hail came from without, closer as if the caller had moved to just the other side of the door.

The elder cleared his throat and tried to reply, but his voice broke, refusing to achieve anything louder than a hoarse whisper. Then the door slammed opened, the latch tearing away from the wooden frame as if made of parchment, and two men stood framed in the opening. One, hooded and cloaked stood behind the other, seemingly trying to keep to the shadows. The other was a warrior, and from the markings on his armor, a Benjamite.

Not one of David's men then. Haroeh nearly sagged to the floor in relief, his heart continuing to pound and sweat running down the exposed skin of his face to damp his beard. But then he caught a better look at the warrior—tall, lean, with dark hair that spilled to his shoulders. The scarred, grim face framed by long hair was known to Haroeh. They had met. This was Ishui, son of King Saul.

The next moment found Haroeh on his face in a deep bow before the king's son, even as new worries and fears assailed him. "My lord, my house is honored by your presence."

The warrior snorted. "Not so honored as to answer a greeting."

"Forgive me, my lord. I recognized not your voice and feared those without might have been sent by the son of Jesse."

"And does the son of Jesse bear you ill will then, elder?"

"Would he not? Thrice have I betrayed him into the king's hands. I fear he seeks my life to wrest it from me."

"Perhaps."

Something in the Benjamite's voice caused Haroeh to look up. Both men had moved into the house, the second, hooded one, having closed the door behind him, jamming it into the frame so it stayed closed despite the broken latch. They stood now in the dimmer light facing the kneeling elder.

"Rise," Ishui commanded.

Carefully, Haroeh regained his feet. He glanced around surreptitiously and realized his cowardly servant had fled. He was alone with the two warriors. Unsure, he faced the two men, unconsciously tugging at his long nose. "What would you have of me, my lord?"

Ishui studied the elder carefully, his lips curled in what could be a snarl or could just be the man's natural disposition. Finally, he said, "Would you have an end to the son of Jesse?"

Hope burgeoned in Haroeh's heart. "Aye. Before he makes an end of me. I would."

"Then know, elder of Ziph, my father has forsaken the hunt and returned to Gibeah. David will not be caught unawares when an army is arrayed against him. He is too canny and wary for such tactics to be effective. My father knows that only by subtilty will he be brought down. It is to that end that my father has sent me to you. There is a way to lure the son of Jesse into a trap and slay him. But to do so, we require your aid."

"We, my lord? I do not understand. David has above six hundred warriors, mighty men of valor all and battle tested each. What can we do against so many?"

Ishui leaned forward on his spear, his features turning predatory, like a hawk. "I am not without an army at my command, Haroeh of Ziph. I am not without the means to slay the son of Jesse."

Haroeh swallowed hard. "Forgive me, my lord, but I am filled with fear at your suggestion. Already my life is forfeit in David's eyes. If I remain, he will seek my life to take it away. Surely, the son of Jesse will be wary of anything I do or, forgive me, that you do."

Ishui grinned and gestured to the hooded man who had thus far remained silent, waiting in the shadows. "I have one here who has the means to see the son of Jesse brought down, one with no ties to either you or my father."

The stranger stepped forward and lowered his hood. Haroeh took one look at the large man, the burns on his face, and the missing fingers on his left hand, and staggered back, clutching at his chest in panic. He saw his own death reflected in the other's eyes.

Ishui held up a thin, scarred hand. "Be at peace, Haroeh. Haman the son of Agag is here at my request. This is the man who will aid us in bringing down David."

Haroeh couldn't tear his eyes away from the Amalekite leader. He had once seen the man afar off and had his description told to him on several occasions. To have the enemy warrior here in his house was beyond comprehension. That Ishui, son of Saul, would be allied with this man—an avowed enemy of all Hebrews—defied credulity. He could not imagine how the two had met or how this unholy alliance could ever have come to be in the first place.

"How can this be?" the elder croaked out, his eyes not leaving Haman's face for a moment.

Haman turned and spat on the hard dirt floor. "Know, elder, that I have no love for your people. King Saul invaded my country, destroyed my people, stole our wealth, and drove the remnant into the wilderness to live as animals."[9]

Haroeh looked from the Amalekite to Ishui and then back again, straining to understand. Haman pushed past Ishui and planted himself in front of the elder who cowered away. "Who was it that commanded the attack against my people, elder of Ziph? Who was it that sought our utter destruction?"

Shaking, Haroeh sought to answer, but his tongue refused to cooperate as it should. He managed only to stutter, "Sam—Sam-mu-el…"

The Amalekite's lips curled back in a snarl. "Aye. Samuel, the Great Seer of the Hebrew people. It was he who commanded Saul to lay waste to my homeland."[10] Haman crowded closer, driving Haroeh up against the wall of his house. "But it was Saul who sought to spare some of my people too. Yet when my father begged for his life, Samuel hewed him into pieces to appease your bloody God."[11]

The large warrior shook with rage, his entire body quivering. Ishui watched it all dispassionately, uncaring. Haroeh didn't know what to think or what to do. Finally, the big Amalekite spat on the floor again and spun away from the Ziph elder.

"I can no longer have my revenge upon Samuel," Haman said, looking away. "But his heir is another matter. Did Samuel not anoint another to be king over Israel? I beheld this man, a demon filled with the evil spirits of your precious God. If I may not slay Samuel, then

---

[9] 1 Samuel 15:4-9.
[10] 1 Samuel 15:1-3.
[11] 1 Samuel 15:32-33.

surely I will slay this son of Jesse." He turned back to confront Haroeh. "And you, elder, will help."

Haroeh could do nothing less than nod in agreement. He perceived that if he answered any other way, he would be struck down on the instant. Better to let David's blood be spilled than his. He didn't believe Haman's version of events in the slightest, but in truth, it mattered little. If Ishui and Haman could rid him of David, then he would give them whatever they needed. By Abraham's beard, he would kiss the ground they walked on if he must!

"Have you a plan?" he asked, looking at Ishui. He didn't want to hear anymore from the Amalekite. The man was like a mad dog, but then Ishui didn't seem much better to Haroeh.

Ishui grinned again, making him look like a contented cat. "I do."

20

D avid studied the four men standing without the camp. They were Ziphites, sure enough. A surge of anger rose in David's breast, but he beat it back down, saying a brief prayer to God for strength. "What do they seek?" he asked Joab.

His nephew frowned. "I know only that they desire to deliver a message to you, my lord. They would not reveal the nature of the tidings to me or any other."

"And they come from Haroeh, the elder of Ziph?"

"So they claim." Joab grinned. "They are very frightened, my lord."

David pursed his lips, thinking. "Then they likely know we have divined their betrayal. Think you that they seek peace?"

Joab spat onto the ground. "They deserve it not."

"Yet if it is in our power to grant, then it would do us well to have peace. I long for a place, Joab. A place we might call home. I tire of this constant fleeing." This turn of David's heart and emotions surprised even him. Just recently, he would have doubtless marched on Ziph and laid waste to the city. But since confession of his sin and seeking deliverance from his wrath, a new spirit had infused him. Despite Haroeh's betrayal, David didn't feel anger. He felt sadness.

"It is better than being slain or enslaved," the other protested.

David grunted his agreement. Still, peace would be preferable. "Have them come. I will speak to them."

Joab raised a hand and gestured. The guards watching the four messengers parted and pointed up the hill to where David and Joab stood at the edge of the encampment. David had chosen to camp to the west of Ziph this time. He knew his presence would cause consternation with the shepherds and farmers, but after his narrow escape from Saul, he no longer wished to be trapped near the Jeshimon desert. The rolling hills provided a more temperate solution than the jagged clefts and ravines of Jeshimon—especially for the flocks and herds David had gained from his marriage to Abigail. To protect them all, David had established a network of scouts ranging all the way to Bethlehem. If Saul came south again, David would have plenty of notice.

The four men, all above middle age and gray of hair, approached David and bowed when they neared. David recognized all four as elders of Ziph. Their nervousness bled off them like heat from a fire. They glanced around uneasily and bunched together like sheep, trying to draw strength from their meager numbers.

"Be at peace," David said stepping forward. "I am David, the son of Jesse. What is it that you seek of me?"

One stepped forward. "I am Etam, the son of Anub, an elder of Ziph." His voice, though gravelly, carried well to those listening.

Curious, many of David's men, along with women and children, began to gather around. A touch on David's arm announced Abigail and Ahinoam's arrival. His two wives stood behind him, giving him space to address the elders of Ziph.

"You are well come, Etam, son of Anub. Speak your mind."

"A grievance has been brought to us within the gates of Ziph," Etam announced. "The book of the law has been violated, and the grieved seeks resolution."

David folded his arms across his chest. So, they had not come to seek peace then. His deep scowl of disappointment drove the four elders back a step.

Etam cleared his throat, eyeing the warriors standing around, taking in their dark looks and how they fingered sword hilts and spear shafts. "Will you hear my words?" he asked, a call for safe conduct.

David bowed his head. "I will. Say on."

The elder took a deep breath, still watching carefully the gathered warriors. "Haroeh is near kinsman to Nabal and claims the right of redemption according to the law of Moses. Yet Nabal's wife and possessions have been claimed by another. Upon my journey to this camp, I have seen the flocks and herds once possessed by Nabal." Looking at Abigail, he added. "And his wife does reside within this camp, more evidence of this truth."

"Abigail chose to become my wife," David replied, tightening his tenuous grip on his anger. "We are wed before a priest and in the eyes of God. This cannot be undone."

The elder bowed his head in acknowledgement. "This is so. But the right of redemption was not yours, son of Jesse. It belongs to another. What you have done is perceived as theft, and Haroeh seeks recompense."

"Haroeh has betrayed me to my enemies at least twice. He is not worthy of recompense."

The elder smiled tightly. "Then you do not dispute that you have usurped Haroeh's right? That is well. We call upon you to stand in judgment, David, son of Jesse. Let a judge decide between you and Haroeh. We find that according to the law of Moses, Haroeh's claim is just, his grievance right. Will you stand in judgment?"

David quivered, his grip on his anger slipping. It rose and fell like waves on a windy sea. However, pain in his broken fingers, not yet healed from the events of a week ago, reminded him of the consequences of losing his temper. He clamped down on it, determined he would not give in this time. He closed his eyes, praying for deliverance from his anger. God answered. A peace fell upon him all at once, shunting aside his anger. He breathed deeply, calmly. Curiosity rose in the stead.

"And who will stand in judgment of me?" David asked, focusing back on the elder.

The elder looked relieved. "We know that the Great Seer Samuel anointed you to be our next king. We know that this is a grief to King Saul. Therefore, we would not presume to ask the king to stand in judgment in this matter. But there are two, judges like unto Samuel, who have been called upon. They will arrive in two days. In three days, son of Jesse, we call upon you to return to Ziph and be judged in the gates of the city."

"Who are these two judges?"

"We have asked the sons of Samuel to come and stand in judgment. They come from Beersheba. Know you of Joel and Abiah?"[1]

David did, though he had never met the sons of Samuel. He had seen them while watching Samuel's burial from afar, but he knew little other than that they had made the southernmost city of Beersheba their home. Samuel hadn't talked about them much, and David had never had the desire to seek them out or to learn more. He knew that Samuel's sons had been passed over as judges of all Israel in favor of a king. He didn't know why other than they walked not in the way of their father.

"I have heard of them," David responded.

The elder's shoulders visibly relaxed. "Then you know that they judge Beersheba and have for over two score years. Absent King Saul's judgment on the matter, will you abide by their decision? Will you stand in judgment?"

Strangely, the decision was easy for David to make. The core of his worship and love for Jehovah was the law of Moses. Abiding by it was the central principle of David's life, and he didn't deem it a hardship to be judged by it.[2] If anything, he relished the opportunity to stand before the light of the law, to let it shine on his deeds, his actions, to be held accountable to the will of God.

He had only ever seen the entire written law a few times. Only the king and the priests had entire written copies. Most cities had some portion of it written down, and David's father had various

---

[1] 1 Samuel 8:1-2.
[2] Psalms 40:8.

parts of the law carved into the wood of the doorposts of their house and in the stones of the walls. As a result, David could recite much of the law from memory—especially the Shema.[3]

All of that coupled with Saul's promise not to seek David's harm anymore had strengthened his resolve and confidence that the LORD would see him through any obstacle.

"I will stand in judgment," David agreed, his hesitation gone. Even if he lost, it would be worth it. The people would see that he did not hold himself above the law but was subject to it like any other Hebrew.

The elder blinked. "Truly?"

David smiled. "Why should I not? Let the LORD be my judge. I have walked in my integrity, and I have trusted in the LORD. I cannot lose. Let the LORD examine me and prove me. Let Him try my heart. I ask for nothing else but to plead my case before the God of Israel."[4]

The elder blinked more rapidly. "Ah...then let it be so. On the third day at noon, stand in the gates of Ziph. Prepare yourself for judgment."

David bowed to the elders. "So be it."

Returning his bow, the elders then left, moving more rapidly than their age would dictate.

Murmuring sprung up among the people. Some cast dark glances David's way. They likely did not appreciate that David might lose the herds and flocks, their main source of food. It didn't matter. He had to do this.

Abigail appeared at his side. "My lord, will you heed my words?"

David gave his wife his full attention. "Always, my wife. Say on."

---

[3] Deuteronomy 6:3-9. Verses 4 and 5 are cornerstones of the Shema and were likely the most frequent parts of the law that were carved into doorposts of a Hebrew home.
[4] Psalms 26:1-2.

"I know something of Samuel's sons. My former husband had dealings with them when he traded with the inhabitants of Beersheba. My lord, Samuel's sons are known to take bribery and to pervert judgment."[5] Her face reflected her concern. "My lord, if Haroeh has given them money, they will not judge fairly."

Shammah, having obviously overheard, barreled his way close to David, the beads in his beard clanking together, his bald head glistening with oil. "Your wife speaks truly, my lord. This is the reason the people chose a king instead of Samuel's sons to judge them. They walk not in the way of the Great Seer."[6]

David held up a hand to still everyone. When they had all fallen silent, he turned about and faced the hills, looking far over them as if seeking someone. After a long moment where the silence settled over everyone like fog on a damp morning, he said, "Fear not. My help comes from the LORD who made heaven and earth. He will not suffer my foot to be moved."[7] The words carried weight that pressed into each soul within earshot. It smothered any protest and defeated every objection.

"Go," he added. "Go about your tasks. We have yet three days to make our testimony strong. Then I go to stand in judgment, and we will let the LORD decide."

The third day dawned still and clear, not a cloud could be seen from horizon to horizon, and not a leaf moved on any of the trees that grew on the hills. The spring air maintained only a hint of chill, and the afternoon promised to be comfortably warm. And David's spirits were sufficiently buoyed that he itched to depart for Ziph. That he should so look forward to standing in judgment bothered everyone but Abiathar. The priest approved of the entire affair. But then the fussy priest would. After all, standing in judgment before the law was only proper.

---

[5] 1 Samuel 8:3.
[6] 1 Samuel 8:4-5.
[7] Psalms 121:1-3.

So, David had invited the priest to attend, and Abiathar had readily agreed. But David had decided to take only ten warriors to accompany him as an honor guard—over Joab's most fervent protests. David had no intention of trying to sway the judgment by arriving with six hundred warriors. All would learn of the judgment given and David's response soon enough.

Abigail appeared at his elbow. She carried a pack wrapped in wool atop her head, flattening her dark hair. "My husband," she began, her full and rich voice sending a shiver down David's spine, "I am ready."

Two days ago, she had won a concession from him to attend the judgment as a witness. The law was clear that in the mouth of two or three witnesses would a matter be established.[8] Joab and Shammah would also act as witnesses. It was generally agreed that Haroeh would bring forth his own witnesses, but Abigail's testimony would bear the most weight as the former wife of Nabal and inheritor of all his wealth. She alone might force Joel and Abiah to render a just judgment—if what they said about the sons of Samuel were true.

In truth, David didn't care if the two men were corrupt. He felt confident that the LORD's will would prevail, and the law would side with him.

Turning, David placed his hands on his wife's shoulders and kissed both of her cheeks. "It is well that you go with me today, my wife. I will have need of your wisdom and your words."

Her smile lit her face like a rising sun. "Then we had best be going. Arriving late would not be prudent."

David grinned again. He would never understand women. After learning that Abigail intended to be a witness against Haroeh, Ahinoam had pleaded to also go and stand as witness. It had warmed his heart, but he also feared that arriving with two wives, both of whom had once been connected to Haroeh, would not be perceived

---

[8] Deuteronomy 17:6, 19:15.

well. David wanted things to work out as they should, and he didn't want to prejudice the trial before it even began.

So, he had bid Ahinoam to remain in the camp, and for the first time since their marriage, she had expressed her displeasure. David didn't understand why she would be so insistent in this matter, but he still had forbidden her going. Even Abigail had gotten involved, arguing that Ahinoam should be allowed to testify. No, he would never understand women. When faced with such a wall of feministic disapproval, he wondered how he had ever escaped his tent without being singed right down to the roots of his hair. Being married was complicated enough, but when faced with two wives united together was like trying to batter down a whirlwind with naught but bare hands.

"The others await at the base of the hill," he told his wife. "Come."

They set off. David was arrayed in full armor as were the other ten warriors waiting for him below. He wanted to make a show of divesting himself of armor and weapons when he stood in the gates of Ziph, so arriving armed would suit his purposes well. Besides, he still had enough enemies that traveling anywhere with armament was simply a matter of prudence.

He and Abigail joined up with Joab, Shammah, Adino, Eleazar and seven other warriors, including David's other two nephews, Uriah the Hittite, Elhanan the son of Dodo, David's brother Abinadab, and finally Benaiah the son of Jehoiada. These were some of David's mightiest men, lieutenants, and powerful warriors in their own right.

Abiathar waited with them, slightly off to one side. The young priest would never allow himself to be perceived as one of the common men. He wore his ephod like the warriors wore their armor, and it set him apart, but David doubted Abiathar would want it any other way.

The company of thirteen set off, winding through the spring grass and shrubs that filled the troughs between hills and making their way to Ziph. A cart path led to the city, so little impeded their easy progress. Abigail maintained the pace, easily balancing the supplies of food atop her head, and the men fell in around her, unconsciously becoming a buffer to ward off any harm to David's wife. From afar, it would look as if they escorted her. The priest followed behind, using a walking staff to aid his pace.

They walked steadily for three hours. Because David was in such high spirits, his mood infected everyone else. They laughed, joked, and teased each other. No one looked back at the priest or included him in their banter—not that Abiathar would have joined in anyway, and his frown of disapproval said all anyone needed to know about what he thought of the merry mood that had fallen upon David and his men.

And that is perhaps why David was caught off guard when the attack came.

They were traveling along the base of two opposing hills, just out of sight of the city of Ziph when Amalekite warriors boiled up out of the tall grass like ants and a flight of arrows stabbed unexpectedly at them from the tree line atop the hills.

"Ambush!" Shammah roared, yanking his war club from the hook at his side and charging headlong at the attacking enemy warriors.

An arrow struck Benaiah in the thigh, spinning him around and dumping him into the tall grass. He hit with a grunt of pain. Another arrow glanced off David's breastplate and a second sliced across his right bicep leaving a red trail of blood. Miraculously, no one else suffered a serious wound, though an arrow did lodge itself in the wool pack Abigail clutched to her head.

That was all David saw before the enemy descended upon them, and he found himself fighting desperately for his life.

21

Despite the unexpectedness of the attack, David's men reacted with the precision and discipline of trained veteran warriors. Instinctively, they formed a circle, pulling Abiathar into the middle with Abigail and the wounded Benaiah.

All accept Shammah. The bald warrior smashed into the attackers, bowling over three and smashing in the head of a fourth with a powerful swing of his iron-studded war club. Such was the ferocity of his retaliation that the Amalekite warriors split around him in an effort to keep their distance.

But that didn't spare the rest of David's men, and they were beset upon from all sides. David killed two of the attackers, but three more pushed in on him, nicking his cheek and staining his knuckles with blood. His fingers, not yet fully recovered, throbbed, and he worried his grip would give out on his sword long before the fight ended.

Then Joab went down. A spear catching him in the side and spinning him all the way around to crash into Eleazar, knocking the swordsman off balance. Eleazar took a shield to his face, laying him out flat on the ground.

Too many! Over a hundred Amalekites rushed upon David and his men. Surrounded and without even the benefit of good ground upon which to fight, David knew they could not win.

Not unless the LORD intervened. Like the meadow when Adino slew over three hundred men and like the barley field where David,

Shammah, and Eleazar had defeated the might of the Philistine army, it would require the Spirit of the LORD to win this battle.

"Abiathar!" David shouted, avoiding a spear thrust that scraped along his armor, ripping a hole in his tunic. He countered, ending the spear-wielder's life with a thrust to the neck. "Call upon the LORD! We are in sore need of aid!"

The startled young priest cowered near Abigail. His face reflected his uncertainty.

David yelled again, "Call upon the LORD!"

The priest gulped, fell to his face, and began a prayer for deliverance.

And that's when David saw Ishui. The lean son of Saul was unmistakable, standing halfway up the hill to David's right and urging the Amalekites on. At the Benjamite's side stood another man David recognized—Haman, the son of Agag.

"Ishui!" David roared, anger and fear surging through him.

The man laughed. His rough voice, tinged with madness, rose above the cacophony of the battle. "You will die this day, son of Jesse, and my father will be free of you at last!"

David kicked an enemy warrior away, taking another wound, this time a long scratch on his leg. "You betray Jehovah!" David cried, incensed and almost at the edge of losing control of himself. "You betray Israel!"

"Your blood will water the earth this day," Ishui shouted back, "and a new kingdom will spring from it!"

But then Abiathar's voice rose above the noise and din of battle. "Deliver us, O God, I pray, from these Thine enemies!"

Like a clarion call, the words washed over the combatants and swirled around on a sudden powerful wind that cut right through the heart of the battle. Grass, rocks, leaves, and sand blasted the men, flailed their flesh and blinded everyone, driving them apart.

David fell back, a cry of fear on his lips. The wind picked up speed and power and dark clouds formed rapidly from nothing out of the clear sky above, diming the sun and casting a dark shadow across the land. Such was the force and suddenness that the few who still tried to fight broke off, and everyone struggled just to keep from being picked up by the wind and borne away.

Men screamed and flung themselves on the ground, clutching frantically at anything to keep themselves grounded. Spears, caught in the swirling wind, went spiraling up and away, ripped from fingers. The force of the gale flattened grass, and two nearby trees toppled, their roots breaching the earth like a whale would the ocean water.

David crouched over Abigail, trying to keep them both solidly on the ground. Only Abiathar seemed unmoved. He knelt in the eye of the storm, hardly a hair of his immaculate beard moved so still and calm was he.

Then the wind died all at once as if it had never been, leaving everyone staring about with tear-filled eyes and stricken faces. A rumbling from above caught everyone's attention. The dark clouds continued to boil forth as if poured out of some cosmic jug, spilling out across the horizon like water onto a table. They spread outward, growing low to the ground even as more ominous rumbles shook the earth.

Men picked themselves off the ground slowly, peering about fearfully, knowing in their hearts more was still to come. Only Haman, the wily Amalekite leader, had the presence of mind to try and continue the battle.

"Slay them!" he screamed. "Slay them all! Call upon Molek! Fear not the Hebrew God!"

Lightning shot out of the clouds, striking the earth with enough ferocity to blast men into the air, their bodies flung away like so much chaff in the wind. Dirt and rock exploded outward, peppering anyone in range. David, still trying to shield his wife, felt the blast strike his armor and bite into his neck, head, and other exposed skin. The accompanying thunder deafened everyone, causing their teeth to rattle. David had never heard anything so loud before. His ears rang from it, and his entire body felt compressed beneath it. His insignificance was manifested before the might of Jehovah in ways he never dreamed possible.

Three more lightning strikes hit among the Amalekites, flinging men and rock far and wide. The cries of the wounded and fearful filled the air. So much power! David tasted blood in his mouth where he'd inadvertently bit his tongue while his body rattled and shook from each blast.

It was too much. The remaining Amalekites broke and ran, screaming for their gods to save them, desperate to get away. Soon, of the enemy, only Haman and Ishui remained on the field of battle—along with the wounded and dying. The large Amalekite picked himself up, leaving a stunned Ishui lying prostrate on the ground. Haman's chest rose and fell with deep, ragged breaths, and his face was contorted into a mask of such utter rage that David recognized himself reflected in the other. Surely, this was what he himself must have once looked like when such battle lust had consumed him and why his own friends and family had looked upon him with horror.

Haman screamed, his rage and madness pouring forth in a palpable way. He snatched up his sword from where it had fallen and charged across the broken hillside littered with the dead and dying of his men.

David stepped away from Abigail and his men to meet the charge. Only a few of his small company could stand. All bore wounds, some serious. They could not help David, but even if they could, he would not permit it. This was his task alone.

The two men met with a clash of metal. The powerful Amalekite, his anger turning into a berserker rage hacked away at David with the ferocity of one possessed. David backed away, using every ounce of strength and skill his battered body possessed not to be hacked to pieces in that first few moments.

Haman was beyond caring. He was beyond reason. And David came to believe in that moment that the man was indeed possessed of one of his false gods. The Amalekite screamed his rage as he delivered blow after blow with his sword, driving David back a step with each one.

David had never encountered such speed, such rage before—
except when he himself had fallen prey to the same berserker rage.
He parried, just barely, each blow, but his strength drained from him
with each parry. In moments, David would be unable to counter the
enraged Amalekite.

Desperately, David backed up, trying to find space and relief,
but Haman followed him step for step. Bloody spittle flew from the
big warrior's mouth as he spat out curses and abominations at David,
and his feverish eyes, touched with insanity, followed David's every
move. David swallowed, fear rising in his breast, his strength nearly
gone.

In mere moments he would be dead. He knew it. He could read
it in Haman's eyes. So, he cried out Abiathar's prayer, shouted it with
the force of desperation and fear, "Deliver me, O my God!"[1] He
stumbled and collapsed to his knees, the relentless attack nearly
tearing his sword from his still damaged fingers. But he held on,
determined to sell his life dearly.

Haman, triumph replacing rage in his eyes, stepped forward to
deliver one more overhand blow that could not fail to smash through
David's weakened defenses and cleave David in two.

Unable to do anything else, David raised his sword high to try
and parry the blow. The moment he did, strength flooded into every
muscle as the Spirit of the LORD descended upon him in a rush, like
the wind that had first come before the lightening. It filled very fiber
of his being and cleared his mind of all fear and uncertainty.

When the swords met, Haman's broke in half—exactly in half.
The narrow end flipped away over David's head to embed itself in
the rocky soil where it quivered upright like a snake robbed of its
prey. Haman stepped back, staring at the remainder of his iron sword
in astonishment.

He looked then at David his rage spent. "What evil is this?" he
whispered.

---

[1] Psalm 71:4. (Over 92 times the Psalm writers write about and speak of deliverance.
It is a principle theme in the Psalms and in David's life.)

David didn't try to enlighten or correct him. He surged forward, coming off his knees like a catapult and rammed his sword all the way to the hilt in Haman's chest. The large Amalekite never made a sound. Blood fountained out of his mouth, staining the front of his armor red. His eyes never blinked as they slowly glazed over and fixed, staring at David.

Yanking out his sword, David let the body of his enemy fall. He gasped then as the Spirit of the LORD departed, and he stumbled and fell back to his knees, his strength gone. He struggled to breathe, trying to suck in great lungfuls of air—and failing. His body began to shake with the aftermath of his exhaustion. Unable to prevent it, his sword slid to the ground from listless fingers.

Adino reached him first, followed closely by Abigail. His lieutenant bore several wounds, one of which bled fiercely from his scalp. He wiped away the blood and knelt next to David. "Are you well, my lord?"

David took another shuddering breath, trying to control his shaking and failing. "Aye, Adino. What of Ishui?"

"The king's son has fled the field of battle," the thin man drawled. "As should we." He looked back to where most of David's men had begun to tend to the wounded—which appeared to be everyone except for Abiathar.

David found his wife's concerned eyes. "My lord," she whispered kneeling in front of him. "Let me tend to you."

He nodded and winced as her fingers probed his wounds. "Have mercy upon me," he grunted.

She smiled tightly at him. "You must give yourself over to my ministrations, my lord." She looked around at everyone else. "You all must."

Not that he could stop her if he wanted, so he gave himself into her care. While she worked, he spent time in silent prayer, giving praise to Jehovah for His wondrous deliverance.

The sun had descended far by the time David's small company trudged up to the gates of Ziph. Joab had to be carried on a makeshift litter, and several others had to be supported. Most of the others limped along as best they could. Not a one had escaped injury, and they all needed better care, so they had come to Ziph, the city being much closer than David's own encampment.

And there was still the business of the judgment that the elders of Ziph had called him to stand for. The gates stood open, and the elders sat in a half circle just inside when David and his weary squad trudged in. David studied the men arrayed before him, picking out Haroeh in their midst. Sweat rolled off the man freely. Fear radiated from the entire town.

And David knew.

There was never to be a judgment. It had been but a ruse to lure David away and into the ambush. Indeed, glancing around, he found no evidence of Samuel's sons anywhere. Stepping forward, he addressed the elders. "I call upon the elders of Ziph to stand in judgment!" His voice, though coarse and raw, nevertheless carried authority and power.

The aged men flinched before it.

"Ziph has conspired with the enemies of the LORD," he accused them. "False witnesses and betrayers have you become. As the LORD lives, you are all worthy of death." He stared at them hard. "How do you answer, elders of Ziph?"

Haroeh fell on his face, bowing deeply before David. The other elders followed not far behind. "Have mercy!" Haroeh cried, his body shaking like prey caught in the mouth of a lion. "We were prevailed upon by the son of Saul to conspire with the Amalekites. Ishui, the son of Saul, came to us having already made an accord with the Amalekite, Haman. He prevailed upon us to send messengers to lure you out. Our women and children were held hostage against this deed. Have mercy, O King!"

The last word echoed throughout the courtyard. It was the first time someone had granted him that title—king. But no, it wasn't his yet, not as long as Saul still lived. And not being king, David let his anger drain away. He would not give in to it again. Not this time.

But Ishui's involvement and Ziph's constant betrayals had convinced David of one thing. Saul, whether directly or indirectly, would never stop hunting him. David would one day perish by the hand of Saul unless he escaped. He knew already where he would go—the one place Saul dared not follow—the Philistines.[2] Achish, king of Gath, would deal with him, particularly when he brought an army of six hundred trained warriors to his doorstep.

David knew that Achish, above all else, was a greedy man, an opportunist that could not fail to see the advantage of having David in his service. Saul would be blunted from any further pursuit and perhaps in the land of the Philistines could a place be found to await the LORD's will to come to pass.

He sighed, looking over the prostrate elders. "Rise, elders of Ziph and face me. Hear my judgment."

Slowly, they stood, trepidation and fear etched into every face and into those who watched from afar. All Ziph had turned out for this.

"Here is my judgment," David said, sweeping his gaze across everyone. "Let there be no more war. Let only peace be between us. For I and those with me will leave this place and trouble you no longer. We require only that each family of Ziph give of their sustenance for our journey." David fixed Haroeh with a stern look. "And let there be no more talk of redemption of Nabal's possessions. I have married his wife. Abigail is mine. Nabal's possessions belong to me. I have spoken. Let it be so."

Haroeh was already bowing before David had even finished. "You are most gracious, my lord! We will, each of us, give freely for your journey. And to this end, I forsake my claim upon Nabal's possessions." He bent down, unlaced his sandal, drew it off, and tossed it before him. "By this token is the agreement sealed. You are all witnesses."

The elders echoed, "We are witnesses."

---

[2] 1 Samuel 27:1.

David bowed then himself, feeling both relieved and vindicated. Showing forgiveness and mercy when it was within his power to do so, felt right. It felt a just recompense for all the LORD had already done for David. This was something David could do. As the LORD had delivered him out of the hands of his enemy, it seemed only right that he offer the same deliverance to Haroeh and the people of Ziph. It mattered not if they were worthy of it.

It only mattered that David give it.

For the first time in a long time, he felt whole and at peace.

Epilogue

"Your father is dead." Hammedatha, son of Haman, son of Agag, heard the words spoken by the aged Amalekite warrior standing before him and felt no shock, no surprise. One of the tent walls had been rolled back to let the sunlight of the spring day flood the interior. Hammedatha studied the old warrior who had once served his grandfather and then his father and who now served him. He studied the man with something akin to a boy who discovered some exotic and unusual bug for the first time.

So, his father was dead. For seventeen years, Hammedatha had lived in the shadow of his mighty father. He had little love for his father, who had shown little interest in his smallish son. Hammedatha was not the warrior his father had been—would never be. He was a thinker. A man who wielded his brain better than a sword. But it wasn't something his father had ever understood or appreciated. Hearing now that his father was dead had little impact on Hammedatha.

Yet his father had given him one thing. Hammedatha had inherited his father's pathological hatred of the Hebrews, but especially of Samuel, the Hebrew magician who had murdered Hammedatha's grandfather, Agag. Such hatred had led Haman to try and destroy Beersheba because he had learned that Samuel's sons lived there. The attack had been doomed to fail from the start, but that hadn't kept Haman from trying. Other than being partially burned, some sheep and goats plundered, and a few stray Hebrews killed, the raid had accomplished little.

"How did he die?" Hammedatha demanded of the warrior before him.

The older man spat to one side. "He died at the hands of that devil, David, the son of Jesse. Great evil befell us on the field of battle, my chief. The devil called forth lightning from a cloudless sky and an evil wind that drove us away. Try as we could, we could not reach your father. He was trapped, alone with the son of Jesse who slew him without mercy. We were helpless before such power, my chief. I swear this upon the blood of Mot. We could not save your father."

So, this son of Jesse was a magician too. As a student of history, where knowing your enemy could mean the difference between survival and defeat, young Hammedatha knew that Samuel had twice called upon his magic to do something similar. The first had been to destroy the Philistine army at Mizpeh long before Hammedatha had been born.[1] The second had been when Samuel had chosen Saul to be the first Hebrew king, a puppet that the magician could use to control the Hebrews.[2]

But Saul had slipped his leash, had defied Samuel and had tried to break away from the magician's control, and so Samuel had chosen another successor, this son of Jesse, this David. And it seemed that this new magician was every bit as powerful as Samuel had been.

And now David had killed Hammedatha's father.

He rose slowly to his feet, his body lean and wiry, so unlike his heavily muscled father. "This must not go unanswered," he told the warrior before him. "Vengeance must be met. Go. Find a priest and sacrifice unto Mot. For we will not rest until we bring this David's head down to the ground."

The warrior puffed up his chest. "Do you wish for me to gather the warriors?"

---

[1] 1 Samuel 7:6-11.
[2] 1 Samuel 12:17-18.

"Nay, not yet. In time we will avenge the blood of our people with the blood of David. But we need more intelligence and knowledge that will show us this magician's weaknesses. Only then may we slay him. As my father learned, direct confrontation is not the answer. The evil God of the Hebrews must not be confronted directly. We will find other means to achieve our ends."

The warrior, a man of action after his father's stripe, stared at Hammedatha in confusion. But he bowed before his new chief anyway. "As you command, my chief. So will it be done."

After the warrior had left, Hammedatha turned to his young Egyptian slave. "Khurn, there are four women, virgins of childbearing age in this camp. Know you of them?"

"Aye, Master. I know them," the Egyptian replied. The slave was a gift from Hammedatha's father, a sickly young man who had been taken in a raid against a merchant caravan. His father had given the slave to him so as to shame Hammedatha, since Haman had disdained slaves himself.

Hammedatha didn't care. The slave had his uses.

"Go then. Select one—I care not which—to be my wife and bring her to me."

The Egyptian's eyes furrowed in confusion. "Master?"

"I will need a son, Khurn. I will need an heir to carry on after me. I feel that vengeance upon the Hebrew people will be long in coming. We may discover some means of destroying them in my lifetime—perhaps a way to slay this David—but if not, then I will need a son, and my son's son, to keep our name alive, to prevent our hatred from waxing cold. One day, Khurn, a way will come where every last Hebrew may be slain and cast from the earth."

Khurn shuffled from the tent, his face looking pale and wan. The slave wasn't the most reliable of messengers, but all knew to whom he belonged. He would return with a woman, one to bear him a son. He would call his son Haman, a name he intended to pass down to future generations. For only when Amalek was a nation again could the name Agag once again be claimed. Henceforth, they would be known as Agagites.[3] Until then, he would see to it that his father's legacy of hatred continued.

Vengeance would one day be his—if not his, then some distant son's. Alone, he contemplated ways he might find and kill David, the son of Jesse.

The End

Thus ends book four of the Davidic Chronicles. In book five, King, *David prepares for his final confrontation with King Saul as he looks to finally take his place as king of Israel.*

---

[3] Esther 3:1. Haman of Esther's day was known as an Agagite. Scholars presume that he was directly descended from King Agag, whom Samuel killed. This part of the story is meant to provide some insight in how that might have come to be.

Additional Biblical and Historical Explanations

Facts Versus Interpretation to Discover Truth

Stating a fact and interpreting the fact are not the same. By themselves, facts don't represent truth; they are merely facts. *Truth* is a fact that has purpose and meaning—often what we call a *philosophy*—that gives the fact a means to interact with your life and become relevant and meaningful to you. This then becomes a *truth* for you.

For example, take a fact: dinosaur bones. This fact coupled with either the philosophy of evolution or creationism will give two entirely different and opposing truths. Each side considers theirs to be true and their opposite to be false. But the core "fact" is still a bone. The interpretation of that fact leads to one's perspective, views, understanding, and ultimately truth.

Jesus said that He is truth. This means that when we see life through His eyes, we find purpose and meaning that cannot be found unless we can view that perspective. Jesus is indeed truth— my truth, and I trust your truth as well. But even among Christian circles, that perspective varies enough that our "truths" are often not quite aligned with someone else's. Welcome to individual soul liberty.

I say this to explain that, though I try to incorporate *all* the facts that the Bible speaks of in these stories, I will still interpret what those facts mean for the characters and events described. Not everyone will agree with my conclusions. For example, a fact: Michal, David's wife, lied to her father about David's supposed threat to kill her if she did not aid in his escape. This is the fact. *Why* she lied is supposition. We can likely extrapolate that she did not want to face the wrath of her father and so lied to protect herself from him. But is that an accurate interpretation of the facts? Perhaps not. And that is the dilemma of interpreting the facts. We cannot know with certainty why someone did something unless God explains it.

When you interpret the fact, your "truth" of the event shifts. Your understanding of it changes. And how you relate to the fact and how it becomes meaningful to you also changes. This becomes your truth and understanding of the stories mentioned in the Bible. Preachers do this all the time.

These novels represent my interpretation of those facts into a cohesive and, hopefully, noncontradictory story that will entertain but also spark your fascination for the Bible, the characters, God's interaction with men, and ultimately your own relationship with Him.

I do not expect everyone to agree. But I do hope these novels will inspire you to delve into God's Word in a much more personal way and to see that the characters in the Bible lived real lives, and God wanted to introduce you to those lives.

Old Testament Morality

Morality is born from a culture's understanding of right and wrong. This understanding comes from our interaction with divinity—a higher morality. For Christians, this interaction is mainly based on our interaction with the Bible, which we believe is the embodiment of God and Jesus Christ. For the Hebrews of David's day, it was the law of Moses and God's direct intervention in the lives of His people. For other people and lands in David's day, divinity was ascribed to phenomena beyond man's understanding, the supernatural, the spiritual. Thus, morality took on the aspects of the phenomena's consequences in the lives of those touched, whether good or bad. If the effect is negative, for example, then a moral imperative not to duplicate the effect is put into place.

This explains why some cultures would offer human sacrifices to appease their angry gods, for they saw a flood or a famine as evidence of their god's displeasure. In some cases, a people's false god was in fact an evil spirit, a demon who may have actually taken possession of idols and performed miracles to establish a warped sense of right and wrong.

Many of David's actions, when held up against modern-day cultures, seem evil. For example, when David lives among the Philistines in Ziklag (see book five of this series), he often attacked cities and towns of other nations. To prevent word reaching back to the king of Gath of his actions, he slaughtered everyone—man, woman, and child. To us, this would be the height of immorality, but God never chastises David for this deception or slaughter. Indeed, God seems to bless his deeds. Taken in that light, it is hard for us to attribute morality to God or to David.

But morality in David's day was based on a different understanding of divinity than ours is. It was generally perceived by the Hebrews that anyone who did not follow Jehovah God was thus an enemy of God. Slaying such enemies was not immoral. In fact, in many cases, such slaughter was seen as a duty, a way to purge the land of evil and immorality and to preserve God's blessings upon the people and the land. This mentality still exists today in certain cultures and religions.

Seen in that light, David's actions in slaying men, women, and children are not immoral, but necessary to prevent the propagation of evil and to secure a better future for the people of Israel. But judged by our standards of New Testament morality, David would fall woefully short and be labeled immoral. Thus, it becomes hard to judge David because the standard we live by didn't exist in his day. However, David's love for God and his sense of duty toward the law of Moses far outstrips the level of devotion expressed by most Christians this day. Doubtlessly, he would judge our lack of devotion and count us among the evil, perhaps even the enemies of his God. That is truly a chilling thought.

David was a man after God's own heart, but he was still a man—a man with a wandering eye for the ladies and a man prone to sudden anger and vengeance. He was not above allowing his passions to rule him. But to that end, his sense of morality was highly acute—when based on the standards of his day.

David's Anger

This novel explores a flaw in David's character brought to life by the story of Nabal. Nabal's insults tipped David into a killing rage. This, in light of the rest of the story about David, seemed out of character to me. I realized then that such anger would likely have been born through much more than that one single instance of one man's insults. To get to the point where David was willing to murder everyone to avenge Nabal's insults, David had to have been building up to it.

Fear of Saul and fear for the lives of those he loved most likely played a part in David's building anger. I began touching on this in book three of this series and explored it thoroughly in this book.

David was not a perfect man. We know this mentally, but we tend not to realize that his character flaws, much like our own, are hardly isolated instances. For example, David's adultery with Bathsheba is a result of a flaw that likely existed in David for much of his life. We like to claim that his adultery was the result of his decision to stay home from battle (2 Samuel 11:1), but in truth, his adultery was likely the result of lust that had existed in him for years.

The same is true of David's anger. He led a hard and difficult existence where his life was in constant jeopardy. Constant fear would have plagued his mind and heart, and anger could have been born from that. It would have shown up in other parts of David's life, not just in that one single instance regarding Nabal.

Old Testament Polygamy

Marriage to more than one woman was not uncommon in David's day, but was typically reserved for the rich and powerful as they were the ones who could best support more than one wife and afford the dowry to be paid the woman's family.

Samuel's father had two wives. Saul had a wife and at least one concubine. David ended up with at least six wives, and of course Solomon had a thousand wives and concubines. Based on the number of children that Jesse had, it is very plausible that he also had more than one wife. Polygamy stemmed from the time of Jacob, who had two wives and two concubines, a tradition that never truly left Hebrew society until at least the Babylonian conquest. Even then, there are hints that the practice continued well into the New Testament era.

David's position and influence afforded him the opportunity to take multiple wives. By the time this novel ends, he has taken no less than two more above his first wife, Michal. During David's life, he did not restrict his wife-taking to Hebrew women. Absalom's mother was a daughter of Talmai, king of Geshur (2 Samuel 3:3). This marriage was likely a political alliance to seal a peace treaty between the two nations—a not uncommon practice—or she was part of the spoils of conquest.

In fact, while David was in Hebron, he had six sons—all by different wives. Abiathar, in this novel, rightly points out that God, foreseeing the coming of kings and what they would do to secure alliances—warned of the danger of multiplying wives to themselves (Deuteronomy 17:17). The intent was to avoid having their hearts turned as Solomon did his. David could easily justify taking more wives by making sure that the majority were Hebrew girls, thus, in his mind, satisfying the purpose and intent of the command given in the law.

David took more wives and concubines when he set up Jerusalem as his capital. In fact, Absalom defiled ten of David's concubines in 2 Samuel 15-16. Polygamy, in fact, may have been a mark of status among the Hebrew people. The more wives and concubines one had, the more important and powerful he was.

Overall, I hope to have portrayed an accurate way of life that reflected the character and life views of the period.

Fictional Characters and Events

I try to use characters of whom the Bible already speaks. The story is already in place, and I believe the main characters should remain the main characters of the story. Where possible, I use characters the Bible already mentions.

Still, several fictional characters have been introduced into this story. Haroeh is by far the most prominent among these in this novel. He is entirely fabricated and is meant to represent the city of Ziph and their role in David's troubles. Haman, the Amalekite, is another completely fictional character. I borrowed his name from the Haman of Esther's day since Esther's Haman was an Agagite, very possibly a direct descendant of King Agag. I use Haman to tie the two stories together, for the Amalekites play a significant role in David's life. They are the ones who destroy Ziklag and steal away David's wives. An Amalekite reports Saul and Jonathan's death to David. I also needed an enemy to insert into the story to verify the shepherd's story that David was a wall—a defense to them while in Carmel. Shobal is fictional, representing the sons of Belial who joined up with David and occasionally caused him grief.

The story of Ishui joining with Haman is purely fictional. The purpose of this part of the plot was to explain why David would feel he must flee to the Philistines even after Saul vowed to no longer hunt David. Something had to convince David that Saul would break his word, so the events around Ishui's and Haman's union are an attempt to suggest how David's feelings could have come about.

The story of the spider spinning a web across the cave entrance is actually a Jewish legend I discovered during my research. There is no biblical evidence of such a thing happening, but I adopted the story to explain how Saul could have failed to search the cave wherein David was hidden.

Many of the real people mentioned in the story also performed fictional roles. In effect, they constitute my best guess as how a person could logically get from point A (a biblical fact) to point B (another biblical fact). The fictional part is often what happens between point A and point B.

For example, I made the claim that Nabal was cousin to my fictional character Haroeh. This dual role helped explain certain things as to how David was able to marry Abigail. Ishui is only mentioned once in Scripture as having died with his father. I made him a villain in this story, but his role is entirely fictional. Ahinoam's relationship to Haroeh is fictional. She was of the city of Jezreel, a town somewhere in southern Judah, but never mentioned in the story. Since David, it seems, met her around Ziph, I explained how this might have come to pass.

Most all the characters mentioned take on some form of fictional role to explain how the story may have played out based on what we are told in Scripture.

Timelines and Timeframes

The biblical account is often vague on the actual timeline of events presented in this novel. Perhaps if there is any area that I take the most liberties, it would be with the timeline. For example, there is no indication whatsoever of how much time elapsed between when David won his battle at Keilah and when he goes to Gath with his small army. It could have been months or years. We simply don't know.

All we know for a fact is that David was thirty years of age when he was crowned king over Judah in Hebron (2 Samuel 5:4). If David was roughly seventeen or eighteen years of age when he killed Goliath, then there are some twelve years that must be accounted for.

The only other timeframe given is found in 1 Samuel 27:7, which states that David was in Philistia for a year and four months when he was hiding from Saul.

I leave it to the reader to decide what is right and pray you have mercy on my decision.

Sources and References

Much research goes into a novel like this. I wanted to stay true to the biblical account but also stay true to the era and times. This meant I had to learn how they built their houses, what their clothes were made of, and many other customs and facts. The sources below represent the majority of the information about customs, manners, and geography that I incorporated into this novel. Those not mentioned only corroborated what I found in the sources below.

Disclaimer: Undoubtedly, there are many facts about ancient life that I missed or didn't learn, and so the astute reader may discover historical and geographical errors. Feel free to write me about them, as long as you corroborate them with sources, and I will attempt to incorporate them into future editions of the novel.

Sources:
- The King James Bible
- www.biblicalarchaeology.org
- www.ancient-hebrew.org
- en.wikipedia.org/wiki/Salix_viminalis
- www.gci.org/bible/hist/weapons
- www.chabad.org/library/article_cdo/aid/3942715/jewish/Who-Was-Amalek-and-the-Amalekites.htm
- www.enotes.com/homework-help/in-the-bible-who-was-the-god-of-the-amalekites-69937

- www.globalchristiancenter.com/christian-living/lesser-known-bible-people/31360-agag-king-of-the-amalakites
- www.gotquestions.org/Jehovah.html
- www.theoldtestamenttimeline.com
- www.israelbiblicalstudies.com & blog.israelbiblicalstudies.com
- www.jewfaq.org
- www.bible-history.com
- www.netours.com/content/view/241/26/
- www.jpost.com/Arts-and-Culture/Food-And-Wine/Wine-Talk-Ancient-wine
- www.biblewalks.com/info/Winepresses.html
- blog.adw.org/2014/07/what-was-the-climate-and-weather-of-israel-like-at-the-time-of-jesus
- www.fromthegrapevine.com/slideshows/nature/10-desert-animals-israel
- Jan H. Negenman, *New Atlas of the Bible* (New York: Doubleday & Company Inc., 1969).
- Rand-McNally Bible Atlas - Published in 1910.
- Smith Bible Atlas - Designed and edited by George Adam Smith, 1915.
- Richard H. Hiers, *Transfer of Property by Inheritance and Bequest in Biblical Law and Tradition* (University of Florida Levin College of Law, 1993).
- Fred H. Wight, *Manners and Customs of Bible Lands* (Moody Bible Institute of Chicago, 1953).
- A. Van Deursen, *Illustrated Dictionary of Bible Manners and Customs* (Grand Rapids, MI: Zonderzan, 1958).
- Boyd Seevers, *Warfare in the Old Testament* (Grand Rapids, MI: Kregel Publications, 2013).
- Chaim Herzog and Mordechai Gichon, *Battles of the Bible — A Military History of Ancient Israel* (Barnes and Noble Publishing, 2006).

Commentaries and Dictionaries:

- James Orr, M.A., D.D., General Editor, *International Standard Bible Encyclopedia.*
- John McClintock and James Strong, *Cyclopedia of Biblical, Theological and Ecclesiastical Literature* (1895).
- Canne, Browne, Blayney, Scott, and others, with introduction by R. A. Torrey, *Treasury of Scriptural Knowledge* (1834; public domain).
- *John Gill's Exposition of the Bible* (1746-1766, 1816; public domain).
- *Jamieson, Fausset and Brown Commentary - A Commentary, Critical and Explanatory, on the Old and New Testaments* (1871; public domain).
- *Adam Clarke's Commentary on the Bible* (1810-1826; public domain).
- *Joseph Benson's Commentary on the Old and New Testaments* (1857; public domain).
- *Albert Barnes' Notes on the Bible* (1847-85; public domain).
- *Matthew Henry's Commentary on the Whole Bible* (1708-1714; public domain).
- W. Robertson Nicoll, *Sermon Bible Commentary* (1888-1893; public domain).
- *John Wesley's Notes on the Bible* (1755-1766; public domain).
- F. B. Meyer, *Through the Bible Day by Day – A Devotional Commentary* (1914; public domain).
- W. Robertson Nicoll (Editor), *Expositor's Bible Commentary* (1887-1896; public domain).

About the Author

Greg S. Baker has been writing novels for over twenty years. His books are widely read and enjoyed. His primary focus lately has been on his stellar Biblical Fiction novels and his engaging young adult adventure novels. He has written a number of other helpful books for the Christian life. He has a passion for expanding the Kingdom of God within the kingdom of men.

He lives in the southwest with his wife, Liberty, and their four boys. Much of his writing has been for them, desiring to provide entertaining stories that teach and inspire.

He attended Bible college in the late 1990s, pastored a Baptist church in Colorado for thirteen years, and now works as a writer, a freelance Christian editor, and a programmer from his house. He remains active in his church, serving God in a variety of capacities, but focusing mainly on teenagers and young single adults.

He loves chess, playing sports, and rearing his teen boys.

You can connect with Greg through his website GregSBaker.com. He loves hearing from people and engaging them as an active part of the writing process for his future books. If you love reading, then stop on by.

Printed in Great Britain
by Amazon